Old Farts and Pop Tarts

Old Farts and Pop Tarts

Annie Mick

Copyright

ANNIE MICK

Table of Contents

Old Farts and Pop Tarts   **2**

Copyright   **3**

Dedication   **11**

"Be careful what you ask for."   **13**

Chapter 1   **15**

  Millicent   15

Chapter 2   **21**

  Millicent   21

Chapter 3   **29**

  Millicent   29

Chapter 4   **35**

  Millicent   35

Chapter 5   **39**

Colby   39

Chapter 6   **43**

Millicent   43

Chapter 7   **51**

Colby   51

Chapter 8   **61**

Millicent   61

Chapter 9   **75**

Colby   75

Milwaukee, WI   77

Chapter 10   **89**

Millicent   89

St. Louis, MO   93

Chapter 11   **99**

Colby   99

Little Rock, AR   99

Chapter 12   **107**

Millicent   107

Chapter 13   **113**

Colby   113

Chapter 14   **119**

Millicent 119

Chapter 15 .... **125**

Colby 125

Tulsa, Oklahoma 125

Chapter 16 .... **139**

Millicent 139

The Concert in Tulsa 145

Chapter 17 .... **151**

Colby 151

Grand Canyon 153

Millicent 161

Colby 163

Chapter 18 .... **169**

Millicent 169

Downstairs on the first floor 171

Millicent 175

Chapter 19 .... **183**

Colby 183

The Vegas Stage 187

In the Lobby 193

Chapter 20 .... **195**

Colby   195

  Red Rocks   207

Chapter 21   **211**

Millicent   211

  Omaha - Eppley Airfield   211

  Des Moines, Iowa-State Fair   221

Chapter 22   **225**

Colby   225

  Memphis, Tennessee   225

  Atlanta, Georgia   229

  Imagine Music Festival   229

Chapter 23   **245**

Millicent   245

Chapter 24   **257**

Colby   257

Chapter 25   **265**

Millicent   265

  On the Road Again   269

  Concert Night   273

  The Trip Home   281

Chapter 26   **287**

Colby   287

Chapter 27   **293**

Millicent   293

The End   **298**

Other Books By This Author   **299**

About the Author   **301**

ANNIE MICK

Dedication

To all the talented musicians I spent years on stage with.
May the music continue to flow, your spirits continue to
fly, and your raunchy humor never die.
Stay young at heart and you will never grow old.
Break's over!

ANNIE MICK

12

"Be careful what you ask for."

I had heard it so many times throughout the years.

But had I actually listened?

Apparently not, because if I had, I wouldn't be in the spot I am.

ANNIE MICK

14

Chapter 1

Millicent

Wearing my camouflage pants, one of my popular 70s band T-shirts and clunky combat boots, I should be able to make a formidable impression on these spoiled brats. Watching from backstage for the past two hours I've observed them entertaining a crowd of ten thousand people, preempting it backstage entertaining themselves by sticking their tongues down groupies' throats as well as their hands down those same groupies' panties – making promises of delivering *(ahem)* full satisfaction upon return after the usual encores.

It seems their last two managers suddenly up and quit after the first one developed a severe gastrointestinal disorder and the second an inexplicable case of alopecia. After two hours of observation, I can pretty much guarantee the diagnoses.

The gastrointestinal disorder? Massive heartburn.

The alopecia? Self-inflicted balding brought on by yanking one's hair out due to intense frustration.

These little jackasses are totally out of control; a lawsuit waiting to happen. I watch as they jut their hips in sync, wink, and blow kisses to the young girls in the audience. I know it's all part of the show, but when one palms their crotch and feigns offering the contents like a lollipop, I've hit my limit. These boys range in age sixteen to nineteen. Hence the label 'boy band'. Where the hell are their parents!?

I look to one of the security guards off to my left. "Get the groupies out of the dressing room. Check the far corners, closets and behind the couches; they have a tendency to hide."

The pinch of his brow and drop of his jaw reveals his hesitation, but it's the quiver in his voice that exposes his fear as he replies, "They're not going to be happy about that."

Are you kidding me? The guy is six foot two, must weigh close to 250, and he's scared of a bunch of teenagers?

"Ask me how many fuc…" I sigh, reconsidering my overall approach. "Just do it. I'll deal with the band."

"It's your funeral," he mumbles as he saunters towards the dressing room.

Shouting at the top of my lungs so as not to be misunderstood, I call out after him, "As long as they play good music, I'll rest in peace!"

I sit in the dressing room patiently waiting as the boys walk in. Let me rephrase that. There is no walking with these five hooligans. They strut. They're cocky little roosters. And they're expecting the hens to be waiting for them.

Hello, boys. Meet the wolf.

"Where the fuck are the women?" Trent shouts as he glances around the room. He's the oldest of the group, apparently the most demanding as well.

"You kiss your mother with that mouth?" I snarl, my brow arched.

His eyes land on me and momentary surprise flashes before he slowly assesses me from my head to my toes. His mouth spreads in an impish grin. "I could handle kissing you, sweetheart."

"Not a fan of herpes," I reply casually. "Take a seat boys."

"What did you do with the broads?" Trevor asks, eyeing me as if I've stolen the last candy bar. He's the seventeen-year-old whose parents are on hiatus, leaving him with a so-called nanny. She's probably on the second tour bus drinking herself into a stupor so she can sleep tonight.

"The what?" I snap, shooting him a seething glare, daring him to say it twice.

"The tits and ass we had waiting for us," he replies with a devilish grin.

"Broads was disrespectful enough," I sneer. "Call them that again, and I'll make you regret it."

"Really." He laughs cockily. He leans forward as if to challenge me, tips his chin, and enunciates, "Tits and ass."

I stand and walk slowly towards him where he waits, a total babe in the woods. I grab his nipple through his shirt and twist… hard. He yelps, bends in pain and spins to release my grip. As he does, I kick his ass with the toe of my boot and watch as he flies forward and lands on the floor.

"What the hell!?!" he shrieks, sounding like a wounded child.

I glower as I inform him, "That was a purple nurple with a kick in the ass. You're lucky your bruises will be hidden for the next show."

"That was assault!" he yells, pointing his finger accusingly, eyes flaring in anger.

My cell phone in hand, I wave it in the air and offer, "I'll dial 911 for you. I can't wait to hear you explain how a *broad* pinched your *tit* and kicked your *ass*. Get off the floor, tough guy."

I look to the other four, who now stare wide-eyed. "As I said, take a seat boys."

* * *

We board the bus two hours later after having dinner together as well as a meeting where guidelines and rules were discussed. Much scoffing and many protests took place, but in the end, we came to an agreement…somewhat. They follow the rules or else.

They have no clue what the "or else" is, but then neither do I. I'll cross that bridge when I get there.

It's kind of like "shape up or ship out". Question is, ship out to where?

A little like "it's for me to know and for you to find out". Keep them guessing. The fear factor.

"I'll give you to the count of three". Did you ever let your parents get to three? My dad always gave me that little something extra; two and a half, two and three-fourths. He was a good and patient dad…and I was a petulant child. God, I miss him.

Getting these adolescents through the last leg of their tour is going to be hell for me, but if I can recall enough of my own childhood and the tactics my parents used, maybe I can get through this with my sanity intact. And if not? Well…I was halfway to Shitsville, about to cross Never Again Avenue, so I don't have much to lose.

Proceeding down the aisle of the bus, holding out the plastic trash bag in my hand, I look to Trevor. "Stuffed sock. Put it in here."

His eyes flash a deep, heated glare. "What are you talking about?"

"You know exactly what I'm talking about," I tell him as I hold the bag out closer to him. "Pull it out of your pants and put it in the bag. It's not going back up on stage with you again. You and your buddy are having a parting of the ways."

"What buddy?"

I place one hand on my hip and square him straight in the eyes. "Nobody has a ten-inch dong that hangs in one place for two hours. You're done teasing little girls. Put it in the bag, now."

He reaches into his pants, grabs his fake penis, and grumbles, "Jesus."

Smiling, I pat him on the shoulder. "Doobie Brothers, 1972! I'm so proud of you."

He shakes his head as he throws the hideous thing in the bag. "Who?"

"Oh, Trevor. Your horizons really need to be broadened." I

show him a sad smile. "I'll be sure to put on some good music for you boys to hear on a regular basis."

He narrows his eyes and tips his chin. "That's gonna mess with our mojo."

I laugh because I'll never understand how the lingo can be stretched from decade to decade while the music can be left behind.

"Trevor, we gotta get your mojo working before we can mess with it." I wink. "Get to bed."

He heads down the aisle to join the others when I hear giggling coming from the back of the bus. I push him out of the way and make my way back, whipping open the curtain of Trent's cubby.

On the bed lies a waif of a girl, probably sixteen or so, giggling as she tries to wriggle out of her top.

"Up and out," I growl as I take her arm. I shoot a hard glare at Trent whose eyes flit from me to the wall and back again before he shoots me an innocent smile.

"Where is your purse?" I ask the girl.

She giggles once again before responding, "Oh, my friend has it."

I hear whispers coming from the cubby behind me. I yank the curtain on Devlin's not-so port of refuge and see the lump under the blanket on his bed. Not certain of her stage of undress, I pull the covers down just enough to reveal the head of a blonde hiding underneath. She looks up with doe eyes, hiding a grin.

"How many clothes do you have on?" I ask her.

"Um," she whispers as she rolls her eyes and scrunches her nose. "None?"

I pull Devlin out of the cubby, unconcerned about his stage of undress. We had a meeting not an hour ago about bringing nymphettes onto the bus. Apparently, these two morons didn't get the message.

"Go get dressed," I growl in his ear. I look to the blonde. "Put your clothes back on and meet me at the front of the bus. Pronto!"

I look to Trevor. "Where are Calvin and Hobbs?" Yes, I know, you think I'm joking. I'm really not. Those are the other two band members. Brothers with very eccentric – not to mention unimaginative – parents.

"They haven't boarded yet," he answers, shrugging.

"That's it!" I scream. "You're all grounded!"

"Grounded?!" Trent yells. "You can't ground us! We're grown-ups!"

I turn around and point my finger, tempted to jab it into his chest. "Watch me you little peckerhead!"

Before I step away, the girl that was in Trent's bed starts to speak; babble really, it's inaudible.

"What's the problem?" I snap harshly.

"I gt gmmy brs stck im my teeh," she howls through a sob. More a slobber really.

"What?!" I demand, stepping forward to see she has drool dripping from the corners of her mouth…colored drool. It's now mixed with her tears.

"I gt gmmy brs stck im my teeh. Shee," she spits through drool as she points to her mouth.

The boys laugh in unison while I'm failing to find humor in any of this. I study her mouth closer and see the braces underneath the colored goo that coats them.

"She has gummy bears stuck in her teeth," Trevor informs me through his broken laughter. "Must have run out of breath mints."

Trent offers my services without hesitation. "You should probably take her in and help her out. If she flushes her mouth with hot water, it will help dissolve it. There are bathrooms inside the building."

How nice of him to offer *my* services. Did I tell you I'm not stupid? About the time I step off this bus, all band members will be safely tucked inside, and the wheels will be rolling, *without me.*

I reach forward and grab Trent by the ear and pull him off the bed. "Let's go, playboy. Your knowledge will be most useful. Seems to me you may have done this before." I continue to tug on his ear as I scream, "Devlin, get your ass out here! Now! And bring a toothbrush."

Chapter 2

Millicent

My boots clomp loudly across the shiny marble floors of the lobby as I make my way to the receptionist's desk. She smiles brightly, her teeth the perfect shade of white, her lipstick matches the bold red shade of her dress. If I spent as much time on my makeup as she obviously does hers, my day would be half over by the time I got done. Her blonde hair is wrapped in a perfect chignon bun pulled tightly to the back of her head. Why do women do this to themselves? Don't they know if you continue to pull that hair back every day it's going to fall out? Strand by strand, piece by piece into the sink, the bathtub drain, onto the carpet. It gets tied up in the roller in your vacuum and needs to be cut out with scissors; a sharp knife when that doesn't work. But I suppose we do keep the Drano and Shark vacuum companies in business. A messy bun is one thing, but plastered to your head like a skullcap? Nah, I'll pass.

"Good morning," she greets me with a smile. "May I help you?"

"Mortimer Montgomery," I answer. "Would you tell him Millie's here, please?"

She picks up the desk phone and calls upstairs. Her chat doesn't last but seconds when she tells me, "Head on up. His secreta…"

"I'll be happy to deliver her, Rebecca," a deep, smooth timbred voice offers from behind me that literally sends goosebumps rippling up my arms.

I turn to see a rather shy smile lighting the face of a most handsome man. He's tall; six feet something, which compared to my five feet five on a good day, is tall. He has stark blue eyes that aren't hidden under the cutest book-worm glasses and a slightly darker than his mussy blonde hair, well-trimmed beard. He's well built, dressed in blue jeans, a navy Henley, and tennis shoes. *Casual much?*

He shrugs one shoulder when I eye him skeptically and informs me, "I'm headed that way."

"That's quite all right, I know how to get there." I internally chastise myself immediately. My voice is harsh, and his offer is out of kindness, I'm sure. It's not his fault I'm ready to rip Morty a new one for sending me into the depths of hell babysitting Satan's spawn.

Morty's office is on the tenth floor. I've been here plenty of times, but each time brings a new challenge. Today, I'm here to challenge him.

"Would you mind company in the elevator?" he asks, his cheeks blushing the slightest tinge of pink.

I chuckle lightly. "No, I think we'll fit."

He stands with his hands in his pockets on the elevator ride up.

"So, Millie," he starts. "Is that short for something else?"

I sigh and shake my head, acquiescing. "Doesn't matter, nobody uses it."

"Millicent, perhaps?"

"Yeah," I say as the elevator doors open and we step out.

He stops and turns to me before he heads off in the opposite direction.

He smiles and tilts his head. "Maybe I'll see you around… Millicent."

Damn, my name sounds sexy when he says it. And here I

stand in ripped jeans, T-shirt, and combat boots. When's the last time I dressed like a woman? A real woman?

"Oh, I-I don't work here. I mean in…in this building," I stammer, feeling the heat in my cheeks.

His smile broadens into a glow that lights his eyes and melts my heart, or is that my panties? Who knows? It's been so long I don't know the difference.

"I know," he says softly before he takes his leave and walks away.

Nice butt, pal.

* * *

I sit in Morty's office and wait while he finishes a meeting he's currently held up in. I'm not nervous; I'm pissed. I sit back in the chair and kick my feet up; my combat boots making a thumping sound as they land on the top of his desk.

Hey, if he wanted me comfortable, he should have provided me an ottoman!

I glance around the room, admiring the many awards on the shelves; the statues from the music academies, the plaques and record label albums from the artists he's represented over the years.

He's a good guy, my Uncle Morty; a bit eccentric, a little OCD – hence my boots on his desk – and a whole lot pain in my ass; the other reason for my boots on his desk. When I came to work for him fresh out of college four years ago, after a six-year military stint, he insisted I work in the building, in an office, before I hit the road managing the bands. I suffered my penance of indoor air, girly clothes, and heels. I was dying to hit the road and manage the venues, oversee equipment setup, organize photo shoots and interviews.

Never in my wildest dreams did I anticipate babysitting Satan's minions. Nor did I anticipate stooping to itching powder, ipecac, and constipation remedies – had to make them believe they were allergic to alcohol – and confiscating condoms after making them watch STI films and Facetiming with grandmas. There is nothing more embarrassing than emotional impotence. Painting their toenails bright glitter pink while they slept was a good one as well. Let's not forget the Freddy Krueger mask and the fake tarantulas and scorpions while recording their reactions and girly screams to use as ammunition for blackmail. But you gotta do what you gotta do in dire circumstances.

"Hey, kiddo!" Morty greets me happily as he opens the door. Eyeing where my feet are currently propped, he growls, "Get your feet off my desk! God only knows what you stepped in out there on the street."

I look up with a sly smile. "Little bit of spit, a little dogshit. I brought some special, just for you."

He walks quickly to his desk and pulls a bottle of cleaner and a wipe from the bottom drawer and goes to town on the area from which I have removed my boots.

Straightening in my chair I state my case. "You owe me ten years, Morty."

He looks up from his OCD task at hand; amusement dancing in his blue eyes that matched my mom's, his handsome face edged with graying temples. "I owe you what?"

"Ten years of my life back!" I emphasize. "Those little assholes caused me probably fifty gray hairs and twenty wrinkles."

He stops what he's doing, shakes his head and laughs. "Millie, if I gave you ten years of your life back, you'd be in the midst of puberty. You really want to go through that again?"

I shoot him a look of indignance and huff, "I'll be thirty in four months, Morty. It would hardly put me back in puberty. It would put me back in the Army."

"Hmph," he grunts and studies my face in an exaggerated fashion as he tilts his head back and forth, stretching his neck. "I guess you are getting up there in years, aren't you?" He rounds his desk and sits in the chair next to me. "Damn, Millie, that's almost middle age, over the hill." He reaches out and yanks a hair out of my head.

"Ow!" I yell, reaching for my scalp. "What the hell did you do that for?"

He holds it up and examines it against the sun shining through the window. "Nope. Musta just been the way the light was shining on it. Still blonde." He reaches out again. "Here, let me pull another."

"You ass!" I shout as I slap his arm away.

"Smile for me, Millie," he snickers and grins.

"What!?"

"Smile for me," he repeats and nudges my shoulder playfully. "Come on, give it up."

"Knock it off." I nudge him back as I chuckle and a smile spreads across my face.

"There you go," he laughs and lovingly pats my head. "No wrinkles, just laugh lines."

I drop my face in my hands and groan, "Morty, please no more boy bands."

"So," he drawls. "The boys lacked maturity, huh?"

I look up at him with pleading eyes. "Morty, they lacked maturity, morality, manners…" I blow out a deep breath. "They were lovable and loathable at the same time. Give me adults, please."

He rolls his eyes. "You know loathable is not a word, don't you?"

"It is in my dictionary."

"Well, you must have done something right," he tells me, patting my leg.

"Yeah," I groan. "I got them through their tour alive and without killing them myself."

"No really," he says. "They're standing outside my door right now."

"What?"

"They want to see you."

He stands to open his door and lets in all five of the devil's spawn…Trevor, Trent, Devlin, Calvin, and Hobbs.

I really wasn't joking.

After a half hour together, we're ready to part ways and the boys give me something I'll never forget. The memory of four months of hell that I realize wasn't all bad; we did have some good times, but they also leave me with apologies from every one of them. And a thank you for putting up with them. With that thank you comes a beautiful diamond necklace with matching earrings. I'd like to think they are remorseful. And they almost have me convinced, until we do one last group hug and I feel two hands land on my ass and give it a good squeeze.

"Get out of here!" I yell to one and all.

"Purple nurple, on the house any time you're ready," Trevor yells.

"And a kick in the ass free of charge!" I yell back.

"Take care, Miss Millie," Trent says softly and winks.

The boys make their exit via the elevator. I watch as the doors close, and I close another chapter on my life.

* * *

"Okay," Morty says as he shuffles the papers on his desk. "Adults it is. I have a reunion tour I need you to oversee. Starts in a month and it lasts for six, coast to coast. These guys were pretty big in their time."

An ugly sense of apprehension makes me approach with caution. "Revival tour? What do you mean, *in their time*?"

He eyes me with a sharp severity that tells me I bit off this chunk, aka more than I can chew. "You wanted adults."

See page one…"be careful what you ask for".

Oh my God…it's a Geritol tour. MiraLAX, Metamucil, Centrum Silver move over. YeeHaw! Or is that HeeHaw? The underwear thrown on stage is going to be granny panties…with tummy control no less. This is the Spandex crowd. No thongs here people. The ladies in these crowds have spent years trying to find underwear that don't ride up the cracks of their asses. They're not stupid enough to spend money on ones that do.

"Uh, Morty," I hesitate.

"Uh, Millie," he mocks.

"Just how *adult* are these people?"

He smiles wryly. "They're not using walkers, if that's what you're asking." He mumbles quickly, "Not at the present time anyway."

"What?"

"It's the kind of music you love." He grins, his eyes lit, eyebrows arched.

"Old rock?" I ask. "No rap? No hip-hop? I can get lost in the lyrics and hear a story? Actual music?"

"One in the same," he tells me.

"Count me in," I answer, my head dancing like a bobblehead doll. My body vibrates with excitement. I picture myself backstage, hips swaying, my feet moving, fingers snapping, so lost in the music the rest of the world goes away; even if only for four minutes at a time. This is my jam.

ANNIE MICK

28

Chapter 3

Millicent

"Fourplay!?" I look at the papers in my hand again. "Are you serious?"

"Serious as a heart attack," Morty replies. "Is there a problem, Millie?"

I huff and I puff, but I don't blow the house down. "Morty! These guys are like...old!"

He sits back in his chair and folds his arms over his chest, a slow smirk tips the corner of his mouth. "And you were expecting... what? GQ models?"

"At least in the range of AARP prototypes," I shriek. "Maybe Jitterbug phone advertisers. Not representatives for retirement homes!"

"Be careful, Millie. Jumping to conclusions is the only exercise some people get. Don't be one of those people." His forehead creases as he reminds me, "You wanted adults. You got them."

"I asked for adults," I protest. "Not antiques!"

He sits up straight and points his finger while scolding me as if I were a child, "Antiques are worth their weight in gold, young lady. You will do this job and you will give it your best. That is, if you want to continue to work for me. Understand?"

I sigh in resignation. "Understand."

Morty heaves a sigh of his own before he says, "Millie, these are some of my best friends. Life isn't always about the money. Do what you love and love what you do. If you can't do what you love and have fun with it, you don't give it your best. When making music becomes a chore, it just ain't worth it."

Humbled, I meet his eyes and question, "You're talking about them, aren't you?"

"I'm talking about all of you. Have fun with this, listen to the music, let the lyrics tell you a story."

I slap my hands on my thighs as I stand to my feet. "Old farts it is."

"Hey, you little shit! They're close to my age!"

I shoot him a cocky grin. "What's your point?"

Shaking his head, he stands and waves towards the door. "Let's go meet the boys, shall we? They're waiting in the lobby."

"Boys." I giggle. "How many joint replacements are we talking here?"

He flips through some paperwork on his desk and studies the page he's looking for when he finds it. "Three hips, four knees and one shoulder."

My eyes go wide with shock…and fear. "It was a joke! I didn't really expect you to answer that."

He shrugs one shoulder. "Liability. Gotta know these things. C'mon, the guys are getting hungry."

"Lovely," I drawl. "So, do I need to schedule prostate exams, shingles vaccines? Maybe cardiology appointments? I charge extra for providing geriatric support." I giggle. "You did pack the portable defibrillator, didn't you?"

His piercing glare reveals his failure to find me funny. "Lobby…now."

"Lunch is on you today," I say, crossing the threshold.

"More likely in Duffy's beard," he mumbles.

"What's that?"

"Nothing, Millie."

In the lobby stand five gentlemen, all in different stages of the aging process, but none of whom look to be elderly in any way, shape, or form. They actually look pretty damn good . . . for a bunch of old farts.

"Morty!" shouts the one with a long white beard. "How the hell are ya?"

He reminds me a bit of one of the guys from ZZ Top – truthfully, one of two, sans the shades. He has nice eyes; I'd swear I've seen them before. He embraces Morty in a tight hug when we reach the group. The other four men wear huge, friendly smiles. They range in height anywhere from six feet to an added few inches. These guys are tall!

Morty makes the rounds, shaking hands and exchanging manly hugs with each of the men, then proceeds to introduce me to all of them.

"Gentlemen, this is my niece, Millie Trinkett," he proudly announces, his arm laid gently around my shoulder. "Millie, this is Duffy, Grady, Charlie, Bruce, and Dave."

I put my hand forth to shake theirs one at a time. As I get to the fifth one – the ZZ Top double – he pulls me to him in a bear hug and lifts me off the ground as if we're family who haven't seen each other in years – that and an air pillow as it seems effortless.

"Millie Trinkett, huh? I could almost tuck her in my pocket and carry her around. She looks like a trinket." He glances at Morty then back to me and grins. "Which do you prefer, darlin'? Millie or trinket?"

"I prefer you put me back on the floor," I growl. "And Millicent would be fine."

I hear a voice I recognize from weeks ago and suddenly develop butterflies in my stomach. "Uncle Duffy put her down. She's not a sack of potatoes."

He sets me back on my feet, but not before twirling me around and making a production of it. He kisses the top of my head and provokes once more, "She's just cute as a damn button, isn't she?" Before I can kick him in the shin, he looks to the butterfly maker.

"Cheddar cheese! How the hell are ya?" He pulls him into a hug and pats him on the back. "Lookin' good boy. Been workin' out?"

I see the butterfly maker's cheeks pink up as he nods his head and smiles. "Good to see you, Duffy. How have you been?"

Duffy struts around in a circle and slaps his right hip. "Better than the factory original. I can almost dance again." The guys all laugh in unison as they shake their heads.

"As long as you're still playing guitar," Grady says. "You'll do all right."

"Man, it was the only thing that kept me sane during rehab," Duffy replies. "I am so ready to get this show on the road."

"Aren't we all!?" Charlie agrees, a slight southern twang in a timbre so deep it's almost a growl, then he looks to me. "So, you're our road manager, are ya?"

I nod in confirmation as it's the only answer I can give at the moment; the butterfly maker has rendered me speechless.

"Millie," Duffy breaks my thoughts. "Have you met my nephew?"

"Uh…" I clumsily search for an answer. *I have, haven't I?*

"Cheddar, this is Millie," Duffy says as he waves his hand toward me. "She's our manager for the tour." *Cheddar?*

Cheddar holds his hand out to shake mine. "It's Colby." He chuckles and shakes his head as he rolls his eyes. "My uncle has a bad habit of deeming nicknames when given the opportunity. Hello, Millicent. It's good to see you again."

It's now that I realize he hasn't released my hand; from both of his. They feel warm against mine. His fingertips are slightly callused; he obviously works for a living. I feel a tingle in my fingers that works its way up my arm and creates a flushing warmth that envelops my neck and my cheeks. I feel the need to pull my hand back before I feel any more embarrassed than I already do. I shake my head slightly to release myself from my Colby-induced coma.

The guys study our short interaction with smiles plastered on their faces before heading for the door of the office building to make our way toward the restaurant for lunch.

"Is Duffy his given name?" I whisper before following them.

"Actually, it's Darwin," Colby answers with a slight chuckle.

I giggle evilly. "Oh, this could be fun. I'll have to come up with something."

"I love strategizing," he murmurs. "We'll work on it together."

"Over lunch? We won't have very long."

He smiles shyly. "I guess Morty didn't tell you. I'm part of the tour. We'll have plenty of time."

Be still my heart. I may need that defibrillator! Those fingertip calluses are from guitar strings!

Up ahead of us we hear harmony being sung by three of the band members as they make their way down the street. The Flamingo's "I Only Have Eyes for You", Art Garfunkel style. Duffy turns around and winks at us.

Oh yeah, we need to come up with something...good. The 'Grape Ape' was a cartoon around his time, wasn't it? Get ready Darwin.

ANNIE MICK

34

Chapter 4

Millicent

"So, Trinket, tell me what you have in mind for the concert in Atlanta," Duffy inquires as a drip of mustard falls off his French fry down onto his beard. Who dips their French fries in mustard? I eye it as it sits dead center top to bottom and side to side. I couldn't have been more precise if I had been aiming. My hands itch as I fight reaching out with my napkin to wipe it off. I cannot look the man in the eyes as I am homed in on that damn yellow drop of goo in his beard.

I hear Morty laugh as he sits beside me. He knows my pet peeves and he also knows how much I ache to wipe that damn drip off Duffy's beard.

Duffy picks up another fry, dips it in mustard, holds it up and tips it downward until another drop falls onto his beard before he puts it in his mouth.

Duffy looks at me with worry lines in his forehead. "Trinket? Hello, anybody in there?" he asks as he snaps his fingers in front of my face. "I asked what you have in mind for the Atlanta concert."

I feel something hit the right side of my face, then drop to my shoulder. I look to see a paper wrapper from a straw. *Grady.* I feel water splash my face from the left. *Dave.* In my periphery to the right, I see a hand reach over to my plate and snatch an onion ring.

"Sorry, sweetheart. I should have gotten the rings. Those just looked too good to pass up. You don't mind, do you?" I shoot a glare at Bruce, who's stuffing my onion ring in his mouth before I get a chance to protest.

As I'm dealing with Bruce, in my periphery to the left, I see the other half of my corned beef sandwich disappear as a hand removes it from my plate. I watch as Charlie takes an enormous bite out of it and grin.

In the midst of chewing, he holds it in the air. "Did you want it back? You're so tiny I figured there's no way you could eat the whole thing."

I feel Uncle Morty's shoulders rocking against mine as he laughs. I turn slowly, my eyes filled with anger, my jaw clenched as my nostrils flare. "You told them my pet peeves, didn't you?"

1. I am Joey Tribbiani on steroids. I don't share my food!
2. Don't talk with food in your mouth.
3. Use a damn napkin!
4. Don't shoot straw papers; your spit is in there!
5. Don't splash your water from a drinking glass. That's backwash water. Ewww!

He shakes his head, continuing to laugh. "You might as well get used to it."

"You told me they were adults," I growl, sneering at the others.

"They are!" Morty exclaims, giggling like a little boy. "Look at them!"

I eye each man sitting at the table; they grin like clowns. I avoid the eyes of my butterfly maker. "They're overgrown children!"

"You said nothing about maturity, Millie." He puts his arm around my shoulder and kisses my temple. He leans in close and whispers in my ear, "Lose the camouflage pants and combat boots.

Three of these guys are vets. They don't need to be reminded...and neither do you." I swallow hard as my stomach bottoms out.

A fresh plate of my same order arrives at the table. Now I feel like shit. They had it planned all along.

I hold the plate up and offer something to everyone. "Dig in, guys. There's no way I can eat all this." I watch as Duffy wipes his beard with a wet napkin and cleans every last bit of mustard off. I feel one more straw paper hit me in the middle of the forehead. I shoot a glare at Colby, the guilty party.

He shrugs, an impish grin lights his face. "Couldn't help myself. Wanted to know if it was as fun as they made it seem."

"And?" I ask.

He nods and winks. "It was."

Will somebody bring that damn defibrillator, please???

"Morty, you did get those Pop Tarts ordered, right?" Duffy asks him.

"Four cases, came direct yesterday," Morty answers. "They'll be on the bus."

"What?" My eyes flit back and forth between the two of them. "Pop Tarts? Four cases?" *Lovely...Old farts and Pop Tarts. I can see the logo on the bus now.*

Duffy hums, "Two blueberry, a strawberry and a cherry. Gotta have our Pop Tarts, Trinket."

"Would you not call me that?" I huff.

"Why not?" He grins mischievously.

"Why?" I ask, just because.

He shrugs. "A trinket is a treasure." His eyes flash to Colby's and he winks. "And when you find one, you hang onto it." He stands and stretches. "Three days before we roll. I gotta see my urologist and orthopedic surgeon before we leave." He turns to the others who are rising from the table, leaving tips, and gathering their jackets. "You guys all caught up on your doc appointments and have your med refills?"

"We're covered, Duff," Grady tells him. "Morty all but made us sign our lives away."

"See you at practice tomorrow," he tells them with a wave.

He stops before reaching the door. "Trinket, feel free to join us." He laughs loudly and nods. "Old farts and Pop Tarts. Has a nice ring to it."

Oh my God! Had I said that out loud?

Chapter 5

Colby

I shouldn't take it so hard that she doesn't remember me. We'd only met once before, and it was years ago; eleven to be precise. Well, eleven for a normal man, eternity for me. It was her sendoff party before she entered the Army. I pondered for hours finding a way to kiss her goodbye; a proper send off. Everybody else was doing it. Couldn't hurt for me to slip one in. But I never got the chance.

I wasn't terrified *of* her; I was terrified *for* her. I was a software engineering student with two years of college under my belt, back for the summer, ready to spend it doing studio musician gigs for her uncle Morty. There must have been over a hundred people at that party and Millicent was already lost in the crowd. She had a lot on her mind and Morty was trying to ease it by giving her a happy send off with people who loved her. And within two minutes of meeting her, I think I became one of those people.

Morty had raised Millicent for the prior five years after her parents died in a car accident. Uncle Duffy told me all about it and since he hadn't been able to attend the party due to emergency gallbladder surgery, he asked me to go in his absence. Our introduction was cut short by an obnoxious partygoer who interrupted, and we never got back to conversation with each other. I wanted to tell her I would make arrangements to see her whenever she had leave, that I would meet her in any town, in any country when she had time off, but I never got the chance. As I watched her interact with the other partygoers – this beautiful, fiery, pint-sized marvel – I realized she would forever be etched in my mind…and my heart. She was a flavor I never got to taste.

One of my biggest regrets in life was not kissing Millicent Trinkett goodbye before she left for the Army.

Since then, I've spent my years developing software programs and traveling all over the world as a musician; perfectly content being in the background, both as a business partner and part of the band.

When Uncle Duffy called and asked if I was interested in being part of this reunion tour, I almost laughed. In fact, I'm sure I did; just not out loud. I was in Europe finishing a four-month stint and ready to come home for a much-needed rest. I love my Uncle Duffy. You won't find a nicer, or funnier, guy on the planet. But a reunion tour…at his age? The only factory original part left in my uncle is his sense of humor. Well, that and his heart.

Which would explain why I'm here.

My uncle has been through a lot. He's a veteran who's spent a lot of time helping other vets who didn't make it through unscathed by the ravages of war. That's not to say my uncle made it through unscathed. He treats his wounds by helping others; thereby preventing his own scars from splitting open. He was one of the last group of soldiers to come home from Vietnam. The man is solid as a rock, a bit dented and scratched, but one hell of a musician who loves to rock and roll. At the age of 65, he can outdo most 30-year-olds on and off stage despite a few joint replacements and a couple of wrinkles. Okay, maybe more than a couple, but he still looks pretty damn good for his age and for what he's been through. He's a vast table of knowledge and wisdom and would be the perfect research point for writing one of those bathroom books of little-known facts. Trivia is his game and Darwin is his name. And what fun we're going to have. *Poor Millicent.*

She's the other reason I'm here. When Duffy told me she was managing the tour, I was in…hook, line, and sinker. And he knew it.

I was amazed to learn she was still single, not to mention willing to travel with a bunch of old codgers wanting to relive their youth.

That day in the lobby, I knew it was her at first glance. Those ridiculous little combat boots. Hell, I knew it was her by the sound of her voice; airy and sexy, sending goosebumps up my arms. Wild silky blonde hair, blue eyes that pierce your heart with a glare as fast as they melt it with a shy glance, a smile that lights up a room, and that little nose that crinkles the tiniest bit with her smile.

Yup, that's Millicent Trinkett. Talent from her forehead to her chin. Bringing men to their knees since 1991; me to mine since 2010.

Gonna have to get that girl some new boots. Damn, I'll bet her toes are pretty.

ANNIE MICK

Chapter 6

Millicent

"This should be everything, Millie," Uncle Morty reassures me, handing over the black Amex and an envelope of cash. We're standing at the door of the bus loaded to kingdom come with every luxury a person could ask for. A second bus sits behind this one; full of equipment and roadies. Morty must be bankrolling this and I'm sure it's costing a fortune.

He places a reassuring hand on my shoulder. "The guys have done this a million times. They know what they're doing. If you have any questions, don't be afraid to ask."

I shake my head and roll my eyes. "I've done it a time or ten myself, Morty. I know what I'm doing, too."

"I have no doubts, sweetheart." He nods encouragingly. "I just want you to know you can trust every one of these guys with your life. All concerts have been set up with as short a distance in between as possible and plenty of time to travel. The longest distance is from Nashville to Atlanta; and I have you set up in a hotel for two nights. One night before and one the night of."

"That sounds fantastic." I sigh with relief. "No hopping on the bus immediately after. I can crash in a comfy bed."

"What are you talking about?" he asks, his brows furrowed.

"You've got the master suite at the back of the bus. The best mattress money can buy."

"The private bedroom…in the back?" I point to the rear of the bus.

"Yes, Millie."

"But Morty," I protest with a whisper. "These guys are old! I shouldn't be sleeping in luxury and leaving them in the equivalent of bunkbeds." I wave my hands before I run them through my hair. "They're going to be too stiff to perform. Their backs are going to give out." I finish on a mumble, "Hell, their bones probably creak."

Morty heaves a sigh and narrows his eyes. "Young lady, if you make it three days into this tour without having your ass paddled…"

It's a joke. I've never been spanked in my life.

I gasp. "They wouldn't dare!"

He lifts a single eyebrow. "I've never seen you like this. What has you in such a tizzy?" His eyes light with a smile. "Or should I ask who?"

"I have no idea what you're talking about." I glance around us, pretending to assure things are in place and ready to roll.

He tips my chin up between his thumb and forefinger and grins. "Millie, I could assign you an ass-paddler."

Slapping his shoulder and frowning, I groan, "Not funny, Uncle Morty."

"Millie." He sighs. "Would you just breathe? Enjoy this. The guys put you in the back for privacy…and because they snore like freight trains." He laughs and shrugs. "And fart… a lot. What can I say?"

"Oh my God," I groan. "I'd better go before this gets any worse."

He kisses me on the forehead and hugs me goodbye. "Be good, baby girl. Call me if you need anything. I love you. I'll meet you in Atlanta."

"Thank you, Morty. I love you, too." I step onto the bus and look back one more time.

"Hey, Millie," he says, grinning. "I'm not privy to his ass-paddling skills, but I'd check out his ass-kissing skills first. You deserve the best. Don't you dare settle for less." He winks before the door closes.

I've spent the last few weeks gearing up for this trip. No more camouflage, no more combat boots. Yes, I can dress like a woman; I simply prefer comfort. I can manage that with leggings, T-shirts, a couple pairs of sandals and tennis shoes for travel. But I also found I can maintain a certain level of comfort with a few sexy outfits paired with low heeled ankle boots for show nights. I even brought make up and a curling and flat iron. Proud of me? Don't hold your breath just yet. I still have my hairbands to throw in a messy bun on lazy days and shorts and tank tops for PJs. Nope, no sexy lingerie. Okay, okay, only three sets to go with my sexy outfits…maybe four. Or was that five? Whatever the case may be, it's all brand new.

Sandy, our bus driver looks up with a smile. "You ready?" He's a friendly sort, about 40 or so, trim, clean cut. He and John will be sharing the load of carting us from place to place.

"As I'll ever be," I answer and make my way down the middle of the bus where I find the table surrounded by six men sitting together, laughing, and talking excitedly about the first concert coming up in five days.

Milwaukee, Wisconsin.

Ticket sales already at 6800.

Maybe they haven't been forgotten.

"Okay," I address them, eyeing each of them one by one. "Just one question before we get this show on the road."

"What would that be, Trinket?" Duffy grins, testing my reaction with his chosen nickname for me.

Ignoring his teasing, I pose my question. "Fourplay. I get the play on words, sexual innuendo and all, but there are five original members. Can none of you count?"

They all look to one another and laugh. Grady starts with, "One, two, three, four."

All five voices boom together as they sing Pink Floyd, "We Don't Need No Mathematics".

You caught that, right? Play on words?

I roll my eyes and smirk. "Apparently you don't need no education either, huh?"

"Ohhh," Bruce hums as he waggles his eyebrows. "We were educated all right. Weren't we guys?"

"Best damn math teacher a boy could ask for," Dave sighs, his eyes twinkling, chin in his hand. "Lois Carmen Denominator. 36 double D…"

"Twenty something waist with the cutest little belly button," Charlie interrupts.

"And…" Duffy adds, "…those little bulldogs that wrestled with every step."

I see Colby lower his head to avoid eye contact and watch Grady's mouth twitch at one corner.

"Bulldogs?" I inquire.

"Butt cheeks," Duffy quips, cupping his hands, palms up, mimicking motions of balancing a scale. "Honest to God. When the woman walked, it looked like two little bulldogs wrestling in a gunnysack. What do you call those mini bulldogs?"

"Frenchies?" I reply without hesitation.

He groans, "Well, now you make it sound dirty. That's just not right, Trinket. Way to spoil a young man's fantasy." He shakes his head in disappointment.

My cheeks grow hot with embarrassment as my jaw goes slack. Did I really ruin a young boy's memory? I see five mouths spread in huge grins before these overgrown children break out in laughter…at my expense.

I reach out and pull the bandana off Duffy's head. Underneath lies a balding scalp while the lower half nurses a braid that reaches halfway down his back.

"When's the last time you had a haircut?" I growl.

"I ain't cut this hair in twenty years!" he snaps.

"If you can't grow it on top, *Darwin*," I narrow my eyes, "you've lost the battle. It looks like a monkey's tail."

He smiles, his teeth a glowing shade of white, his eyes twinkling. "Sassy. I like it. Would you prefer I call you that instead?"

I glare.

He smiles.

I glare harder.

He smiles brighter.

I narrow my eyes.

He winks.

I growl.

He laughs.

The man is contagious. He's like sprinkles on ice cream, a rainbow in the midst of a storm. He's sunshine and lollipops.

Try as I may, I can't hold my giggle in. "You're impossible," I tell him once I've calmed. "There aren't many like you."

"Sure ain't. I'm from hell. Population 317. You should visit sometime," he tells me. "My mama's there."

"Duffy!" I gasp. "That's a terrible thing to say about your mother!"

He shrugs. "What? She loves it there. Peaceful, quiet."

"Hell is not a quiet place, Duffy. And I'm sure the population is greater than 317."

"I didn't say hell," he says slowly, "I said hey-ll. Hale, Iowa. Population 317. And yes, my mama is there and very happy." He grins as he tips his chin. "Ornerier than a gnat on a monkey's butt, too."

Once again, I hear laughter from the group around the table. I take a few deep breaths and blow them out slowly.

I pat him on the shoulder. "Well, we all know where that gnat landed, don't we? Hope he doesn't bite you too hard, Darwin." I turn to make my way back to the bedroom to unpack my things.

"Hey, Trinket," he calls after me. "How do you know hell isn't a quiet place?"

I spin back and shoot him a wry smile. "You guys make too much noise."

"You're gonna grow to love us!" Charlie shouts.

My eyes meet Colby's, and something happens in that very moment. I'm not sure what it is. Could be hunger, but I don't hear my stomach growl. Could be thirst, but my mouth isn't dry. Could be heat, but I'm not sweating. Could be cold, but I'm not shivering. Ahhh…it's tingles. It's a spinal rush that spreads from the base all the way up and over the top of my head. It almost makes me dizzy.

My eyes never leaving his, I nod slowly. "Anything's possible." Colby winks and smiles, making my heart flutter. I brace my hand on the wall in order to maintain balance and turn slowly to make my way back to my room, fanning my face once I'm out of their sight. "Holy crap," I mutter to myself. "Where did they pack that damn defibrillator?"

* * *

"Millie!" Bruce yells from the short passage leading back to my room. "We're stopping for dinner. You hungry yet?"

"I'll be right out," I reply, gathering my sandals from the side of the bed.

Upon arriving to the middle of the bus moments later, I see them gathered around the table again, and feel the bus pulling to a stop. We're four hours into our destination and surprisingly, my stomach is calling for food. When Morty indicated our longest leg of the journey was from Nashville to Atlanta, he actually meant once the shows started. Our longest jaunt is from our starting point – Los Angeles – to Milwaukee. Now, by my calculations, that is virtually three-fourths of the distance across the country. Over 2000 miles of travel, seven people on the same bus, nine if you count our drivers, and five days to get there. All about acclimation. We become accustomed to the travel, get used to each other, and work out any kinks in the system.

After four hours on the bus, I'm becoming well aware the only one needing acclimation is me. These guys blend better than bread and butter. They finish each other's sentences, their harmonies are spot-on, they each know the others' histories. If I didn't know better, I would swear they're brothers. Brothers who don't argue. I've yet to see one of them frown. If one hits the wrong chord on the guitar, another will correct in a round-about way that never insults the other. They build each other up, brick by brick, and loyalty is the mortar that holds them together.

"So, Millie, you like Mexican food?" Dave inquires, rising from his seat at the edge of the table.

"Mexican food?" I ask slowly. I hear my own low whimper as I recall Morty's warning, 'and fart…a lot'. I think about the two windows I have on the back of the bus in my private room. But there's no cross ventilation, and if they open one on the side of the bus while it's moving, it will push all that air towards the back, forcing it to waft through my room on its way out. My room will become the quiet place where farts go to die, to rest in peace, and I, Millicent Trinkett, will spend the next six months in a gas chamber. Talk about crapital punishment! Maybe I can put a towel across the threshold to prevent it from seeping in.

"It's our favorite," Duffy cheers. "Hot sauce too. Keeps the pipes clean and the blood flowing freely."

Oh my God. What else is it going to make flow freely?

"Uh, I would have taken you all for the steak and baked potato types." I wince, my hopes dwindling as I watch them exchange glances.

Charlie pats his stomach. "We save that kind of food for show nights. Don't want to be too gassy up on stage. It's hard to sit at the drums when your belly's bloated."

"But you're okay with being gassy on the bus?" I frown, hoping he'll take a hint.

Dave laughs. "Honey, this is home away from home. When you gotta blow, you gotta blow. Otherwise, you get all crampy."

I feel Colby's hand reach for the back of my neck, and he gently leads me towards the front of the bus. "Let's go, Millicent. The longer you indulge them, the worse it gets."

I get lost in the feel of his hand on my neck. It's not controlling; it's almost protective. I want him to tug on my hair, lean my head back and kiss me. I don't care who's watching. He leans down close – *I think he's going to nibble my ear!* I feel his warm breath tickle my neck and I nearly melt before he whispers, "I stashed some Beano on the bus."

Well, there went that lady boner.

I nearly groan out loud in frustration. But instead I snap, "We're still stopping for Gas-X. I'm taking no chances."

I nearly hop to get a few paces in front of him as I rush to get off the bus and head to the restaurant, pulling the door open and stepping inside.

"The Gas and Bass Company" Best Mexican food and fish tacos north of the border

Chin up Millie. At least it's not a combination restaurant/ bait and tackle shop.

Chapter 7

Colby

What?! I was trying to ease her unease. I wanted her to know I was thinking ahead. I know how bad it can get with a bunch of guys on a bus; uncouth, lax in manners, ass and ball scratchers, belchers, breaking wind without a second thought. My uncle and his buddies will be considerate, but let's face it, every single one of them – no pun intended – have lived alone for a long time. Having a woman around is not something they're accustomed to. Not that I'm an expert. I was raised with two sisters and there was always my mom, but she's not around to snap me with a dishtowel to prevent me from screwing up on this trip. Don't get me wrong, my mother did it only with love in her heart and a sense of obligation to the woman I would someday spend the rest of my life with. She still does it on occasion, just for shits and giggles, but the woman can snap a dishtowel faster and harder than an expert chef and you don't want to be on the receiving end of it.

She's my uncle Duffy's sister and she can put him in line with a single glare. If you want to see a man brought to his knees in ten seconds or less, watch my mother put Duffy in a headlock. Duffy's mantra? "Unhappy ladies make for a life in Hades".

And yes, I do hail from Hale, IA. Population 317. At least it was in 2018. Not sure what it is today. One bar where the farmers come in for lunch wearing boots that smell like pig shit, a feed store, one itty bitty grocer, a community center, etc. etc. But the people are friendly; or were years ago. I haven't been back there since I can't remember when. We moved when I was fifteen and I see my grandmother as often as possible on Facetime and when they drive her to Des Moines for family reunions.

No, I've been alone and on my own for a long time, traveling the world as a musician and sowing all those wild oats everyone talks about. I'm no saint but I'd like to think I'm not the devil's spawn either.

Telling her I stashed Beano on the bus. Could I have been any stupider? I had my hand on the back of her neck. I was touching Millicent Trinkett! And my topic of conversation was prevention of farts. I may as well have said, *"stick with me, I'm fart-free"*. Maybe *"You want to go for a walk in the morning and get coffee with me? They should have the bus fumigated by the time we get back?"*

Smooth, Colby, real smooth. Even in my head, feeling like an idiot, I come up with flatulent pick-up lines. My inner child is laughing while the cupid on my shoulder is calling me a dumbass. I can't get far enough away from the thoughts of gastrointestinal functions to chastise myself for being a total klutz around Millicent. I palm-slap my forehead and groan before opening the door of the restaurant.

"What's the matter, Norway?" Grady asks as I hold the door open for him.

"I…uh…forgot something on the bus," I stutter as I hand off the door to Charlie who follows him.

"You sure they're on the bus, boy?" Charlie grins knowingly. "Check both your pants pockets. I usually find mine sittin' somewhere in between them."

That's Charlie for you. Gruff, to the point, but charming in his own way. Hair as white as Santa Claus with a short beard and mustache to match, but he still looks to be in his fifties. Fit, healthy, takes no shit from anybody, and a voice that sounds like he breathes fire.

Standing at the door of the bus, I take a few long, slow, deep breaths. Why does the woman make me so nervous? Because she's perfect, that's why. Well, perfect for me anyway. Fine. Fish tacos it is, no hot sauce, no beans on the side.

Oh, and Norway? My father was Norwegian; last name Jarlsberg, just like the cheese. I'm an American slice of Colby and a block of Norwegian Jarlsberg. And yet, Duffy calls me Cheddar and Grady calls me Norway. Yeah, these guys are a laugh a minute.

Upon entering the restaurant, I hear my name shouted from the back corner where I see the entire group sitting at a table, drinks in hand and chips with salsa in separate bowls spread across the table.

"I already ordered you a beer, unless you want a fru-fru drink like Trinket here," Duffy says as I take a seat next to Millicent, which just so happens to be the only open seat left.

I glance at the drink in front of the gem next to me and see a giant margarita with salt on the rim.

"Fru-fru?" I laugh. "Duffy, there's more alcohol in there than you'll be getting in four of your beers. That's tequila."

He looks to Millicent and winks. "I know. She's got about three to go so they can get to the bottom of the bottle. They're saving the worm for me."

Millicent rolls her eyes and groans, "There's no worm, Duffy. I specified Patron."

"I had them transfer the little critter while you weren't looking," he informs her. I know he's joking but Millicent eyes him warily. Three more of those and I'll be carrying her back to the bus…comatose. I pick up the menu and scan for the fish tacos. *I hate fish tacos.*

"What are we eating?" I ask, studying the menu. God knows why I bother; there are only two choices for fish tacos. *Blech and blech.*

"I'm getting the enchiladas," Dave tells me.

"Same here," Bruce chimes. "Super-size. I'm starved."

The guys converse back and forth, discussing appetizers.

I watch Millicent break a chip in half, dip it in salsa and

place it in her mouth. She chews slowly as if not to make any crunching noise, and I see her swallow. She reaches for her drink and sips from the rim, washing down the remnants of chip. Every move is deliberate and dainty, and I find myself lost in Millicent Trinkett's world of mastication and drinking. I'll bet her salty lips with a touch of margarita would taste fantastic.

Breaking everyone's train of thought; the waitress appears at the table. "What can I get you gentlemen to eat?"

"Millie, ladies first," Dave tells her as he directs a frown at the waitress. I hadn't been paying attention, but apparently the waitress wasn't following protocol.

Blushing, the waitress answers, "Oh, I didn't see her over there."

"How'd you miss her?" Grady huffs. "She's the cutest damn thing at the table?"

"I'd have to agree." The whispered words spill from my mouth like whiskey from the bottle.

Millicent's cheeks flush as she rolls her eyes and spots us all a wry grin. "Guys, the competition isn't all that stiff." She hands the waitress her menu. "The trio special please, with extra guac and a side of sour cream. And don't worry about it; I'm a little fish in a big pond."

The waitress winks at her. "Quite a lake you're swimming in, honey." She turns to me. "How 'bout you handsome?"

I hear Millicent growl softly next to me, "Little fish still have big stingers, *honey.*"

I spread my arm across the back of her chair. "I think first up, Millicent needs another margarita and I'll have the fish tacos." *Chivalry is not dead.*

Millicent's head whips toward me. "Fish? No one should eat fish in a Mexican restaurant." She grins mischievously as she waves her finger from one end of our table to the other, circling back to me. "You realize no one's going to know who the guilty party is come morning, don't you?"

Matching her smile and nodding, I turn back to the waitress and place my order. "Put a two by hers. We're having the same thing."

OLD FARTS AND POP TARTS

* * *

The first night sleeping on the bus is a piece of cake for me; I'm used to it. We have two drivers assigned to each bus. Federal law limits the number of hours each can drive in a 24-hour period so Morty assured travel was safe, within legal limits, and we have plenty of time to rest easy in between each concert.

I exit my cubby to find no one else awake yet. I detect snoring coming from two of the cubbies: Bruce's and Charlie's. I head to the bathroom to relieve myself, elated to find I don't have to fight for a spot as the others haven't risen from peaceful slumber. Millicent was gifted a bathroom of her own. None of us minded…at all. We're guys. We can pee into a bowl at the same time if forced to. Mind you, if the bus were moving, it might be a bit of a challenge – cross streams and all – but sharing for us is no imposition. And this bus is pure luxury. I've never been on one quite this comfortable. Morty really went all out.

Finding my way around the kitchen area, I'm able to make coffee in the special 12-cup machine encompassing a thermal no-spill pot and find the infamous Pop Tarts to place in the toaster. Grateful for generators to power the machines on the go I'm able to enjoy coffee, and the thermal pot keeps it hot while I wait for the late sleepers to rise and shine.

In my periphery I catch motion as Millicent's door opens and I see her walk towards me. She's in a tank top and shorts and her hair is wild – a perfect display of bed head and *Too Many Margaritas*.

"Coffee?" she groans, her voice even raspier than usual.

I can't hide my smile.

"Is that your hair of the dog?" I ask sympathetically. "I could come up with a better remedy. We have some whiskey and cream and I saw some honey in the…."

"Coffee," she rasps. "Black, hot. No hair, no dog. Please hurry."

I pour her half a cup so as not to spill it and carefully hand it to her. As I do, I glance at her bare feet. Just as I thought; *Millicent Trinkett has very pretty toes.*

"What is that godawful…" She wrinkles her nose in disgust as she raises her free hand to cover it.

Since I've slept in the same quarters all night, I must have become accustomed to whatever unpleasant odor has struck her olfactory sense.

She turns to rush back to her quarters, and I watch that cute little butt bounce with every step. She yells over her shoulder, "Tell the driver to find the nearest KOA campgrounds and pull over. Open some windows!" She slams her door shut and I hear her scream of frustration from the other side as well as some awfully nasty swear words. Who would have thought Millicent Trinkett had such a potty mouth? Odd as it may sound, it makes the pint-sized little fireball even more attractive than she was five minutes ago. Odder still, I think I'm finding grumpy Millicent rather hot.

I walk to the front of the bus, open the partition, and ask our driver, Sandy, to search for the nearest KOA and make a pitstop.

"I heard her loud and clear." He laughs. "It's half hour away. Close the partition, please. In kind of in a hurry myself."

Approximately thirty minutes later we pull into the KOA campground in Utah where Sandy finds our reserved area. Arrangements had obviously been previously made as there are four spots marked reserved and they are all ours, accommodating space for both buses.

* * *

All windows on the buses are open. Water hookups were done once the roadies got the lines in the campgrounds flushed to be assured the water ran clear from the spigots.

All the guys are having coffee at the table, and I've already fixed the third pot. Pop Tarts are finished, and Duffy, saving half of the second one, as always, to take outside to feed to the birds. Don't ask me why…it's his ritual.

The eggs and bacon are almost ready, the toast sits in the

warmer. How I ended up being the cook this morning is beyond me, other than the fact that I really want to be the one to take a plate back to Millicent and make her smile. I heard the water to her shower shut off and felt the water pressure increase in the kitchen a while ago so she should be dressed and ready to eat soon. I plate hers first and fill a fresh cup of coffee.

Looking to the five bright-eyed, grinning faces as they watch me turn towards Millicent's room I say, "Serve yourselves. You have cleanup duty." Pausing one last time, "There's Febreeze in the closet. Use it."

Upon reaching her door I realize my hands are full and I can't knock so I tap the bottom of the door with my foot. It's more of a thud, but it works.

"Millicent, I have breakfast for you. Would you open the door, please?"

She still sounds a bit grumpy, but her volume has come down a few decibels. "Cherry, strawberry or blueberry?"

Chuckling, I answer, "Cheesy, porky and toasty."

She opens the door slowly and takes in the sight before her. "And more coffee?" she asks sheepishly.

Her hair is wet, no makeup, she wears a T-shirt, shorts and sandals. She a natural beauty. But when those blue eyes fly open my way, I nearly drop the plate in my hand. She reaches for the coffee first.

"Oh my God! I love you," she groans as she raises it to her mouth. Realizing her blunder, she blushes and fumbles, "Y-you… you know what I mean. I mean the coffee. I-I was dying for coffee and…I usually drink like three cups before I even breathe and…I couldn't breathe out there and…"

My mouth twitches as I do my best not to laugh at her. It's nice to know I'm not the only one who can trip over their own tongue. I want so much to let her babble. It's quite the picture; the contrast of the pink in her cheeks to the hue of sapphire blue in the brightest eyes I've ever seen.

"Well, if coffee can make you love me…" I hold out the plate and smile, "…let's see what breakfast can do."

"Have you had yours?" she asks, taking the plate from me. "No, not yet."

She worries her brow as her mouth twists. "You need to eat, Colby."

"I will. I needed to make sure you got yours." I turn to head back to the main area.

"Wait," she says, stepping over to the nightstand, setting the plate and cup down. She rushes back to where I wait, stands on her tiptoes, reaches behind my neck and pulls me down to leave a soft kiss on my cheek. My hands automatically land on her hips, but it's over much too soon. She pulls back and looks up at me and my hands fall back to my sides.

She smiles, her eyes twinkling. "That's for breakfast."

Stunned, I nod and rub the back of my neck. "Uh, the bus is aired out so it should be safe to come out when you're done… anytime."

I see her shoulders sag as she blows out a breath. "Yeah, okay. I'll see you later."

She kisses my upper cheek and I gotta talk about what blows between the bottom two. Flatulence! Beans…the musical fruit. Way to go, Colby. I wonder if my uncle and his buddies like tofu?

Arriving back to the kitchen area, I see two asses trying to hurriedly slide back into the seating area and five sets of eyes studying me.

Charlie is the first to speak. "Apparently you didn't check them pockets like I told you."

"Colby, when she thanks you like that for breakfast you tell her you'll bring her lunch and dinner. What the hell's wrong with you?" Dave snorts and rolls his eyes.

"Lighten up, gentlemen. He's a rookie," Bruce tells them. "He'll learn."

"Not at this rate," Grady grumbles. "Norway, when they offer you ice cream you gotta take a lick."

"Did you take her a Pop Tart?" Duffy asks, amused.

I glare as I answer, "No, Duffy, I didn't take her a Pop Tart."

He lifts his hands and laughs. "There ya go. Problem solved.

Take her dessert."

"What I'm going to take is a run." I grab my duffle bag from my cubby. Turning back to the group of disheveled men still laughing at my expense. "And when you've finished cleaning up, I would recommend you all take a shower. It smelled like an outhouse in here this morning." I toss my duffle bag at their feet. "Bring this with you. I'll grab my shower when I'm done with my run."

"Hey, Colby," Charlie calls out when I'm about to step off the bus.

"What?"

"I'll bet you can find them in the shower if you look hard enough. There's a pool cue sits right above 'em that…"

"Screw you, Charlie."

I can still hear the raucous laughter when I'm many steps away from the bus as I hang my head in shame. Well, not shame as much as embarrassment. I'm not shy, I'm not even an introvert really. I simply cannot gather my bearings whenever I'm around Millicent. And when she reached to give me a kiss? It was totally unexpected. So now I'll know; expect the unexpected.

ANNIE MICK

Chapter 8

Millicent

"The bus is all aired out. You should be safe to come out anytime," I sneer like a whiney child as I mimic Colby. I throw my wet towel over the shower rack to dry out and put my soap, shampoo and conditioner back in the case, so they don't roll around during travel.

Let them use the community showers! I hope they all slip on a bar of soap. The bus smelled like rotten eggs this morning. Mexican food is now a verboten menu item for the rest of this tour unless they will be spending the night in a hotel room – or tents. The rest of this tour. HA! We haven't even started it.

For guys who are so nice and polite, not to mention complimentary, they sure do have gastric problems. First on my to-do list: change their dietary habits. Second: stop thinking about Colby Jarlsberg as anything more than a friend. How could I have been so stupid as to kiss him? Talk about shell shock. The poor man looked like he'd been attacked by his cousin. Cousins toss their arms around your shoulders like buddies. They place their hand on your neck like they're leading a horse to water. They lay their hand on the back of your chair just to get comfortable. They study your face to see if your table manners are up to par. Oh my

God! That's all it was. He was just a guy spreading out to get comfortable. He's tall, his arms are long, as are his legs. He wasn't touching my shoulder or gently caressing my skin. I am such an idiot. I will never pick up a romance novel again for the rest of my life! Alpha males be damned. You don't exist in real life. Not in my life anyway. I may be small but I'm tough. I can handle myself quite well. Who needs tall, blonde and handsome with a smile that sends signals to my nether regions? Not to mention that butt like granite. Well, I need it but…

I wait until they've all exited the bus before I slip on my running shoes and leave my room. I'm going for a quick run before we have to hit the road again. The park and campground are perfect for it. Tall trees, fresh air, a nice path that's even and smooth. I take off at a medium pace, intending to work up to a fast run, slowing down to a walk before I'm done. I'm nearing the men's shower house when I hear Charlie's booming voice ring all the way outside:

"I love to go swimming with bowlegged women
And swim between their legs"

Colonel Potter from M*A*S*H* sang that song once. I remember seeing that episode. I laugh to myself. I don't want to picture a naked Charlie, but somehow, I can see his face, smiling and bobbing his eyebrows.

The next voice I hear is Bruce's. Don't ask me why I've stopped pacing my run, why I've stopped moving completely.

"I saw her snatch…
Her suitcase from the window
I held her but…
A moment in the rain
I kissed her ass…
She started for the station
To see her boyfriend…
Jack off…
On the train"

That has to be one of the crudest ditties I've ever heard. Yet, if someone tried to call him out on it, he could deny it wholeheartedly…with a cocky smile.

I shake my head, my jaw nearly unhinged. My Uncle Morty has some really crazy…and dirty… friends. Why did I not know this until now?

I feel an arm come around me from behind and a finger near my chin. Automatic reflex kicks in and I hit with a hard elbow to his ribs and before I take him down with a spin kick, I realize it's Colby.

"What the hell are you thinking, Colby?" I shriek. "Don't ever sneak up on me like that!"

The poor guy is bent in half trying to catch his breath while he holds his ribs. He's in a T-shirt and running shorts, apparently coming back from his own run in the park. He's sweaty, his shirt is soaked, and his skin is glistening.

"Holy shit, fireball!" he grunts through heavy breaths. "I was gonna close your mouth before a fly got in. It was a joke." He winces when he looks up. "I forgot you're military. I should have known better."

I step forward and place my arm around his waist. "C'mon. I'll help you."

He steps away from me, trying once again to catch a deep breath, and holds a hand up. "I'm fine. Need a shower."

I watch as he walks slowly toward the showers, still holding his ribs, until I do the only thing I can. I take off in the other direction and run.

I'm mad at him for being so stupid as to approach me from behind without speaking. I'm mad at myself for not being more aware of my surroundings. I'm mad at me for kissing him this morning and thinking he might be the slightest bit attracted to me. I'm mad at me for being stupid, stupid Millie Trinkett who's never had a boyfriend and doesn't have the slightest idea how to be or act like a real woman. I hate the fact that I've had to watch You Tube videos to know how to apply makeup and how to put my hair in a messy bun the proper way, research the best birth control; not that I've ever needed it. I'm just glad my mom was still alive when I got my period. Imagine the horror if my Uncle Morty had had to deal with that. I had to look up the latest fashions to know what to buy for this stupid, stupid tour because I had to throw out my camouflage. I'm traveling with three veterans that don't need to be reminded of the hell they went through.

And before I realize it, I'm wiping stupid, stupid tears away from my eyes because the breeze won't dry them up fast enough. And the faster they fall, the faster I run.

I've gone off the beaten path, into the woods along the rim of the park, and making my way back to the trail meant for walkers and runners when I hear panicked voices.

"Trinket!"

"Millie!"

Duffy is calling from one direction while Grady is calling from another. Good grief, I've only been gone an hour.

Then I hear Colby shout, "Millicent! Where the hell are you?"

"I'm right here," I quicken my pace and call out. As I appear from the edge of the woods, I see Grady scanning the area, worried and breathless. "My God, would you guys stop screaming?"

"She's over here!" Grady yells to the others before he grabs me and lifts me off my feet, squeezing the air out of me with a hug. "Jesus! Just tell me you're okay."

"I'm fine, Grady," I mumble into his shirt.

"What in the Sam hell did you think you were doing?"

"Going for a run," I grunt. "Put me down!"

Duffy and Colby reach us at the same time, both out of breath, Colby slightly bent over and near growling.

"What are you doing off the trail?" Colby screams, pointing to the woods with one hand, holding his other arm close to his side. "You don't know who or what's out there. There's a reason you stay out in the open in strange places. Damnit, Millie! What are you thinking?!"

Duffy puts his hand on Colby's shoulder and sighs deeply. "Chill out, Cheddar. She's okay." His eyebrows furrow as he dips his chin and fixes his eyes on me. "She ain't going out on her own again like that though, are ya, Trinket." It's not a question but I'm not one much for orders either. I did my six years of taking and following orders day in and day out. I'm militarily trained and I'm not stupid.

Humiliation washes over me as I stand beneath three tall man shadows, being scolded like a child. I square my shoulders, puff my chest a bit, and storm off toward the bus. I've learned to hold my tongue, keep my mouth shut, to grin and bear it. Not because I'm a little girl or weak, but because I'm a soldier.

You don't stay out in the open, Colby. That's the worst place you can be.

"Thank you for your concern, guys," I toss over my shoulder. "Sorry if you were worried. I do appreciate you *saving* me from whatever or whoever might or might not have been out there. We should probably get back on the road."

I watch several people approaching the buses at the same time I am, and realization strikes. They've all been out searching. I can guarantee you, right now it really sucks to be me. I'm waiting for Utah to develop one tiny sink hole to open up and swallow me into the depths of hell. The proper thing to do would be to walk over and apologize and say thank you, I suppose. But instead, my chin takes a dive toward my chest as my feet take me closer to the bus and I climb the few steps it requires to get me inside.

"He was worried about you, Millie," Dave says softly as I pass where he and Bruce stand just inside the bus.

Charlie takes my elbow as I pass him to get to my room. "Said he spooked you before you took off." He lifts a brow as he holds my gaze. "We had reason to be worried, Millie."

I nod and turn to head to my room where I throw myself on the bed. I can't find the words to protest or agree. A nod is neutral, isn't it?

We spent two days in that old, burned out building – Jordy and me – waiting, terrified, not willing to come out to see if they had left, if our men had shown up to rescue us. It was safer not being out in the open where you're a target. It's why I came home two years early, why I went through therapy, why I like fresh air. And apparently these guys know all about it. Thanks a lot, Uncle Morty. My life shouldn't be an open book.

And so much for Millicent. Colby called me Millie. Just like everybody else does. Except for Duffy, who calls me Trinket. I kinda like it really. It sounds dainty, feminine, ladylike. And he smiles when he says it, and he knows I don't hate it. Yeah, I like Duffy. Actually, I like all of them. Still a little iffy about Bruce; he sings really dirty songs in the shower. I haven't made up my mind about him yet. Dave is soft-spoken and kind; tenderhearted. Charlie is ornery but lovable. The way Grady grabbed me today makes me think he's lost someone before, as if he held on tight enough, he could keep me safe. As cheerful as he may seem, I think his heart hurts.

I smell smoke coming through my windows as it permeates the air around the buses. It's barbecue smoke so I don't panic. I assume it's one of the campsite dwellers getting ready to grill hotdogs or hamburgers. I stand and close the windows on the back of the bus and peer outside to see a group of people firing up BBQ grills. It's our group of roadies as well as my own bus mates standing around the grills and tables with a layout fit for the finest of campers.

There's a knock on my door and I hear Colby's voice from the other side.

"Millicent? Can I come in?"

Okay...I am no longer Millie. I think I feel a little better.

I open the door and see a long-faced, very handsome Colby standing with his forearm leaning on the doorframe, eyes downcast.

"They decided there's plenty of time for a barbecue. Burgers should be ready in about ten minutes. Care to join us?" he asks, his voice soft and timid.

I'm hesitant to face the same people who spent time this morning searching for someone who decided to take the path less traveled and wander into the woods, only to scare the living crap out of people who care about her.

"Um, I'll probably grab something out of the fridge later."

"Please?" His eyes meet mine and I want to cry as he apologizes. "I shouldn't have snuck up on you. And I had no right to yell at you. I'm sorry." He winces slightly and whispers, "I hate it when you're mad at me."

"It's okay." I press my hand to my forehead, avoiding his gaze. "I'm sure my whole story has been laid out for you now, so I'll be sure not to do it again."

"Nope," he replies, popping the P. "They wouldn't do that. It's not their story to tell, any more than theirs was for someone else to divulge. Come and have lunch with us, Millicent. There's no judgment out there. I promise."

I take a deep breath and blow it out slowly. "Okay."

He holds his hand out for me to take and we walk to the center of the bus.

"Hang on." He stops and holds up a finger. "Gotta change my shirt. I spilled lighter fluid on this one."

He reaches into the cubby, opens his duffle bag, and grabs a T-shirt. Whipping off the one he has on; he reaches for the one he's set out. My eyes are glued to the broad shoulders that lead to pecs that my hands want to reach for; a six-pack my fingers could run through the ridges, the V with a wisp of hair that leads to the promised land…. *Holy crap!*

"Colby." His name is but a shocked whisper on my lips as I take note of the bruise developing on his right rib cage. My hand has a mind of its own as it reaches out and ever so lightly touches the deep purple mark over his ribs which unfortunately resembles the approximate size of my elbow. He doesn't flinch or move away; just closes his eyes and takes a deep breath.

"I'm so sorry."

"It was my fault." He shakes his head, his eyes still closed, his breathing increasing.

"What can I do?" I whisper, desperately wanting to make it better.

"Honestly?"

"Yeah."

"Kiss it and make it better." A boyish grin appears as he taps his bottom lip. "But it hurts more up here."

He wraps his hand in my hair and lowers his head until our mouths are mere inches apart. "Millicent Trinkett, I wanted to do this eleven years ago. Back then it was to say good-bye. I'm glad I didn't. Because this time it's to say hello."

He captures my mouth in the most delicious kiss a woman could ever wish for. He tastes like mint and his lips are soft. The kiss is commanding yet giving. He tilts my head, so his mouth fits mine perfectly. It's a kiss dreams are made of.

Take that Hollywood! Screw you romance novels! He could give alpha men lessons. And this is only lunchtime, in broad daylight no less.

When the kiss ends, I feel like I've lost a limb.

He leans his forehead on mine and whispers, "Hi."

My voice is but a squeak as I respond, "Hi."

We hear throat clearing from the front of the bus as Grady makes his presence known and I jump back from Colby in embarrassment.

"We ran outta mustard. Came to get some more," he announces, arching a brow. "Seems I interrupted."

"Uh, no, no," I stammer, feeling my cheeks flush. "We were, uh, just getting ready to go out."

He eyes Colby as he heads toward the cupboards to grab the yellow spread. "Where's your shirt, Norway?"

"It's right here, Grady," he tells him, rolling his eyes. "I spilled lighter fluid on the other. It's a fire hazard so I was changing."

Grady holds the mustard in his hand, a grin on his face as he points the bottle back and forth between us. "It would seem there's more combustibles in here than there is out there." He laughs loudly when he reaches the door and turns. "Put your damn shirt on and get out here. Gotta admit, Little Bit," he says as he looks at Colby's ribs and then to me. "You throw a hell of a punch."

I stare at my shoes and mutter, "I didn't mean to…"

"Hey," he interrupts. "Yeah, you did. I'm proud of you. Now I know why Morty told us to watch our step. I thought it was for your sake." He laughs. "Hell, it was for ours. Nice to know." He winks before he steps down off the bus and walks toward the group gathered around the barbecue and yells, "Got the condoms! Whoops, condiments. Eat up, Milwaukee's ears are burnin'. Let's go give 'em the real music!" We hear cheers and hollers as another pep rally takes place. The closer we get to opening night, the more revved up everyone seems to feel.

"Hey," Colby says as he takes my cheeks in his palms. "We good?"

I smile. "We're good." *Kiss me, Colby, one more time.*

And he does. And it's wonderful. I could do this every day, for a very long time.

"Yes! Millie!" I hear Bruce scream. I rush to the window and see him holding his cell phone in the air, waving it around. "Call Morty. Duffy got sticky whiskers!"

The entire group outside begins to yell as disruption and chaos seems to erupt. Duffy, Dave, and Grady walk toward the bus at a hurried pace.

I look to Colby. "I think Duffy got something stuck in his beard. He's heading this way. You'd better see if he needs help. Bruce said something about sticky whiskers."

Colby doesn't move from his spot. In fact, he tucks his hands in his shorts pockets and rocks on his heels; his mouth held tight in a straight line, his eyes not meeting mine.

"Colby!" I scold as I grab his elbow. "See if your uncle needs help."

Throwing my hands in the air when I see he's still not moving; I head to the front of the bus to check what type of medical attention might be needed. Maybe Duffy scorched his beard getting too close to the grill, maybe he got lighter fluid on it like Colby did on his T-shirt, maybe sap from a log. Who knows?

As the three men enter the bus talking rapidly, I rush to get to Duffy – the second one climbing aboard.

Checking his beard by patting it down and flipping it upward, therefore virtually turning inside out, I ask, "What happened? Are you okay?"

Duffy looks surprised, blinks fast, and places his hands on mine to halt my search of his facial hair. "Whoa, Trinket. It's not a stuffed animal. It's actually attached to my face." He laughs. "Be gentle."

"What did you get in it out there?" I ask, reaching for his beard again. "Do we need to shampoo it? Bruce said it's sticky. Why do I need to call Morty? Is it serious?"

Grady spasms with his laughter while Dave chokes on his.

"Colby!" I shout behind me. "Why aren't you worried about your uncle?!"

"Millicent…" he groans as he blows out a deep breath. "Duffy is fine. You, on the other hand might not be when you…"

"What are you talking about?" I glare at Colby, then snap my eyes back to the three grinning morons at the front of the bus.

"Cheddar, where the hell are your clothes?" Duffy asks him, grinning.

"Don't change the subject, Duffy," I insist. "What is going on?"

"You like him with that shirt off, don't you?" Grady laughs and winks. "I told him to put it back on eons ago."

I narrow my eyes and snort. "You're just jealous of his six-pack."

"One, two, three," Grady counts slowly as he studies Colby, then points and twirls his finger. "Turn a little, Norway. Can't quite see the other side."

In my periphery I see Colby quickly slide his T-shirt over his head. *Damn them!*

Colby rolls his eyes and heaves a deep sigh. "Would you get it over with and explain to Millicent what's going on?"

"Oh, yeah," Dave chirps, his eyes lit with excitement. "You gotta call Morty. Tell him we got sticky whiskers."

My eyes flit from musician to musician, my face twisted in confusion. "And this impedes your playing capabilities how? Can't you just wash it off? And why on earth do I need to call Morty?"

Duffy chuckles. "That explains why you were pawing my beard. Sticky Whiskers is a band. They're going to meet us in Milwaukee. Just call Morty and let him know."

"Who is Sticky Whiskers and what happened to The Impotents?" I still shudder when I think of the name of the front band. The long vowel sound? The short vowel sound? Are they im-pottants or are they im-potents? I watched the video. They're a damn good band. But the name….oh the name. Turns out they use the stressed vowel sound. Is it a lack of libido…or ability? Talk about self-inflicted punishment. Maybe they're all married, and their wives have them on short leashes. You'd think a better name and Lorena Bobbitt posters tacked up all over the bus would be stronger incentive and less humiliating.

"We did tours with Sticky Whiskers years ago," Grady informs me. "You couldn't find a better front band. We all know each other. They're looking forward to it. Just got off the phone with two of them and the guy who's going to manage it. All set up as long as Morty puts his stamp of approval on it."

We're three days away from opening night. The advertising and tickets have been out for the last month. I puff my cheeks and hold my breath while thinking about it before Grady pokes my cheeks with his index fingers and says, "Let it out, Little Bit. You're turning blue."

I release an exasperated huff, "But the posters and signage and…."

"Just call Morty. He'll take care of it," Duffy says. "We'll wait."

"So," I start. "You want this billed as Fourplay with Sticky Whiskers or Sticky Whiskers with…Oh my God!" I shriek. "Ewww! No! No! No!" My hands fly through in the air as if to shake something off them; like you would when there are no hand towels or air dryers in a bathroom. But this isn't water…this is just plain dirty.

"Millie," Dave says slowly. "Don't take offense. It's just stage presence. They're fantastic musicians and the names together is a crowd draw."

"For what?!" I howl. "Sex club perverts and the BDSM crowd?"

A burst of laughter breaks behind me. "You know what BDSM is?"

I turn to face the culprit and scowl. Colby's laughter dies immediately as he clears his throat and mumbles, "Sorry. Just didn't expect that."

Shoving my way past him to get to my room I growl, "I read romance novels, you idiot." I yell back to all of them, "I'll call Morty."

"I'll bring you some lunch," Colby calls after me.

"No!" I stop and glare at him. "Let Grady do it."

"Why Grady?" he asks defensively.

"Because he's not you!" I yell, slamming my door behind me and prepare to call Morty. I really need to go easy on this door or I may pop the hinges and end up with a curtain to separate all of us.

* * *

"Come on, Morty," I sigh into the phone. "Fourplay with Sticky Whiskers. You do realize how disgusting that sounds."

"Millie." His voice is condescending as he tries to calm me. "And a rose by any other name…"

"Would smell a hell of a lot sweeter," I interrupt, "and less…crotchy. Don't you dare try and quote Shakespeare to me. William would roll over in his grave."

"We care about the success of this concert," he tells me. "Sticky Whiskers is a great warmup band. You're gonna love them."

"Really," I drawl snidely. "Do they go out on stage with glistening facial hair giving the impression that they've just been…"

"Millie!" he chides. "Young lady, you're going to drive me to drink."

"I get dibs on the tequila." I sigh heavily. "So, it's a done deal, huh?"

"I'll get everything taken care of on this end," he reassures me. "Don't worry about the tickets or the advertising. Just show up in Milwaukee. And Millie?"

"Yeah?" I grumble.

"I love you."

"Love you, too, Uncle Morty." I press end and toss the phone on the bed.

I really do love him. He's been my rock for so long. Morty stepped up to the plate without hesitation when I needed him most. He put his life on hold and came to my rescue. He didn't hire a nanny to take care of me; a 13-year-old basket case of a girl who had suddenly lost her parents. No, Morty stayed with me for three solid months before he went back to work in the office. He worked from home, was at my beck and call 24/7 in person, until he felt I was comfortable enough to be driven back and forth to school by his chauffeur instead of him, able to function on my own for a couple hours a day without being hovered over, had made some new friends in a new environment. We took vacations twice a year meant for teenagers, not adults, and he made them educational as well as fun. Yeah, I owe Morty a lot.

But what I will always feel most indebted to Morty for? Coming to Germany after I was injured, both physically and emotionally, and staying until I was on that plane and on my way home. He found me the proper therapy, an excellent therapist, and monitored everything to assure it was being done correctly. He's never treated me like an invalid nor a victim. He's never treated me as anything or anyone other than…Millie.

ANNIE MICK

Chapter 9

Colby

"Norway," Grady groans. "How in the hell you manage to put both feet in your mouth at once, I'll never know. I'm gonna go get the lady something to eat. I'll get her the hamburger. Shall I grab you some crow as long as I'm out there?"

I run my hands through my hair and yank hard. I couldn't help myself. Hearing Millicent say BDSM was too much. Face it, it was funny. The girl drank two margaritas and woke up with a hangover. She hesitated with a kiss, for crying out loud. It was a damn good kiss, but it had innocence written all over it. I know she reads romance novels; I saw it on her nightstand when I took her breakfast to her. Yes, she's tough; my ribs are proof of that. But on the inside, she is sweetness personified. Admittedly, I probably shouldn't have asked her if she knew what BDSM was. Welp… there went my kiss goodnight.

"Cheddar," Duffy starts. "You never laugh *at* a woman; you laugh *with* a woman. Your mama would be whipping you with a dishtowel right now. Do I need to bring her on board?"

"Depends, Duffy," I sneer. "You in the mood for a headlock?"

Dave snickers. "Damn, now that's something I'd love to

see. Matter of fact, I'd kinda like to see both of those things."

In unison we turn to him, "Shut up, Dave."

Grady walks on to the bus balancing two plates full of food in his hands and passes one to me.

"You get the hotdog," he says. "Loaded it with onions too. I get the feeling the only thing you're gonna be kissing for a while is her ass. Pucker up, son."

I watch as he walks to the back of the bus and taps on her door. "Little Bit, got you some lunch. Open up."

Millicent opens the door, Grady walks in, and the door closes. What the hell? And what's with "*Little Bit*"? Now Grady has a nickname for her?

"You ain't jealous are ya, Cheddar?" Duffy eyes me, smiling mischievously.

"What?" I snap. "No. He's old enough to be her father."

"Yeah." He nods. "She's like a daughter to all of us; the one we never had. Did you see the way she tried to take care of me? She's special. Don't treat her with kid gloves, but don't treat her with boxer's either. Just be Colby and let her be Millie. You'll do fine."

I think of that kiss. I was being Colby…and she was being Millie. And it was just fine. Hell, it was great.

Milwaukee, WI

I can't believe I almost turned this gig down. I also can't believe the setup. Massive stage, a light show that would give the Fourth of July a run for its money, two sets of drums, (you know, just in case Charlie breaks the skin on one of the heads) B3 complete with Leslie, as well as Rita; my Uncle Duffy's Fender guitar. He named it after my aunt, the love of his life. It's his prized possession. It was packed away on the bus and never left its case during travel. He was saving her for performances only.

I watch Dave as he plays the B3. His fingers dance across the keys like ocean waves wash across the beach on a moonlit night. He's smooth as silk. No wavering, no hesitation. He's at home behind those keys. It's hard to decipher if he was made for the keyboard or if that keyboard was made for him.

I observe Bruce on bass guitar. He's so relaxed he plays with only his left hand at times, so lost in the music and keeping rhythm with the drums. His eyes closed as he loses himself in times that once were, in a life he once lived, and relives tonight and will live for the next six months with the men he spent the most enjoyable times with.

I see Charlie keeping everyone in time with one another while he beats the living shit out of those drums; one foot beating the bass pedal, the other clapping the hi-hats, his hands moving sticks from one drumhead to another as well as the cymbals while he pounds a mighty beat.

Grady and Uncle Duffy switch back and forth from lead guitar and rhythm guitar as well as entertaining the crowd, their fingers moving through licks so fast they fly and become a blur. These guys haven't lost a thing.

I see the same characteristics they showed in the videos I watched of their performances from years ago. They hold their guitars the same way, their posture is the same, the fingering of their strings is identical, their smiles are as golden now as they were thirty years ago. It's like watching a life reborn.

I'm honored…playing with them. I've played with some of the best bands across the world. I've filled in, I've played backup, I've played lead, and I've always been on stage. I feel like I should take a step back tonight, let these guys show the crowd what they're made of.

I'm fascinated… and I'm a musician.

Humble pie should be my dinner for the rest of my life.

Who knew sixties was the new sexties?

The ladies in the crowd are enamored; absolutely mesmerized. Some almost swoon they're so dazzled. They sway and shake their booties, as well as their boobies, their eyes fixed on my uncle and his buddies. I'm sure they're wearing push-up bras; those that haven't been surgically altered. They throw panties up on stage, some throw thongs. I doubt my uncle is going to collect them. God, I hope not. When a pair lands on his head and he lets them sit there for more than what a head-bob or shake would take to toss them off, it initially causes me concern. But when he blows a kiss and waggles his tongue at the sender, I laugh so hard I nearly piss my pants.

The men in the audience are a virtual potluck. You have a choice of clean-shaven business types, blue jeans and chambrays, overalls and flannel, chain wallets and leather vests, Hell's Angels' lookalikes, hippie throwbacks, and your everyday T-shirt and jeans with a backwards cap on their heads or man buns. The biggest surprise is the age range. The music being played tonight spans a few decades – five actually – and so does the crowd. Which may explain why some of the men look like grandfathers of some of the young people. Probably because they are…or could be.

We are, tonight, the music of generations. And it would seem every generation out there is enjoying themselves.

We perform Fourplay's originals, tributes to CCR, Joe

Cocker, Eagles, Stevie Ray Vaughan, Lynyrd Skynyrd…and the list goes on and on.

When we play Bob Seger's "Old Time Rock and Roll" the crowd goes crazy – big surprise. What band under the sun doesn't play this song? Who hasn't played it…a thousand and one times, give or take a hundred. "The Fire Down Below"? It's pretty much a tribute to prostitutes. Does it make a difference? Not a tinker's damn. Sometimes it's the lyrics, sometimes the beat, but always the music that accompanies it. The crowd roars just as loud, they dance just as hard, they sweat just as much.

I watch this crowd show more energy tonight than I have seen in any concert I've played in the last eight years on the road. More importantly, I watch these men on stage – my Uncle Duffy and his cohorts – come to life in a way I never thought possible. We've practiced for weeks on end; it sounded good, I knew it was doable, but I hadn't a clue how phenomenal these guys really are.

Age has done nothing to hamper their abilities or speed. It's done nothing to make them feel less than. If they're feeling older or aching at all, it sure doesn't show. Their smiles are like high beams on a highway. Their loyalty to one another is evident with the last song of the night, after the second encore:

Joe Cocker's "With a Little Help from My Friends".

The song is calmer; a good one to close out the evening. The audience sways   shoulder-to-shoulder, arm-in-arm, friends gazing at one another, singing along. When the song is over, I'm thinking this is it, we can pack it in, go back to the bus, take a breath, celebrate success.

Duffy speaks through their cheers and foot stomping, the hollers for "one more song!"

"Folks, thank you for coming. Drive home safely. Let the other guy have your lane if he needs it. Nobody's in that much of a hurry."

"Just one more," the crowd screams.

Duffy looks to the band. "What do you think, boys? One more?"

Grady smiles. I take a deep breath. This isn't practiced!

What now?

"Grady, Charlie, you ready?" he asks them. They both nod and respond, "Yup."

"One more real short one, folks," Duffy tells the crowd as he snaps fingers in 4/4 time. "But you gotta listen real close. This is what's known as our closing song…and this is why."

Duffy starts acapella with a very drawn out…

"Becaauuse…."

And Grady and Charlie join him, acapella, fingers snapping at the sides of their mics.

"Now I gotta go, I gotta take a pee,
I can feel a trickle runnin' down my knee,
To form a puddle on the floor,
And it's a growin' so fast
I just don't think I can last
Until the end of the song
So I'll just quit."

The lights go out at the exact moment the song ends and the stage is left in darkness…as is the audience, mentally, until the words have sunk in. Laughter rings throughout the auditorium.

"We love you, Milwaukee!" Duffy shouts. "Goodnight!"

Millicent stands in the shadows offstage and I see her slap her forehead with the heel of her palm as her shoulders rock with laughter. I do believe she had a good time.

We haven't spoken much in the last three days. She's been ignoring me; still mad about my not so funny (*sorry but it was*) comment about BDSM. I've been sure to be the first one up in the morning to fix coffee, therefore providing her with a fresh cup when she wakes. I flip a damn good pancake, I toast an awesome waffle, and I'm the best at warming a Pop Tart. Just ask Duffy.

There wouldn't be any point in asking Millicent; she's insisted on fixing her own food.

That is until this morning when I gripped her hip from behind and growled in her ear as she reached into the cupboard to grab anything other than what I had prepared. "Eat the damn pancakes. I fixed them for you." I left a soft kiss on her temple immediately after. It must have worked because she sat down at the table and ate four of them.

I'll kiss her ass, but I'll spank it too if she insists on being stubborn.

She wears the sexiest little red dress with ankle boots. When she stepped into the dressing room earlier this evening, she literally took my breath away. I've seen her in shorts, but I've never seen her in a skirt. There's something about Millicent in a dress that changes her presence. Her hair is down in soft waves, and she wears makeup tonight. She doesn't need the makeup; she's a natural beauty, but it does enhance the blue in her eyes. And those legs…

Fact: Millicent has curves where other girls don't even have places.

"What did you think, Trinket?" Duffy asks as he picks her up and twirls her around. He's running on adrenaline, the rush will probably last for a couple hours, but when he crashes, he's going to sleep like a baby.

"You guys were outstanding," she tells him. "You literally blew me away." She hugs him tightly around his neck and kisses his cheek, and I see the gratitude in Duffy's eyes. I feel a pang in my chest. I can't possibly be jealous of my Uncle Duffy, can I? Besides, I wanted to be the first one she hugged. Duffy is sweating profusely and I'm going to suffer the consequences. Duffy's cologne and body sweat mixed with the sweet scent of my Millicent is not my ideal reward. Wait a minute. *My* Millicent? Slow down, Colby. She's not yours. Someday though…

Grady, Charlie, Bruce, and Dave stand in line for hugs. *What the hell?* What am I…chopped liver? I played my ass off out there! I see their shit eating grins as they watch me fuming as each one takes their turn at a quick hug. *They're trying to piss me off!*

Grady steps back to where I stand. "Go for the upper cheeks, Norway. The onion breath should be gone, and I'd be surprised if she ain't got bruises on her ass by now from you kissin' it."

Charlie slaps my shoulder as he passes on his way to the dressing room. "Still think the old farts ain't got it?" He laughs, his devilish goading echoes in my ears. "Gonna have to up your game, boy. Better check them pockets."

Lovely…first night on the road the bus smelled like an outhouse. First concert, my Millicent is going to smell like a sweatbox; whisker burned by old farts. This ought to be good: Nautica, three different scents from Old Spice, and God only knows what Bruce uses. My bet is he buys it at Dollar Tree. Like I said, they've been single for a long time. I'm hard pressed to believe they're really okay with that, but Rita was my Uncle Duffy's one true love. Him, I understand, because Rita understood him. And I don't know as if anyone else could. I'm unaware of the others' histories. If they're anything like Duffy's, it might well explain their singledom.

If my armpits weren't soaked through, I'd toss my arm over Millicent's shoulder and walk her to the room, holding her close to my side the entire way. As it is, I'm not sure my own Mont Blanc has lasted through the sweat I worked up on stage.

"Hey." I smile as I reach to tug one of the soft curls that falls gently in front of her shoulder. "Not bad for a bunch of old timers, huh?"

She pats me on the chest and grins. "Oh, Colby, don't feel bad. With the right diet and enough exercise, a little more practice, you'll be able to keep up with them in no time."

My jaw hangs slack as I stare at her. She giggles before she places a finger under my chin and tips my mouth closed.

"You were fantastic," she whispers.

I narrow my eyes and arch a brow. "You kissed my Uncle Duffy."

She shrugs. "Shock value."

I place my hands on her hips and bring her closer, our faces mere inches apart. "I get the first kiss, always," I inform her, testing the waters for making demands.

"Then you'd better get your butt over here first…always." She tips her chin in defiance. "You snooze, you lose."

I rub my nose softly against the side of hers. "You made his night, you know. You're the daughter he never had."

"I know," she answers softly. "He told me."

"You can make my night, Millicent," I whisper. "You're unlike any woman I've ever met." I lower my mouth to hers and take it in a kiss I don't want to stop. Sweat be damned. It's why we have showers…and laundromats and dry cleaners.

* * *

We board the bus an hour and a half later, after cheese and crackers with fresh cut meats and a platter of various fruits. I shouldn't fail to mention that Millicent took special care to serve each plate and forced each one of us to eat a cup of yogurt in the name of digestive health. This was also after she forced each one of us to eat half an apple, half a pear, and half an orange. The grapes and apricots were optional. The prunes were individually wrapped in airtight packages for freshness and will be available at any given time, as she had purchased an abundant supply and they will be kept fresh in the refrigerator on the bus. I believe the word she used was yummy. It wouldn't be gentlemanly to disclose the words used by the rest of us. Of course, Millicent didn't hear them; we'd all like to keep those things between our pockets.

The adrenaline effects are wearing off, slowly but surely, as the guys make their way to the cubbies. I don't much care what anyone sleeps in at home, but we all wear lounge pants or shorts for sleeping on the bus in the name of respect for an angel that deserves it.

"One hell of a night, guys," Charlie says dreamily. "I haven't had that much fun since the last time we did it and that was thirty years ago. I feel like a new man."

Bruce props up on an elbow, a shit eating grin plastered on his face. "A new man, huh? Did I miss something? I was under the impression you were into women all this time. I did see a couple of slackers hanging around the depot though. If you want, I can see if they're still there."

Charlie picks up a boot at the side of his bed and throws it in the general direction of Bruce. "Asshole. Always spoilin' a genuine moment."

"Bruce," Grady warns. "Too early in the tour to get the shit beat outta you."

"I'm a year younger than you guys," Bruce protests. "The little brother that gets away with everything."

"Noogies in the morning, Bruce," Dave pacifies him. "Good night, little brother."

"Nobody's gonna tuck me in?" Bruce pouts.

"I'll be happy to knock your ass out if you don't shut up," Charlie offers.

"God, it feels just like home," Bruce hums.

"Ain't that the truth," Duffy sighs. "It is like home, isn't it?"

"'Night grandpa, 'night John boy, 'night Mary Ellen, 'night Jim Bob," Dave teases.

"Wait!" Bruce flashes his classic grin. "Which one is Mary Ellen?"

Grady groans as he rolls over, "Shut the fuck up and go to sleep."

* * *

The bus is rolling and the hum of the wheels against the harsh concrete of the interstate mixed with the dark of night lulls everyone into a soft slumber.

I've given them all ten minutes to pass out when I hear snoring from two of the cubbies and figure I'm safe taking my chances.

Slipping out quietly, I make my way to the back of the bus and tap lightly on Millicent's door when I see the light coming from under the threshold.

"Come in," she answers groggily.

I open the door slowly and step in, closing it behind me. Her makeup is gone and she's in PJs. This is my favorite Millicent. Fresh faced, natural.

"Hey," I whisper, making my way to the side of her bed and kneel. "Just wanted to tell you goodnight. All tucked in?"

"Yeah," she replies. "It's been a wild day. Good thing we get a few in between to recuperate."

I chuckle softly, reaching out to brush her hair away from her face. "You want to run with me in the morning?"

Her face lights with a smile. "I'd like that."

"I'll have Sandy find us a nice park with a trail." I lean down to plant a soft kiss on her mouth, and she places her palm on my cheek, brushing her fingers in my scruff. I've never felt anything like it. It sends a tingle up my spine but gives me comfort at the same time. I murmur against her mouth, "I hate it when you're mad at me."

"I hate it too."

"Let's not do that anymore. I'll do better," I promise her.

"I'll try to not be so sensitive."

"You're perfect." I place another soft kiss on her mouth, savoring the moment to fuel my dreams. "Goodnight, Millicent."

"Goodnight, Colby."

Closing the door quietly behind me, I lean against it, taking a deep breath. How easy it would be to slip in beside her and hold her all night long, breathe her in, feel her wrapped around me. Eleven years and I'm still as crazy about Millicent Trinkett as I was the day I met her, even more so. You don't find that every day. Hell, you're lucky if you find that any day. I breathe a deep sigh and head back to the cubbies.

"I had ninety seconds left on my watch before I was gonna come drag you outta there, Norway." Grady's low warning rings out from his cubby as I near my bed.

"Ninety?" Duffy huffs. "Hell, I only had sixty left on mine. Were you gonna make me go in there all by my lonesome?"

I hear a phone alarm going off in Dave's cubby as Charlie rises out of his. Bruce and Dave appear at the same time behind him. All five pajama-clad men stand with their arms folded across their chests, hair mussed – those who have a full head of it – dark circles under their eyes, and scowls on their faces.

"What the hell is this?" I ask, irritation quickly building as I throw the blankets back on my bed, getting ready to crawl back under them.

"Just makin' sure you ain't lookin' to do any funny business," Charlie says.

I snort. "Funny business? Is that what you kids are calling it these days?"

"Actually," Bruce chirps, "we called it backseat boogieing, but this is a bus and there are no backseats per se…"

"Go back to bed, Bruce," Charlie growls.

Bruce's face twists in confusion and then splits in a grin. "We're not going to tie him to his bed? No toilet swirlies? No threats of castration if he doesn't behave himself?"

Dave whips his head toward Bruce. "You want those Noogies now?"

"I'm going, I'm going," Bruce mumbles. He turns before slipping into his cubby. "Go easy on him. Believe it or not, they're grownups." He nods once at me and disappears.

I eye the men standing around me, legs spread wide so they don't stagger as the bus moves under their feet. I move my gaze from each one to the next, then tilt my head in the direction of Bruce's cubby.

"Yeah, what he said," I grunt, incensed at their lack of faith in my integrity. "Goodnight gentlemen."

"Cheddar," Duffy sighs. "We're just…"

"Don't, Duffy." I take a deep breath and roll my shoulders. I know they're looking out for her, but damnit, so am I. Pretty sure they know her history as well, but she'll tell me when she's ready. "I don't need you watching my every move and you don't need to protect Millicent from me. And if you think for one minute that you care about her more than I do, you're wrong." I whip my T-shirt over my head, tossing it to the foot of the bed, and turn toward them one last time. "And if and when we decide we're having sex, believe me, it's not going to be where a bunch of old geezers can hear us. Again, goodnight gentlemen." I lie down on my bed and pull the blanket up over me.

"I'll be damned." Charlie laughs as he slaps Duffy's shoulder. "He did find 'em. Shall we smoke a cigar in celebration?"

Bruce pokes his head out. "Can I have a puff?"

"Just one," Grady tells him. "Don't inhale though. You'll puke again."

"Hey, Colby," Charlie says. "Any matches around?"

I sit up and square him right in the eye. "I know of two."

"Let's have 'em." He holds his palm out.

"My ass to your face and your breath to a buffalo's fart. Have Sandy pull over, smoke it outside, and blow the smoke away from the bus. Goodnight."

Chapter 10

Millicent

Sticky Whiskers was not at all what I was expecting. About a decade younger than Fourplay, handsome, well built, clean cut, denim clad, four-piece band. They seemed respectful, classy. That is, until they hit the stage. To say they shined would be an understatement. They were shining alright…as in glistening…and grinning; mischievously. Their facial hair was glossy wet, little sparkles sprinkled throughout, and the lewd sexual innuendo was definitely present.

The ladies swooned, the men laughed, the crowd danced. They worked everybody up to the perfect level of, shall we say, pumped? Their music was great. One solid hour of rock and roll to warm up the crowd and ready them for the spotlight band.

My spotlight band. My guys. My "old farts" who proved they can dance rings around any young performers out there.

And Colby. I had no idea. I wanted to be that guitar. I watched his fingers slide over those strings and dance from fret to fret. I want him to play me the way he plays her. The ease of his movements, yet the concentrated furrow of his brow as if his goal was to please her, make her sing with pleasure. Oh yes, I would love to be that guitar.

Ah, but alas, my job is to keep them healthy…and moving. Hence, the prunes on the table when the show is over.

"You're gonna make us eat these, Little Bit?" Grady asks, his face crinkled in sour expression. You would think I just held up a spoon of castor oil.

"I won't force them down your throat," I tell him. "However, I've been studying the digestive health of sixty and older adults. Prunes are highly recommended for regularity and overall clearance of the digestive tract." I sound like a biology professor schooling them in class, as if that should be the end of the discussion.

"I think she's trying to tell us we're full of shit," Duffy injects with a laugh. "Trinket, you know Mexican food works the same way, don't ya?"

"Do you like sleeping under the stars, Duffy?" Narrowing my eyes, I threaten, "Because that's where you'll be the next time you eat Mexican food."

"Now what makes you think that was me?" he asks. Playfully winking and smiling, he adds, "It could have been Cheddar for all you know."

"Duffy," Colby scowls. "Eat the damn yogurt, choke down the prunes, and quit bitching. We all know who the culprits were."

"I love prunes." Dave smiles as he slides another bite in his mouth. "You know they're just wrinkled plums, don't you?"

Bruce snorts and laughs loudly. "You always did have a thing for the old piano teacher, Sr. Mabel."

"Ah…" Dave holds a finger in the air. "Until she rapped my fingers with that ruler."

"Hit the wrong keys?" Grady asks.

"No," Dave explains. "It was in the middle of study hall. I was writing a poem to little Miss Fanny. Talk about poetry in motion. That girl had one of the cutest little asses. Asked her if she'd meet me that day after classes." He sighs as he reminisces. He looks up with raised brows. "You know where this is going, don't you?"

In unison they answer, "Uh huh."

"A shadow cast over my desk from the harsh fluorescent

lights above and I knew I was already in trouble and I thought, what the hell, just go for it. I finished the last stanza," he uses air quotes, "'this poem is getting bolder and bolder, and now there's a nun looking over my shoulder'. Next thing I knew, thwack!" He slaps his hand on the table. "She nearly maimed me for life, you know." He holds up his hands and wiggles his fingers. "These golden boys almost met their demise that day."

"And you liked this teacher?" I ask, aghast that he would approve of such methods of discipline.

He laughs heartily. "She wasn't my music teacher. My folks had me taught outside the system. No, I grabbed her ruler and snapped it in half; then informed her that she should never mess with a musician's *digits*, fingers or otherwise, and left the room. She never used that ruler again, or any other as far as I know."

"What does that have to do with prunes?" I laugh, not understanding how this conversation got off track.

He stands and walks to where I lean against the counter. "It's what we called her. 'The Prune'. That day was my biggest win. I dropped my poem on Fanny's desk on my way out."

"Did she like it?" I giggle, trying to picture a young, brown-haired, blue-eyed Dave in high school writing poetry about cute little asses.

"She did," he says with a wink. "Enough to mess with *my digits*. I married her..." His face falls as he acquiesces, "...and buried her three years ago."

I feel the burn in my nose and the sting behind my eyes as I hold back a sob. Sometimes saying nothing is better than struggling to say something. But a hug is worth its weight in gold; wordless but says everything, so that's what I do. I reach out and give him a hug.

His chin rests on my head as he says, "I think the bus is ready to roll, Millie."

The Band: "The Weight"

Makeup off, PJs on, butterflies slowing down, limbs aching as the adrenaline rush wears off, I finally manage to lie down in bed.

My emotions are running all over the place. Poor Dave. Marrying his high school sweetheart and losing her three years ago. How his heart must ache. It's no wonder he's quiet and reserved.

Colby kissed me tonight after the show. Thank God! Now I can be done being mad at him. I was actually done being mad at him days ago, but I didn't know how to tell him that. Besides, what was I supposed to do…jump on him and smother him with kisses? Not that I wouldn't be happy to do that but traveling with the five Millie-sitters makes it impossible. The first time we kissed, Grady needed mustard and the second time was interrupted by finding out we were going to be touring with the simulated crotch seats. Well, you know what I mean. Okay, that does sound rather crude and… unfortunately, a bit stimulating.

Good God, I need some sleep.

A light tap on my door brings me out of my drifting thoughts of cunnilingus.

"Come in," I croak. I'm half asleep, trying to shut off the part of my brain that wants to relive the evening.

"Hey," I hear my favorite voice whisper. "You all tucked in?"

Colby asks if I want to run with him in the morning, kisses me once, informs me he hates it when I'm mad at him, tells me I'm perfect, and kisses me again before he leaves. The perfect ending to a perfect day.

St. Louis, MO

"You ever been up in the Arch, Trinket?" Duffy asks as we walk past shops in the downtown area. Colby and I walk side by side while the rest of the guys walk ahead or behind, dependent upon who has stopped to window shop. We have today and all day tomorrow before the concert in the evening.

"Oh, yes," I reply. "Morty and I were here a long time ago. And before you ask, I have no interest in going back up."

"I hear ya, Millie," Grady tells me, shaking his head. "I've never been one much for heights myself."

"It's not the heights so much as the closed in space," I explain. "Getting stuck in something like that would…" my words trail off into silence. I've gotten better over the years…being reminded without freezing up and slipping into darkness. I reach for my right side out of habit though. The scar from the shrapnel wound is my constant reminder. It healed, I healed.

I feel Colby's hand reach for mine and take hold, fingers intertwining with mine.

"Been to the zoo?" he asks lightheartedly as he bumps my shoulder with his. "We could visit Duffy's relatives."

"Hey, you little shit!" Duffy exclaims, rushing Colby from behind. "You're one of my relatives."

Colby's eyes go wide with feigned worry. "Mom didn't tell you?"

"Tell me what?" Duffy asks, eyes filled with curiosity.

"You're adopted. Jane Goodall dropped you off at the door." Colby's face breaks in a grin. "I think one of your cousins is still housed at the zoo though. You want to go say hi?"

Duffy growls as he closes in on Colby. "I think somebody needs a noogie."

He grabs Colby in a headlock while the others join in enthusiastically, tackling, and rub the top of his head with their knuckles, all the while shouting, "Noogie!"

I watch the spectacle before me, shaking my head in wonderment of the patience Colby shows with the overgrown boys. I pick up his baseball cap from the ground and wait. When they're done with their antics and have released him, I make my way over to a slightly frustrated, flushing Colby, place his cap on his head backwards, wrap my hands around his neck, and pull him down to me for a kiss.

"All better?" I ask as I break the kiss.

His smile beams as he lifts me off my feet. "Five more of those and you can ask me again." His mouth seizes mine in a kiss that probably shouldn't be taking place in front of the band.

"Ah geez," Grady groans. "He's not mortally wounded, Little Bit."

"Better she lick his wounds than make us do it," Bruce tells them.

"Talk about milkin' it," Charlie grumbles.

I feel one of Colby's arms leave my waist as he grips tighter with the other.

"Hey, hey!" Duffy scolds. "That bird's for special occasions only."

I giggle against his mouth. "Did you just flip them off?"

"I did," he mumbles, his lips millimeters from mine. "Now kiss me one more time before they pry us apart." One lip-lock later and I'm set back down on my feet.

Sliding my arm through Duffy's and tugging him forward, I urge, "Come on Darwin. You'll have to introduce me to this cousin of yours. I'll bet he's a real ladies' man." I snap my fingers and quip, "Hey! If we can get him groomed quickly, teach him not to scratch in unseemly places and keep his fingers out of his nose, you can bring him to the concert tomorrow."

He narrows his eyes, but his tone is affectionate. "You been hangin' around Cheddar too much."

* * *

We spend the afternoon at the zoo, take pictures of each of the men (boys) with the gorilla at the entrance, and visit the monkeys for posterity's sake. We settle on Greek food for dinner and a nice walk after. The Ubers have picked us up and taken us back to the campground where the buses sit ready and waiting our arrival.

There's a fair taking place in the distance, the lights bright and colorful. The carnival music can barely be heard, but the shrill screams of the people on the rides are quite audible as they're being lifted, twirled, and spun so fast their heads will feel dizzy or they'll puke once being let off. Well, that's if the crowd is lucky. Not so lucky if the puking takes place while that one sick passenger is still in the air.

I learned a long time ago, *by observation fortunately*, to never walk under or too close to the rides. Always walk on the midway. I watched as a large number of people started patting the tops of their heads, suspecting raindrops to be the pitter patter they felt. *No, people, it does not rain under a clear blue sky.* It was the idiot in the twirly swingy things way up high leaning over the seat sharing the contents of his stomach. I left the carnival that day, early, as in right then, never to return to one since. I'll visit amusement parks where you're given a wide berth between rides and walkways. But traveling carnivals? I'll pass.

We all sit outside on picnic benches, beers in our hands, not ready to let go of the day. It's been peaceful and relaxing. No wheels under our feet, no cramped spaces, fresh air (with the exception of the monkey house).

"I remember the last carnival I was at," Bruce sighs. "Back in those days I was so high."

Charlie slaps the back of his head and groans, "That was the Ferris wheel, dumbass. And you screamed like a girl."

"Ah," Bruce chuckles as he holds up a finger, "but I took home the girl."

"You took the girl home," Charlie corrects him.

Bruce shrugs. "Potato, potatah."

"And you had to get your man voice before she'd go out with you…a year later," he reminds him, grinning.

"I wouldn't have been able to sing Flo and Eddie properly before then," Bruce explains cheerily. "It had to be perfect."

"So, you were a late bloomer," Grady adds, laughing as he lowers his head.

"Only with my vocal cords," Bruce snaps. "And once I polished those and serenaded her, there was no turning back."

Charlie chokes on the drink he's in the midst of swallowing and spews it on the grass in front of him. "Seems to be me you turned back pretty damn quick when her daddy showed up at the window with his shotgun."

"One piece of buckshot!" Bruce shrieks, his arms flailing.

Charlie snorts. "It was a wood chunk ricocheted off the edge of the garage implanted in your ass. And it was worth every last splinter and you know it."

By now we're all giggling, enjoying the banter between these two. I'm not sure if any of it is true or if this is a night of too many beers and tall tales.

Bruce smiles, his eyes glassy. "You bet your ass it was. Ellie snuck out her window that night, tracked me down, pulled out the wood, and bandaged me up. Did it every day for a week until I was healed. That girl knew my ass like a roadmap before we even kissed. It was my best pair of Levi's too. She even repaired the tear for me. I cut the repaired patch out of them and framed it years later when the jeans wore out. It's all I have left of her other than a few pictures." He turns to face Colby and me. "No man should ever have to bury his wife." He takes a deep breath and lets it out slowly. "But I'll see her again. She'll be there waiting for me."

For the second time in a month, I feel my heart shattering for someone who has become near and dear to me. What do you say to pain like that? I stand slowly and walk to him, wrapping my arms around his waist in a bear hug…just like I did with Dave. It's not an expression of sympathy. That's not what I want to convey…I want to offer comfort.

I look up at him and whisper, "You'd better be ready to introduce her to me when I get there."

"I look forward to it, Millie. She's going to love you," he whispers back. He arches his brow, and his voice is stern. "Eighty years from now."

Turtles: "Elenore"

ANNIE MICK

Chapter 11

Colby

Little Rock, AR

Good God, I thought the British accent was irritating, the French language a little too over the top, the Aussie accent a bit cocky. But Southern twang is enough to make your ass cheeks clench. One mile outside of Mexico, Missouri and you'd think you were in Louisiana. Yes folks, there is a Mexico in Missouri. There's also a Columbia in Missouri. Just like there's a Moscow and a Paris in Iowa. I don't know if it stems from a lack of originality or dreams of grandeur surrounded by cornfields. Maybe it's wishing you could be anywhere other than the Midwest.

But I digress. Down here in the south, I get confused when I'm by myself and I hear someone say, "Ya'll come back now." Do they see more than one of me? Who exactly is ya'll?

I thought fetchin' is what dogs do when you throw a ball. No…apparently it's what kids do when they want a "whoopin"… at least that's what their mother told them while in the convenience store.

We aren't washing our clothes at the laundromat today… we're "worshin" 'em.

Double negatives are a way of life here.

Ain't got none…*so you must have some?*

I didn't steal nothin'…*so you did steal something?*

I ain't never seen nobody do nothin' like that…*so you have seen somebody do something like that?*

But their love of music is profound down here. Southern Rock is its own entity. And once it's found its way to your ears, it grips your soul.

* * *

The amphitheater is near capacity tonight. The weather is good, 70 degrees, a bit balmy, pretty typical for Arkansas in late June.

Sticky Whiskers has another half hour to play when Charlie sees one of the stagehands walking around backstage wearing a Groucho Marx mask on his face.

"What the hell you got that on for?" he asks the skinny, scruffy, ripped jeans wearing, blonde. Blonde hair and black eyebrows equals fashion faux pas, I guess.

"Uh," he hesitates, sliding his hands into his pockets, glancing around warily. "I'm kinda going incognito."

"You got a badge on your shirt, a stage pass around your wrist and you're kinda going *incognito,*" Charlie growls, emphasizing the last word. He crosses his arms over his chest, looking quite fearsome. It's not hard to do at six foot three and a voice that sounds like you eat gravel for breakfast. "Explain yourself, son. You got one minute, starting now."

"I-I might have made a mistake this afternoon," he stutters.

"Keep goin'," Charlie says as he glances at his watch.

"I met up with this girl and we went to her house and… and…"

"And what?" Charlie snaps.

"Well, we got naked and, I-I thought it was her house but turns out it was her parents' house and then they pulled in the driveway, and she freaked out and she fainted on the couch and…"

His words are rushed as his hands fly in the air in defense.

The rest of us are taking in the story, doing our best not to roll on the floor in laughter.

"Finish," Charlie tells him. "What did you do?"

He shrugs. "I grabbed my clothes and ran out the back door."

Charlie nods slowly as if in thought. "Okay, I can understand that," he says slowly. "What are you not tellin' me?"

Stagehand chuckles. "I might have grabbed a plastic banana out of a fruit bowl on the coffee table and put it in her hand before I left." His voice is raised as he defends his actions. "Thought it'd throw her daddy off the scent and give me enough time to get away."

Charlie scowls. "So why the mask?"

Grimacing, he answers, "Pretty sure she's in the audience."

Grabbing the nose on the mask and pulling hard before releasing it, Charlie lets it snap back hard.

"Ow," stagehand yells as he grabs his nose.

Pulling it once again, this time tearing the elastic band off, Charlie growls, "Man up, Groucho." He throws the mask on the floor behind him. "You better hope only she sees you and her daddy doesn't. Those racks on the pickup trucks down here are for shotguns and they're legal. Dollar to a nickel says she wasn't. Dumbass. Stay outta sight."

* * *

There's nothing like getting Charlie pumped up before a show. He is on fire tonight. He laughs out loud, twirls his drumsticks, and even stands while playing a couple times because he gets so into the music, and his excitement is hard to contain while sitting on his ass.

When one musician is on fire, the others follow. When the others are lit, I find myself lost in the fun, the fury, and the magic that takes place on stage with them.

I glance off to my left, backstage, and see some members

of Sticky Whiskers standing close to Millicent. Extremely close to Millicent. They chat; it's friendly, as in very friendly. As in arm over her shoulder friendly, whisper in her ear friendly.

She's in another sexy little dress that highlights all her feminine features. It's blue, follows every curve, every dip and angle, and makes her eye color pop. As if her eyes weren't blue enough already to stop a beating heart, she adds to it by enhancing them with makeup. And those damn little ankle boots that she wears. At least I'm the only one who knows what those pretty little toes look like.

The roadies love her. The venue owners love her. The advertising staff love her. But when fellow musicians take advantage of the time offstage to flirt with her while I'm onstage and can't do anything about it? Why am I so bothered by it? It's just flirting, right? I'm not jealous…am I?

Do your job, Colby. Deal with it when the show is over, Colby. Don't be an ass, Colby.

* * *

When the show is over, Millicent isn't waiting backstage for us as is her usual. I check with the roadies headed on stage to pack up and load equipment. No one seems to know where she is.

"Have you seen Millicent?" I ask Duffy, worried after seeing her with the band members from Sticky Whiskers, as none of them seem to be standing around either.

He glances around quickly, as do the others when they hear my inquiry. "No," he answers. "She's usually with you right after the show."

"Where the hell would she go?" Charlie yells above the noise.

Grady takes off towards the dressing room. "Check down the halls," he shouts. "She's gotta be around here somewhere."

Dave approaches one of the female staff and asks her to check the bathroom, describing Millicent to her in the process.

Bruce hollers, "I'll check the bus!" as he heads toward the

exit.

"Found her!" Grady yells, waving us all back to gather together. He rubs the back of his neck and frowns. "She's in the dressing room. And she looks pretty pissed."

"What?" I ask, my eyes wide. "Why?"

"All she said was she wanted all six of us in there…*now,*" he emphasizes.

"Who did what?" Dave eyes us, questioning as if we would have any insight.

I shrug. "I didn't do anything…that I know of."

"Let's go," Charlie orders. "Somebody did somethin'. Think I'll keep my hands in my pockets, though. My reflexes ain't what they used to be."

* * *

Walking into the dressing room one by one, we find Millicent sitting on the sofa, red faced and fuming; arms folded across her chest, one leg crossed over the other, foot bouncing in anger.

"Sit down," she orders as soon as the door closes.

Like children about to be whipped (or is that whooped? This is Arkansas), we all cower as we take a seat.

She stands, examining each and every one of us with very angry narrowed eyes before she inquires, "Which one of you jackasses told Sticky Whiskers and their crew that I am a lesbian?" She glowers at me. "Was it you?"

Slightly amused with the initial information, now pissed at the accusation, I yell, "No! Why would I do that?" Although I must admit I'd like to kiss whoever it was. Ingenuity at its best. That is one way to keep her from being hit on. Who says lesbian anyway? I believe the term is gay.

I look to the others to glean any insight as to who the guilty party is. I see two grins, two mouth twitches and a set of furrowed eyebrows. Damn…could be any one of them…or all of them. If guilty, these guys could all be singing soprano by next week's concert.

"Millie," Bruce sighs. "Why are you under the impression they think you're gay?"

"Oh gee, I don't know," she sneers, tapping her chin. "It could have been the proposition by the woman who put her hand on my ass asking if she could party with me later, *or* the dude who told me twenty minutes of heaven with him would change my tastes forever."

Grady holds his hands out, palm side up. "Maybe they assumed?"

"Or," she drawls, "maybe it was the confession I got out of the guy I put in a chokehold."

"Which guy was it?" I scowl, picturing the asshat that had his arm around her shoulder, whispering in her ear.

"Doesn't matter," she replies casually.

"It matters to me," I snap harshly.

"Thank you, superman." She flashes a snarky smile and winks. "But I can handle it myself." She actually fucking winks. And superman? That's taking it a little too far. I won't be her battering ram when she strikes out. If she wants to get pissed, she needs to find the right target. And I'm not him.

"Wow." I chuckle sarcastically. I stand and wave my hand towards the guys. "Maybe you can punch one of them and get a confession. Superman's going to put his cape to bed. Goodnight, Millicent." I bow dramatically before I take my leave and find my way back to the bus.

* * *

I slam a few cupboard doors as well as the fridge door when I get inside, looking for something to eat. Damn, I'm hungry. I settle on a Pop Tart, get undressed and plop in bed where I snack on Duffy's blueberry breakfast fetish while I sit and stew over the insolent little shit that refuses to be anything but the independent and 'Mighty Millicent'. A chokehold for being propositioned does seem a bit extreme.

I could be inside savoring fruits, cheeses, yogurt, and meats. Not to mention a couple of beers. But instead, I sit here boiling because as much as I want her company, there are times I would much rather be on top of her, pounding into her so hard she'd be screaming my name all the way into tomorrow.

Who in the hell told the band she was a lesbian? Whoever it was, I'm going to shake their hand and buy them dinner. One big fat slab of prime rib.

I toss the blankets off, throw on a pair of jeans, a T-shirt and shoes, step off the bus and make my way over to the bus that houses the Sticky Whiskers band and their crew.

Jake, the guitar player, is about to board when I reach my destination.

"Colby," he greets me in his usual friendly manner. "Great night tonight." He eyes me closer and frowns. "You don't look so good, bud. What's goin' on?"

"Which one of you guys hit on Millicent?" I ask him.

"What?" he asks, holding a hand up in defense. "Whoa, whoa, Colby. She's a little young for us."

"No shit," I bellow. "Which one was it? Which one thought he could get her to swing to the other side?"

His eyes fill with puzzlement and a side order of amusement. "The other side of what?"

"From women to men," I say without thinking. This whole conversation is sounding more ridiculous by the second. I can only go by what Millicent said in the dressing room. Twenty minutes of heaven…who the hell do they think they are?

"So…" Jake's mouth twitches, fighting a grin as he eyes me head to toe. "You must be one of them cross dressers then, huh?"

Chapter 12

Millicent

My heart sinks as Colby slams the door on his way out. Turning my back on the guys, I stare up at the ceiling and take a deep breath, blowing it out slowly.

"Wee bit harsh, don't ya think, Trinket?" Duffy says softly.

Nodding, I turn back slowly. "I screwed up," I whisper, my mouth twisting to one side as I bite my lower lip. "I can take care of myself though."

"So can we." He shrugs. "But you think we don't rely on each other? Colby's got it bad, Trinket. He'd do anything for you."

"I'm the one that did it," Bruce confesses, rolling his eyes. "I thought it would make things easier. I figured if I threw them off the scent from day one, they'd leave you alone and we wouldn't have to beat the shit out of anyone. Just tell us who it was, we'll keep the bruises invisible."

"Damn!" Charlie exclaims. "That's creative, buddy. I'd thought about telling them she's my daughter, but they already knew I didn't have one." He pounds a fist on a flat hand. "But I'm not averse to using a little physical reminder."

"I'm not averse to puttin' his ass in a wheelchair," Grady adds.

"Tell us who it was," Duffy orders.

I shake my head. "Not even sure. Didn't pay that much attention."

He looks to me and snorts. "We ain't that stupid. You know exactly who it was."

"It wasn't one of the band members, Duffy. Those guys have been nothing less than perfect gentlemen and friendly. It was a roadie." I grin impishly and add, "Don't think he'll be lifting anything for a while."

"What did you do, Little Bit?" Grady asks, eyeing me with a knowing grin.

"Look," I explain. "I can put up with only so much. I was trying to give him a pass for being an obnoxious ass and let it go the first time, but he just couldn't keep his mouth shut. He asked me to dance, I told him no. He grabs my ass and says," I lower my voice and mimic the asshole's response, "'Well, I guess a blow job is out of the question'." I shrug casually. "A choke hold and a knee to the balls seemed perfectly reasonable to me."

I wait for a response; any response will do. But I find it's generally easier to talk when your jaw isn't hanging open. Maybe that's why they aren't saying anything.

Charlie's the first to speak, "Damn, Millie, most women slap a man when he gets outta line."

"Why would I make my own palm sting?" I shake my head in disagreement. "The only thing I felt was satisfaction."

Laughter fills the room, and they look to one another and nod.

"Morty was right." Dave slaps his hand on the table. "She is a force to be reckoned with. Those hands and feet are deadly weapons."

I sigh in disappointment. "Yeah, well, I used my tongue as a weapon a while ago and now I have some reparations to make. I need to go find Colby. Eat up, guys."

"Take your time, Millie. We'll be awhile," Duffy says with a wink. "Tell Sandy and John to join us in here for some food. They'll get the bus door open from the outside."

"I'll walk you out the door and make sure you get to the bus," Grady offers.

"I can…" I start to protest but stop myself as I remember what Duffy said. There's nothing wrong with relying on each other, and he's simply looking out for me. "That'd be great. Thanks, Grady."

* * *

After informing Sandy that food awaits him inside and the bus will be occupied while both he and John are gone, I slowly make my way back to Colby's cubby. I stand outside and gather my bearings before I make an attempt to make amends.

"Colby," I whisper softly.

No response.

"Colby," I say louder and wait.

I hear him sigh. "I said goodnight already, Millicent."

"I know," I reply. "I came to tell you I didn't mean it."

"All right."

"That's all?"

"Yup."

Feeling defeated and dejected, I turn to walk away down the short path that leads to my bedroom. Before I get too far for him to hear, "Colby?"

He sighs again. "What?"

"I hate it when you're mad at me."

No response.

Turning the knob, I enter the room and close the door behind me. I tried. Wait! I didn't say I'm sorry, only that I didn't mean it. What good is an apology if you don't actually apologize? Twisting the knob once again with the intention of going back out and correcting my massive error, the door opens, and I find a shirtless Colby standing at the threshold.

For every step he takes forward, I take a step back. He closes the door behind him and locks it without turning around. He doesn't look like my usual Colby. His eyes are a darker shade of blue, his glare is heated. He's not angry per se. He's…he's, I don't know what he is.

"You hate it when I'm mad at you?" His voice is gruff, his tone sharp.

I nod and whimper, "Uh huh."

He narrows his eyes. "And just how mad do you think I am right now, Millicent?"

"On a scale of one to ten?"

He shakes his head, scowling. "Try triple digits."

"Oh."

"Oh." He nods as he takes a couple steps forward. I take a couple back. "Why didn't you just tell him you're mine?" The backs of my legs hit the side of the bed. I fall back onto the mattress and Colby follows on his knees above me.

"Yours?" I hiss, my chin tipping in defiance. "Him who?"

"Mine," he says. "And him is the idiot who is sitting on the Whiskers bus with an ice pack on his balls waiting to see if he has a job tomorrow. Regardless, he will be apologizing in the morning."

"You went over there?!" I wiggle to get out from underneath him, but he slides his hand under my back and scoots me farther up onto the bed.

"I did."

"Why?"

He pins me with a gaze that I can't tear my eyes away from. His voice is deep and rough as he tells me, "To make it clear that you. are. mine."

He takes my mouth in a demanding kiss. It's not harsh; it's overwhelming. It's owning, and for some reason I don't mind it. But Millicent and her mouth…

"Do I get a say in this?" I sass as he feathers kisses down my neck.

He squares me with a frosty glare. "Are you not mine?"

"Are you still mad at me?"

"Infuriated," he whispers as he plants another kiss on my mouth. "Exasperated, *(kiss)* annoyed, *(kiss)*. You're maddening, frustrating, *(kiss)* but so damn kissable."

My hips move of their own volition. Our pelvises bump and grind and it only gets worse as I wrap a leg around his back, simple fabric separating us. Our breaths growing shaky and heavy.

"Colby," I whine, wanting more.

"Millicent," he quietly warns, his warm breath on my neck. "This isn't happening here."

My stomach bottoms out at the realization that he's absolutely correct. This isn't happening here. We're on a bus with five *ahem* senior citizens, all of whom we both deeply respect. And let's face it folks, one throat clearing, one cough, one "Hey, dumbass, I wanted the blueberry Pop Tart tonight" or "Hand me the Beano, Millie's gonna have my head on a platter for that convenience store burrito I had for lunch", and the mood would be gone. And even if they aren't on the bus right now, we have no idea when they might return. Besides, I've never done this before, and I have no idea how loud I might get. Would I scream his name? Would I scream for God? Would I give directions for harder or faster? Yeah, that's a big no for bus sex.

I heave a sigh and whimper, "I know."

"Can you be quiet?" he whispers as his kisses take a trip south.

"I don't know," I answer, my voice shaky. "I can try."

"Good enough for me." He chuckles as he continues a journey to a region no one's ever been.

And man, do I try to remain quiet. I bite the heel of my palm as I try. I cover one hand with the other and muzzle myself to hide my moans and screams.

It must have worked. No one called the police…or an ambulance.

* * *

Colby holds me in his arms as I rest my head on his chest. I'm tucked under the covers in a blissful sated state. He gently rolls me off and kisses me once more.

"Goodnight, Millicent," he whispers.

"Wait." I reach for his arm and pull him towards me. "What about you? We didn't…"

He caresses my bottom lip with his thumb and smiles. "That was probably more for me than it was for you. We'll get there. Now, get some sleep. I'll see you in the morning."

"But I…"

"Millicent," he interrupts. "I've been walking around with the worst case of blue balls I've ever had for the last three months. I'll survive. You're worth the wait." He stands, walks to the door, and turns one more time. "Oh, in case you haven't figured it out, I'm not mad at you anymore. Sweet dreams." He winks and closes the door.

Goodnight, Colby.

Chapter 13

Colby

Jake certainly had his fun at my expense. "So, you must be one of them cross dressers, huh?" I would have liked to wipe that shit eating grin off his face. "Damn, Colby. Had me fooled. I thought you was carrying a set." Ha, ha.

Turned out all the guys in Sticky Whiskers were well aware Millicent and I are together. It also turned out all of them work for Morty and don't care to lose their jobs, or their balls, aka "stay the hell away from my niece".

They were also told by Bruce that prevention is always worth a pound of cure so informing their team she was gay would avoid any problems. Not taking into consideration that any members of their team might be female…well, we see how that didn't pan out.

What Millicent had failed to do was tell the whole story. She did more than a chokehold. The poor bastard is on the bus with an icepack on his balls, probably hoping he'll be able to walk without a limp by the next concert.

Approaching a woman, even propositioning her…it goes with the business, quite often. I'm not saying it's right, not saying it's proper. But grabbing her ass? Out of line, pal. That's my ass to grab.

He didn't have to lift any equipment after the show. No, they made him wrap all the cords. Funny thing about wrapping cords. You can do it sitting down, standing up, on your knees, or bent in half. It's my understanding he alternated body positions to accommodate his pain. If her knee to his balls was anything like her elbow to my ribs, I'd almost feel sorry for him…almost.

And right now, while he's icing those balls, he's writing an apology note and will be delivering it in the morning when the buses are parked. I initially suggested he do it while we're rolling, but I didn't want to chance it blowing away in the wind if I got tempted to throw him under the bus (pun intended).

* * *

I get back to the bus and see Sandy resting, right where I left him fifteen minutes prior.

"Feeling any better?" he asks.

"Not really," I answer. "I'm going to bed. See you in the morning."

"'Night, Colby," he says with a laugh.

"Did you get anything to eat yet?" I ask him.

"Not yet," he says. "John just went in. They always bring me a plate. I'm good, thanks."

Climbing into the cubby, I yank the curtain for privacy, hoping they leave me alone when boarding tonight. I'm still pissed, frustrated, and mildly horny. Did I say mildly? Moderately. Extremely.

I could go take an ice-cold quick shower in that skinny corner standup stall on this godforsaken bus: my usual treatment. I hear voices at the front of the bus and wait for the predictable routine of my fellow musicians after a show i.e.:

Change into lounge pants.
Brush teeth.
Sniff armpits.
Scratch balls.

Take nighttime meds.

Swallow Maalox to offset heartburn.

Call out the Walton's "'night, John Boy" routine.

And lest we forget, "Damn, I forgot to pee. Can somebody go for me?"

Instead, it's quiet. I hear the bus door close, and I wait. John and Sandy must have switched places.

"Colby?" Millicent whispers outside my cubby. I squeeze my eyes closed and ignore her. If I don't acknowledge her, she'll go away. No such luck.

She says my name louder and this time I answer. My voice is sharp, my answers short. But when she says, "I hate it when you're mad at me," it hits me right in the heart. I hate it too. I hated it when she was mad at me. This isn't us. I throw the blankets off, open the curtain to the cubby, hop out and see she's already closed her door. It's only a barrier, one simple door…

* * *

Hmph…that worked out well. I may be sporting the hardest, most painful chub I've ever had, but her glazed over, hooded eyes and blissful smile was all the satisfaction I needed. I will not be taking Millicent in the back of this bus. She deserves better. She deserves a full night – and many thereafter – of being able to release those moans and screams she withheld tonight…sort of… to the best of her capabilities. Millicent is no firecracker. That little lady is TNT waiting to detonate. And I'm itching to light that fuse. I wonder how long it's been for her. I know how long it's been for me. And after seeing her again after all these years, I can't seem to remember a damn one of them.

The bus starts to fill with seven men that have all been taking their time inside the auditorium, unbeknownst to me until Millicent shared that little tidbit when I got back to her room. I still wasn't taking her on this bus. We all have hotel reservations in two weeks for two nights. I can wait.

"Cheddar, you're looking a little less…angry." Duffy grins.

I scowl at him as I pull the curtain on my cubby. "Goodnight gentlemen."

Grady slides the curtain back and leans in over me. "Get out here, Norway."

"I'm tired." I pull the curtain closed again.

"And we're curious." He grins as he pulls it open once more.

I roll over and glower. "Curiosity killed the cat."

He shrugs. "More than one way to skin him."

"Are we killing a cat or skinning it, Grady?"

"Depends on what you did," he replies.

I pinch the bridge of my nose, grateful my glasses are not sitting on it, and blow out a deep breath.

"I'm not telling you anything about what Millicent and I…"

"Whoa, Norway," Grady stops me, his hand held in front of my face. "We ain't asking about Millie, you dumbass. We want to know what you did to the idiot on the Whiskers bus."

Charlie steps forward, finger pointing in my direction. "You ever tell us what you and Millie do and you ain't gonna have the parts to do it with. Understand?"

I glance over to Bruce and arch a brow. "Had it not been for Bruce's master plan, I wouldn't have made a total ass out of myself in front of Jake tonight and this whole mess could have been avoided."

Duffy laughs. "Bruce does stupid shit all the time. It's those wild hairs up his ass that grow too close to his brain. He can't help himself."

Bruce snorts and looks to Duffy. "I still have more hair on my legs than you do."

Duffy shoots him a wry grin. "But you ain't got any hair on your ass, Bruce. You could light up the whole bus with them lily-white half-moons."

"Skin cancer is no joking matter. I keep this bad boy covered at all times." Bruce slaps his ass with both hands, tips his chin and huffs indignantly. "Besides, I come in handy in a power outage."

He turns his back to us and drops his pants, bending slightly. "Anybody need a light?"

Throat clearing captures our attention from a direction none of us want to look. Bruce snatches his jeans quickly and pulls them back up over his ass, fastening them at the waist. He remains frozen where he stands, his back to the rest of us.

Millicent stands in the entryway to our quarters of the bus with her hand in front of her face, palm side out as if shielding her eyes. "Good grief, is there an on and off switch for that thing?"

"Millicent." My eyes flit from her to Bruce's ass. Don't ask me why, I have no idea. Did she see it?

"I came out for a bottle of water." She walks to the fridge, opens it, and grabs a Dasani. She turns back to head to her bedroom, pausing before she gets too far away. Her voice is light, laced with taunting. "Huh, all this time I thought the men's competitions involved tape measures. I guess you learn something new every day. Thanks for the light, Bruce. I'll know who to call when I lose something under the bed. Goodnight guys."

Bruce turns to face us once he hears Millicent's door close, his face flaming red, awash in embarrassment. "Well, who gets the honor of performing the first toilet swirly?"

Dave glares at him. "Covered at all times, huh?"

Raising his hands in defense, Bruce huffs, "Old jokes die hard. Mooning is now off the table. I promise."

Duffy looks to me, grimacing. "Remember when I said Bruce does stupid shit all the time?"

I nod slowly.

Grady slaps my shoulder. "Give him time, Norway. He'll come up with something even dumber."

Sweet Jesus, tell me it won't involve a Full Monty...or a Glow Worm.

Chapter 14

Millicent

"Good morning, sweet cheeks." I lean in and plant a kiss on Bruce's cheek and watch his skin flush from the neck up. Colby flashes me a look of shock, his mouth agape, eyes bulging.

It's Grady's turn to fix breakfast this morning and he stands at the stove turning bacon. I see him smirk at my gracious greeting. The bus is parked at a rest area somewhere between Little Rock and Tulsa so everyone can take a quick stretch and eat while the wheels on the bus are not going round and round.

I didn't spend too much time pondering how to face this morning. I've seen a lot in my years between the military and traveling with road bands; it would take a whole lot more than a bare ass to shock me. Besides, what happened last night was more my fault than Bruce's. I should have announced my pending arrival rather than stepping out the way I did.

He scratches the back of his head nervously, staring at his coffee cup. "Millie, I'm sorry about…"

Patting his arm as I take a seat next to him at the table, I reassure him. "Nothing to be sorry about, Bruce. It's a nice butt."

"Excuse me?" Colby stares as if I've insulted him personally.

I shrug casually. "You don't think so?"

"I wasn't studying it," he snaps, then narrows his eyes. "Apparently like someone else was."

Bruce drops his forehead onto the heel of his palm, wincing. Grady's shoulders rock gently with silent laughter. The door to the bus opens and the three other band members join us, each one taking in the scene before them.

"Breakfast is up," Grady informs us, setting my plate on the table as well as his own. He turns to the others and tilts his head toward the stove. "This ain't no restaurant. Serve yourselves."

"What's for breakfast?" Charlie rubs his hands together as he walks toward the stove. I note he seems to be limping a bit, favoring his right leg.

"Bacon, eggs, and toast," Grady replies. "Don't forget the required yogurt and fruit…" He nods at me, "…thanks to Little Bit. And to help him get a head start, there's a special helping of peach fuzz on the side there for Bruce. Good cover until the Rogaine starts working."

Bruce glowers at him. "Real funny, asshole."

"Bruce with the nice butt," Colby grumbles, rising from the table.

Duffy hands Colby a plate as he nears the counter. "What's that, Cheddar?"

"Nothing," he grunts.

"Watch," Grady whispers, nudging my shoulder as he points to Colby's backside. "Nothin' makes a man flex his cheeks faster than a woman complimenting another man's ass."

Fascinated, I watch the globes of gluteus maximus twitch as Colby serves himself at the stove. I swear there's a dance performance taking place inside those jeans. It's not a ballet, not a samba and not a waltz. Ahhh…that's a fox trot.

Grady nudges me again and winks. "Told ya."

I giggle once, twice, and can't stop. Grady's low chuckle is a welcome sound next to mine.

"Something funny?" Colby asks, setting his plate down harder than necessary.

"Just enjoying the entertainment, Norway." Grady grins.

"Out of curiosity, do you dance?"

I laugh so hard I snort and grab my napkin, holding it to my mouth for fear coffee will shoot out my nose. I stand from the table, snatching my dishes away to set them near the sink. I need to step away, if only for a few moments.

"Where are you going?" Colby asks, obviously irritated. "You didn't finish breakfast."

"I'll grab a yogurt later." Turning to Bruce, my inner smartass surfacing, I smile. "I seem to have lost a sandal. I'm afraid it might be hidden under the bed. Think you could shine a little light in there and help me find it later?"

He laughs, as do the others; all but one that is. Colby scowls as he sets his fork down and rises from the table. His gaze is set, his footsteps don't falter as he stomps his way to his target...me.

I rush down the hall and before I can get my door closed, Colby blocks it with his hand. I've seen this look before. He's amusingly irritated. I take two steps back as he takes two steps forward, I take two more steps back, he takes two more steps forward until he's in the room, shutting the door behind him and locking it. *I think we've done this before.*

He arches a brow, his voice a deep growl. "A nice butt? Really?"

Clearing my throat, hiding my giggle that begs to be released, I tell him, "Not as nice as yours. His doesn't do a fox trot."

"A fox trot?"

"Kinda like those little bulldogs your uncle Duffy talked about, only foxes, and they, uh..." I move my hands like balancing a scale, adding a little sway, "...dance." This time I can't suppress my giggle.

We hear the bus engine start and feel the floor beneath us gently vibrate as the wheels start to roll once again.

He places his hands on my hips and squeezes. "And you think that's funny?"

"Meh...I'm pretty easily entertained."

"So am I." His smirk is devilish as his fingers move upwards and begin to dance on my ribs. "Ticklish?"

I shoot him a glare and clench my jaw. "Colby…"

* * *

After tickles, screeches, and multiple kisses later, we leave my bedroom and enter the main part of the bus where we find the rest of the band seated, playing cards.

"What are we playing, guys?" I round the table as I peek over their cards.

Charlie shelters his cards against his chest. "Apparently not what you were."

I roll my eyes. "So, you're not playing Candy Crush?"

He snorts and looks to Colby. "Is that what you kids are callin' it these days?"

"Charlie," Colby snaps.

"You were playing Candy Crush?" Dave looks at the two of us and grins knowingly. "From the looks of him, I would say you were playing Colby crush."

Duffy looks up from his cards, thankfully changing the subject. "Poker. You any good, Trinket?"

"I've been known to play." I don't bother to add I'm an ace at the game. "You guys ever gamble?"

Grady looks up from his hand, a gleam in his eye. "We could make it interesting. No money. We'll bet on chores."

"Chores?" I ask. "As in cooking, cleaning, that sort of thing?"

"Yup," he answers, popping the P, sounding a little too sure of himself.

I narrow my eyes and glance around the table. "No laundry. I'm not doing anybody's underwear and I certainly don't want you doing mine."

"How about laundry without underwear?" Bruce proposes.

"No dice. I already help you guys and I don't trust anyone else to do mine. That's a lose-lose for me. Off the table. Everything else is up for grabs." Little do they know I already have this in the bag. They didn't call me "little shark" without reason.

"Deal," they agree in unison.

I rub my hands together and take a seat.

"Millicent," Colby warns, shaking his head. "You might want to think twice about this."

With a wink and a bright smile, I reassure him. "I'll take my chances."

He groans loudly, "Deal me in. I may as well get stuck doing half the chores with her."

Five games later and now chore-free, I slap my hands on the table. "You guys care to play for anything else?"

Six sets of eyes glare from their fixed positions.

"No?" I tease, grinning like the Cheshire cat. "We could play for dinner choices, activities while we're off, who gets to polish my nails when we have pajama parties. Ooh, I know. Whether or not Duffy gets a haircut!"

That one earns me a specific glare…and a growl. "I am not cutting my hair, Trinket. And you already pretty much have charge over the dinner menu. No Mexican, remember?"

My shoulders sag as I realize they really have been good to me. They've adhered to the change in their diets, they do get exercise on a regular basis, they drink more water than beer.

"Well, I'll take the winnings I have and be a happy camper then." I rise from the table and start to collect the glasses that are empty.

Grady reaches for my hand to halt my collection. "Uh, uh. We got this, Little Bit. You won fair and square. You are officially a lady of leisure."

"It was just a game, Grady. I'm not going to run out on my responsibilities."

I hear a deep voice whisper in my ear, "Go, we've got this. They called the rules. I really wish you'd agreed to the laundry though. I would have been happy to wash your underwear." He chuckles and leaves a soft kiss on my ear.

I head to the front of the bus and open the partition. "Hey, John. How far to Tulsa?"

"Should be in by seven tonight," he replies. "Looks good."

"Thanks."

Thank God for open WIFI. I find a five-star Mexican restaurant in the area, call ahead for reservations to include our roadies as well as the people on the Whiskers bus for eight o'clock tonight; just in case we're late getting into town. I call Jake, the guitar player in the Whiskers band, to confirm Mexican food is a good choice. *I believe I could have heard the cheers without the phone connection.* I also locate the KOA campground we're headed for this evening. We utilize the campgrounds so that everyone–roadies included–can grab full showers without waiting one-by-one a half an hour for hot water in between, and without smashing an elbow against the shower wall every time you turn. Luxury has its limits on a bus, and noses have their limits for less than daily showers.

We have two days before the concert in Tulsa. Morty scheduled this tour in such a way that there is no rush between performances. There's time for a bit of sightseeing and tourism before and sometimes after the next concert. This entire reunion was never about money; that's become more and more apparent with every day. God, I love my Uncle Morty.

Now, what to do with the rest of our time in Tulsa before the actual concert.

> *Oh, give me a home,*
> *where the buffalo roam*
> *and the laundromats*
> *are open all day...*

Chapter 15

Colby

Tulsa, Oklahoma

Millicent insisted Duffy be blindfolded before we park the Uber van she had ordered to take us for the surprise she had planned. He was a bit reluctant, fearing she would bring out the shears before he could escape, but eventually surrendered to her pleading and promises it had nothing to do with his "beautiful monkey tail". The rest of us were sworn to secrecy or we would be banished to the sandwich shop across the street, ne'er to eat Mexican food again so long as we should live. It was like a burrito vow sent straight to divorce court on the grounds of infidelity with a slip of the tongue.

Upon arriving inside the restaurant, Duffy's head tips back, his nostrils flaring at the smells infiltrating them.

"Is this what I think it is?" His smile is so big, the corners of his mouth nearly reach the edges of the blindfold still wrapped around his head. "Trinket, I'm gonna kiss you!"

Millicent places a gummy in his hand, closes his fingers around it and whispers, "They didn't have a worm to place in the bottom of the bottle, so I brought one for you. I'll let you dip it in my fru-fru drink."

Duffy tears his blindfold off with his free hand, his eyes blinking fast to adjust to the stark contrast of light from the dark as he stares at the gummy worm in his hand. His sudden burst of laughter can be heard throughout the restaurant as he lifts Millicent off her feet and twirls her around in a circle until I see her eyes close; making me fear that fru-fru drink isn't going to seem very appealing.

Duffy finally sets her back on her feet and squeezes her tightly around her shoulders, kissing the top of her head. "Have I told you yet today you're my favorite human being in the whole world?"

Have I ever told you Duffy's eyes smile when he smiles? They crinkle at the corners, they sparkle; there's a light that reflects off them. He's like a leprechaun.

She smiles sheepishly as she looks up at him adoringly. "Your favorite human being, huh? So, who's your favorite animal being?"

He snorts and looks to me. "That'd be Cheddar. Roars like a lion, but he's really all fluffy inside." He winks at Millicent. "Like a kitty cat."

And boom! Make that a smartass leprechaun.

"There's a tent on the bus, Duffy." I narrow my eyes and smile. "Guess who's sleeping outside tonight."

He slaps an arm over my shoulders as he pulls Millicent along with his other still wrapped around her.

"Let's go get our burrito on, boys. Hot sauce is on me." He dips his mouth close to Millicent's ear, "Not literally, Trinket. I'll keep the beard clean."

* * *

"How many of those you gonna have, Little Bit?" Grady asks her as the waitress sets down a third margarita in front of Millicent. She tips back the glass she's currently holding, drains it, and hands the waitress the empty.

Millicent bows her head and hesitates. *I think she needed to release a belch but I'm not sure.* "As many as it takes." She smiles at Grady, her eyes glassy.

The drummer from Sticky Whiskers is at the end of the table. He holds his mug of beer up as if to toast. "She's okay, Grady. A good woman knows how to hold her liquor."

"How does a good woman hold her liquor, Brody?" Millicent asks innocently.

Damn you, Brody.

He wears the smile of the devil and winks. "By his ears."

Every head at our table turns in his direction and shoots him a glare. We knew what was coming.

Millicent isn't fazed in the least. She shakes her head slowly, then shrugs her shoulders. "I wouldn't know about that. I'm a hair puller myself." She takes another sip of her margarita, licks her lips and hiccups. *How many more margaritas is she planning on having?*

All eyes come back to Millicent in shock and slowly turn towards me in a *'what the hell?'* glower. I subconsciously scratch the back of my head – don't ask me why. She didn't pull my hair. Did she? I'm getting tingles on my scalp just thinking about it. Maybe she did. All I remember is being so lost in…

Duffy smirks. "Got an itch, Cheddar?"

"Uh…" I feel my cheeks flush with being caught in Millicent lust.

Millicent pats my leg and leans her head on my shoulder. She tips her head up and whispers in my ear, "I like kitty cats. They're really good with their tongues."

She's going back to the bus…now. Apparently, two margaritas is her limit.

"We should probably get going." I adjust her so she's sitting up straight and place my napkin on the table.

"No, no, no," she protests, swaying in her seat. "We're not going anywhere until Charlie tells me why he's limping."

"I ain't limpin', Millie." Charlie frowns as he turns towards her but doesn't meet her gaze. A pretty glassy gaze, I must admit, but a gaze just the same.

"Yes, you are," she singsongs, waving her finger in the air. "I saw you earlier today and I noticed it again tonight when we came in the door. What is wrong with your leg?"

"There ain't nothin' wrong with my leg." He looks her straight in the eyes, his brows pinched.

She ponders for a moment, her finger tapping her chin clumsily. She's so damn cute I want to wrap her up and take her home forever.

"Aha!" she yells. "Avoidance. It's not your leg. Is it your back? Your hip? Which unruly body part is making you limp?"

"Millie," he sighs. "I'm fine. Nothin' to worry about."

"Your gait is crooked, Charlie. Something's not right."

"My what is crooked?"

"Your gait," Bruce interjects. "It's your manner of walking. I thought maybe you had a stick up your ass."

Charlie reaches over and slaps Bruce across the back of the head.

"Ouch! You asshole!" Bruce shouts.

"Oh, God." Millicent's eyes go wide. She leans over and whispers loudly to Charlie. "Was that code for something? Is it hemorrhoids? We can stop and get some cream."

I get up from my seat, shaking my head as I reach for her arm. If it is hemorrhoids, it's Charlie's problem; not hers.

"Let's go, guys," I say as I pull her towards me. She's wobbly and nearly faceplants as she tries to stand. I hold her under her arms and tuck her against my chest.

"Ooohh," she pitches high as she leans into me. "Those drinks were potent." She looks up at me with crystal blue eyes from under long dark lashes, a goofy grin lights her face as she pets my chest. "Do you ever purr?" Her head drops onto my chest and her legs turn to noodles. Millicent has just passed out, standing up.

Well, now we know. Two margaritas is her limit. And if this time is anything like the last, maybe I ought to buy a tent and sleep out under the stars with her tonight. Damn. She was grumpy after two margaritas last time. Think I'd better have the hair of the dog premixed in the morning. Maybe I could just tuck her in next to me in my cubby....

I reach under her knees and hoist her up into my arms. Her head leans on my shoulder as one arm hangs limply away from her body. Duffy tucks it in, so it doesn't hang freely and to avoid injury. "You're either gonna have to toughen her up or learn when to cut her off, Cheddar."

"Kind of have my hands full right now, Duffy."

He chuckles and pats my shoulder. "Boy, you have no idea. Put a big bowl at the side of the bed. Best plan on being up a while." He heeds a warning with his last bit of advice. "And don't let her sleep on her back."

He takes the lead to get us to the door while the others follow, and we file one-by-one through the restaurant. One-*on*-one if you consider how Millicent is lying in my arms.

On our way out the door, the hostess sees me carrying Millicent. She worries her brow and shoots me a look of pity. "Aw, did somebody have a rough day?"

Grady grins as he looks from her to me. "She'll be all right. Her day's over. His night's just beginnin'."

* * *

As God as my witness, she is never drinking again. I emptied the bowl twice last night, flushed the toilet at least a half dozen times, and held her hair back while she emptied the contents of her stomach.

The worst part? Or maybe the best...I don't know. She whipped off her shirt and bra, shimmied out of her jeans and panties, and tried to put on a tank top and shorts–all while I was in her tiny bathroom cleaning out the vomit bowl. Trouble is, she was sitting buck naked on the bed when I came out of said tiny bathroom, trying to slip one leg into the shorts...and failing miserably. *I only peeked a little.*

I slipped her tank top on her quickly, pulled the shorts up

129

even faster, washed her face gently with a warm washcloth, and put her back into bed. In that order, thank you very much. I spent the rest of the night trying to decide if I was angry, frustrated, worried or just plain horny. In the end, turned out to be all of the above.

* * *

And here I sit at the table waiting for her to wake up and join the living. The bus has been aired out, windows are wide open, breakfast is ready and her treatment of 'hair of the dog' is waiting for her. Should she decide she doesn't want the treatment, this dog is going to bite her in the ass this morning. I think I may have managed two hours of sleep at best and I'm the one who has a concert tomorrow night.

"Don't look so damn grumpy, Norway," Grady says as he sets a plate of pancakes in front of me. "We've all done it."

"Yes, Grady I know." I fork my pancake and shove a bite in my mouth. "I don't usually have to be carried home when I've done it though."

He slaps the back of my head before I can see it coming. "Hey, dumbass. I meant cleaning up after somebody."

"I'll never be able to apologize enough for ruining the floormats in your Dodge, Grady," Bruce groans as he drops his head in his hands. He looks up with an apologetic expression. "Did I ever pay you for those?"

Grady shrugs. "Hell if I know."

"Hell, I still owe Dave for ruining his brand-new boots when he hauled my ass outta that alley one night," Charlie grumbles.

Dave shrugs. "Happenstance."

"Bullshit," Charlie growls.

"You were in a bad way." Dave arches a brow. "Could have happened to any one of us. It's what we're here for."

Duffy holds his finger up to offer another circumstance. "I owe Grady for rolling me onto my side so I didn't aspirate."

Grady looks to Duffy, and I swear I see tears rim his eyes. "And I owe Duffy…for pulling a needle out of my arm before I pushed the plunger…" his voice drops to a whisper "…too far."

My pancakes are cold, my fork was set on the plate long ago. I feel like the world's biggest ass right now. Until I see them all glance at Bruce and watch as Charlie puts his arm around him.

"But this guy, this guy here," he praises. "He's always been the first one to show up; Kleenex in one hand, a bottle in the other, and words that make you believe you will never walk alone. He knew loss before any of us did."

Nope. This world's biggest ass just got bigger.

I knew my Uncle Duffy had a big heart. This is like having four more of him in the same room. I didn't think the world held four more people like my uncle. These are his best friends…and it's easy to see why. They have each other's backs in the best of times and in the worst. They may be old horses but ain't nobody ever gonna put them out to pasture, because together, they are their own glue factory. And God help the man that ever tries to separate them.

The door to Millicent's room opens and she slowly makes her way out to the kitchen area, looking a bit pale and a lot hungover.

She gives a small wave in our direction, not making eye contact with any of us, and walks toward the coffee pot. I get up from the table and open the fridge, grabbing the premixed ingredients to be added to her coffee this morning. I reach for the coffee pot before she can and pour it into the cup. I stir the mixture with a spoon and hold it out for her to take.

"I drink mine black, thanks. I can get it." Her voice is barely a whisper, and she continues to avoid eye contact. She's brushed her teeth; I can smell the minty freshness of her breath. She's combed her hair. She's doing her best to look presentable, but the effects of last night are not easily hidden.

"This one is special," I tell her. "The cure all. And I want to take care of you."

"Colby, I'm fine."

I look out into the room and in a cheerful, raised voice I ask of anyone and no one, "Anybody up for a run this morning?"

She presses her fingers to her temples and shudders with the sound. "Colby, please."

"Headache, Millicent?"

She sighs heavily. "Yes."

I step behind her, pressing my chest to her back and hold the coffee cup in front of her. I lower my mouth to her ear and whisper, "It's called a hangover, love. Drink it, Trinket, or I will be the dog that bites you in the ass."

She finally takes the cup from my hand, but I stay where I am until she takes a sip. I feel her shiver as she forces a swallow. "Drink it, Millicent."

"Do I have to?" she whines ever so softly.

"You do."

"Are you going to watch me?"

I hide a chuckle. "Do I need to watch you?"

Her shoulders slump slightly. "Can I take it back to my room?"

"Depends." I run my tongue from the pulse point of her neck up to her earlobe and nip it gently. I whisper so only she can hear, "Are you hiding a kitty cat back there to lap it up for you?"

Honest to God, she gulps the entire contents in five seconds flat and sets the cup down on the counter so fast I'm afraid she's broken it.

She spins toward her bedroom and tears down the hallway as she calls out behind her, "I'm going to get a shower."

At least now I know she doesn't forget what happens when she drinks.

* * *

The rest of us head for the community showers in the KOA after breakfast is cleaned up. I leave a note for Millicent stating she can take hers out of the fridge and reheat it in the microwave. There's more coffee in the pot, pancakes in the fridge, and the forever available Pop Tarts in the cupboard. She'll be fine. Her shower water had shut off some time ago so it's just a matter of when she decides she's ready to face me. The remnants of last night's aftermath were removed before she woke up. I was hoping she wouldn't remember, but after this morning I'm thinking there's a better chance of August snow in Arizona.

* * *

Bruce is his cheery self this morning as we're all lined up in shower stalls basking in warm water and scrubbing ourselves. Charlie starts with his ever so popular rendition of swimming with bowlegged women. Duffy croons Jailhouse Rock to outdo Charlie. Dave sings Procol Harem while Grady starts singing Heard It Through the Grapevine. It sounds like dogs howling to be truthful.

"What the hell are you doing?" I yell from my shower stall. "The campers are going to call for help thinking there's a wounded animal in here!"

My shower door swings open and standing before me is a park ranger. A female park ranger. "Did somebody call for help?" Her eyes flash as they float to my gender region, and she smiles. My *hands* fly to my gender region, and I don't.

"Excuse me. What?" I scowl at her. "Would you mind closing the door?"

I hear chuckles coming from the other stalls – from, you know, those assholes I thought were my friends this morning. She glances once again at the deep south area and licks her lips. I narrow my eyes and bark, "Shut. The. door."

She rolls her eyes and lets go of the spring-hinged door and it slams shut.

"We heard some odd noises coming from within the building. Thought we should check it out. Wild animals seek shelter in here sometimes," she snickers. "Can't say as if I've seen one like you, but you never can tell. You boys okay?"

"We're fine," I growl.

"I can see that you're *fine*," she says, overtones of playfulness in her voice. "I asked if you're okay."

I look over the top of the stall and curl my lip. "Next time, knock."

"You boys in town for the concert tomorrow night?" she hums.

Bruce doesn't hesitate to inform her from behind his closed door. "We *are* the concert tomorrow night."

"No kidding," she replies, as if she didn't know. There are four buses parked on the sites, two of them plastered with the names of the bands on the sides. Yeah, she had no idea. "Which one are you?"

"Fourplay," Bruce answers without *fore*thought. *Dumbass.*

"That sounds like fun," she teases, her voice playful and sickeningly sweet. "So, in my experience, foreplay usually ends with sticky whiskers. What time do you like your fans to show up? Just asking for a friend."

I slam the faucet off and look over the top of the shower stall once more. "Get out."

She arches her brow and smiles. It's not a pretty smile; it's downright salacious. "My friends and I have front row seats." She winks and blows me a kiss. "I'll be dreaming about it…" she eyes the middle of the shower door as if she can see through it, "…the whole time."

I think my balls just shriveled up inside my taint. I need to see Millicent. She's the only one I want thinking about my gender region. I know she's thinking about my tongue.

Fourplay with Sticky Whiskers…Sticky Whiskers with Fourplay. I knew eventually it was going to catch up with us when we least expected it. Those damn buses and their banners.

"Need to turn on the cold water over there, Cheddar?" Duffy's laugh rings throughout the concrete building.

"I need to get the hell out of here." I reach for my towel – which moments ago was hanging on the door. "Where the hell is my towel?"

I hear the ball-shrinker holler from outside the entrance, "It caught on my belt. Want me to bring it to you or do you want to come and get it?"

Throwing shorts on over my soaking wet legs, I step out of the shower and grab the rest of my things. I stalk to the door and hold my hand out. "Give me my towel and get the hell out before I report you to park services."

She hands me my towel, grins, and winks again. "See you tomorrow night, handsome. Thanks for the early show."

Storming my way towards some of the roadies standing around the buses, I can hear their chuckles and laughter as they stare. Apparently, gossip travels fast. I'm shirtless, dripping wet and pissed.

"Not one fucking word," I growl as I pass. Silence befalls the group immediately. Good. I obviously got my point across.

Upon entering the bus, I find Millicent sitting at the table eating pancakes and drinking coffee. Sandy is holding a paper and having a cup of coffee as well while he and John discuss... whatever. Maybe maps for the road trip out of hell.

"Whoa, Colby." Sandy laughs. "Worked up quite a sweat there. Didn't think it was that hot yet."

Millicent looks up and her eyebrows pinch into a frown. "Did you go for a run?"

I take her hand in mine and pull her up from the table, leading her to the back of the bus where her room is, throwing my items from the shower toward my cubby as we pass. I slam the door shut with my foot after we get inside the room and spin her around to face me, taking her cheeks in my palms, I study her face. These are the eyes I want to gaze into, the face I want to see in my dreams, the lips I want to kiss.

"It's not sweat," I assure her.

She giggles. "I can tell. You smell good. Not that you smell bad when you..."

I drop my mouth to hers, collecting a much needed long, drawn out, tantalizing kiss. I stop for only a moment before taking one more.

"Wow." She gasps. "What was that for?"

I lean my forehead on hers, close my eyes and tell her truth. "For me."

She smiles sweetly and tilts her head. "Can I have one?"

"As many as you want." I kiss her again and again, and

before I get too carried away; I pull back. "I needed my Millicent fix."

She runs her fingertips through my beard. The sense of comfort mixed with the shivers it sends up my spine is overwhelming. "Well, Mr. Jarlsberg, you come borrow my tools any time you need. I'll fix you right up."

"Same here, okay?"

She laughs softly and nods. "Deal."

Millicent Trinkett isn't just a part of my world; she is fast becoming my world. If she said jump, I wouldn't ask how high. I would say, "Come fly with me."

* * *

Everyone is back from their showers and grouped around the table once more when we leave Millicent's bedroom.

"Feel better now, Norway?" Grady teases as we reach the table. Millicent's breakfast plate is gone and now I fear she didn't get enough to eat.

"I feel fine, Grady." I open the fridge to see what I can fix for her. I didn't get a whole lot to eat myself, listening to the conversation that took place this morning.

"It can be traumatizing when a lady sees your tally-whacker when you least expect it," Dave says. "If the water's cold, it can be really embarrassing as well."

Millicent gasps at what she thinks is insinuation that we were doing naughty things in her bedroom. "I didn't see his tally-wonker! We weren't doing anything back there!"

"Tally-whacker," Dave corrects her. "It's a tally can't-whacker if the water's cold. And we would never assume any such thing about you, Millie."

"Colby didn't tell you about gettin' hit on in the shower?" Charlie asks her.

I turn to Charlie and shoot him a scathing scowl as I slice a finger across my throat.

Millicent's eyebrows shoot skyward before she tucks her

chin and laughs. "Some dude hit on you in the shower? Is that why…"

"No!" My eyes flare as I stare her down. She'd better not share what went on back there.

"Is that why what?" Bruce asks.

Millicent clears her throat and shakes her head. "Nothing." She looks puzzled for a moment. "Wait a minute. You got hit on in the shower, but it wasn't a dude?"

"Let's call her…" Bruce taps his chin as if in thought, "… an ardent fan of tally-whackers."

The others laugh and look to me, waiting for my response.

I heave a sigh of frustration. "Can we let this go?"

"No, no," Grady laughs. "Tell her about it, Norway. Didn't I hear something about front row tomorrow night?" He shrugs. "Just asking for a friend."

Millicent stares at me, wide-eyed. "A woman saw your… tally-whacker?"

With a huff of indignance, I answer, "Through no fault of mine."

She sits silent; pondering, before she grins impishly. "Did she like it?"

Another round of laughter ensues and I finally cave. I can fight this or go with the flow. I flash her my sexiest smile and bob my eyebrows. "Says it's what dreams are made of."

* * *

After another hour of ribbing, bad jokes, and numerous cups of coffee with a few Pop Tarts – Duffy taking half of one to the birds outside – we decide to take a couple cars into town and do some sightseeing. When it comes time to put shoes on, Millicent is keenly watching Charlie. She's been keeping a close eye on him for the last couple days; worried about a limp that no one else has seemed to notice. I watch her watching him and see her eyes flash with triumph. She doesn't say a word; she only smirks and I see her hand fist, itching to bump someone else's in victory.

She takes off toward her bedroom and reappears ten minutes later with a smile that lights up the bus. Brighter than Bruce's lily-white ass, I might add.

"Are we ready? Ubers should be here in five minutes. Let's roll," she orders, sounding much like a drill sergeant. "I get to choose the first place today. All set up and they're expecting us. You guys are going to love it!"

"Where are we going, Trinket?" Duffy's a little less guarded with her now after the Mexican restaurant, but it's in his nature to be prepared for what lies ahead.

"Let me pamper you guys today. It's all on the Amex, Uncle Morty style," she says with an easy smile. It's too easy, almost sneaky. She's giving the Cheshire cat a run for its money with the shit eating grin she wears, now lit with a twinkle in her eyes. And half hour later…I know why.

"Toes R Us"

"What the hell is this?" Charlie scowls from his seat next to Millicent. I thought her seating arrangement was a bit odd when she demanded Charlie sit next to her in the car.

She smiles sweetly as she tugs on his arm and pulls him out of the car. "It's my secret indulgence that I'm sharing with all of you today. You get to sit in a chair with a back massager while soaking your feet in a scented bath, and a lovely lady to trim your nails so they don't rub in your boots." She leans her head on his shoulder and hugs him. "I promise, you don't have to get them polished."

I watch as Charlie's chest caves and his shoulders slump. He stares off into the distance and his voice cracks, "Millie, you don't understand."

Chapter 16

Millicent

"Millie, you don't understand."

There's something in his voice that breaks my heart. It's the sound of his breaking as he talks. What have I done? I wanted to help him. I saw his toenails this morning when he was putting his shoes on. It's no wonder he's limping. His toenails are rubbing inside his boots and the pain has to be excruciating. I would have offered to cut them for him, but I didn't want to insult him. I thought if I got all six men to come for a pedicure, I could treat it like a luxury and the problem would be solved. Tada! Stupid, stupid Millicent.

"What did I do wrong, Charlie?" My voice cracks as I look up at the man I deemed to be strong as a rock. I watch as his shoulders sag and his head hangs. I want to wrap him in my arms, tuck him back in the car and take him home.

He wraps his arm around my shoulder and pulls me tight to his chest. He kisses the top of my head and whispers, "You didn't do anything wrong, Millie. I just haven't figured out how to do it right yet."

The others stand outside the Ubers patiently, hands in their pockets, waiting. Charlie turns to them, nods towards the Ubers and says, "Let 'em go. I gotta do this eventually."

He leads me to one of the benches lining the sidewalks around the strip mall where the pedicure salon awaits our arrival. We take a seat, and the others soon join us, taking various places of support, be it on the ground around us, on the bench beside us, or standing next to us.

"I had hip surgery two years ago that impaired my bending and squatting. I can only lift my legs so far, and twisting's a real bitch," he explains. "Sally started clipping my toenails for me after the surgery and always made sure they were trimmed just right. That woman would sit for an hour…clippin', filin'." He takes a deep breath, blows it out and releases a small chuckle. "Hell, I don't know. Maybe she used hedge trimmers. Whatever Sally did, she did it right. She never once cut the skin, never once left a snag or cut 'em too short. I've had to learn to do so many…" he chokes back a sob, then sniffles, "…so many things over the last year. But I can't cut my own damn toenails."

I hug him tightly and feel his stuttered breaths. I feel this rock of man break down in my arms. His wife has been gone a year and he feels the pain like it was yesterday. He is devoted to a memory to the point of agony. That is love.

After a few minutes, the tension eases out of his shoulders and he sits up straight, takes a few calming breaths and nods as if to say he's done.

He looks to me, raises the arch of his brow and in his gravel pit deep voice asks, "You gonna make them get 'em too?"

"Darn right," I sniffle. "We're all in this together."

He scans the semi-circle of guys around us with his eyes narrowed and quips, "Get your pansy asses in there. The boss has spoken."

They all exchange a look that seems to be a special one made only for them. It's in their eyes, the pressed lips that form knowing smiles, the short nods that accompany them. The ones that say, *"We got ya, buddy"*.

He puts his arm around my shoulders as we head for the door and pulls me in for a half hug. "You're in the chair next to me, Millie."

"Wouldn't have it any other way, Charlie." I cup the side of my mouth, so no one else hears. "I think we should make them get polish on theirs, though. What do you think?"

He nods and winks. "Sassy. I like it."

Wilson Pickett: Mustang Sally

"You really painted those little shits' toenails hot pink?" Charlie asks, his shoulders rocking in laughter while the pedicurist tries to hold his foot still while she files his nails after clipping them.

"I did," I confirm. "They had the driver stop at a Walgreen's to get…" I use air quotes "…ibuprofen for a headache. They snuck in a bottle of polish remover, but I filled it with rubbing alcohol when they weren't looking. Imagine how pissed they were when it didn't work. I don't think I slept more than an hour at a time during that tour."

Dave looks perplexed as he turns in his chair. "Rubbing alcohol doesn't take that stuff off?"

I shake my head. "Nope. You need acetone. I was giggling in my bunk listening to them argue while rubbing their toes raw." I mimic the boys in my best baritone imitation as I reminisce hearing them struggle. "'You dumbass, you should have gotten super strength', 'you should have gotten the one that removes glitter, 'you should have gotten the one with the purple lid'." And then I finish with the winner from Calvin. "'I'm gonna have to have sex with my socks on for the rest of my life, ain't I?'" That particular one brings the biggest round of laughter.

We have exchanged stories and antics for the past hour as we've sat in these chairs enjoying our pedicures. It's kept Charlie's attention off the actual task at hand, kept the manly men from feeling girly though I think they're enjoying this as much as any woman could, and it's been relaxing. Really, really relaxing…and fun.

The men roar with laughter while the poor pedicurists once again try to hold their feet in the correct positions while filing their nails. We're nearing the end of our pedicures and three of the guys are already getting their feet toweled off. Some of the girls have enjoyed the banter. They've smiled, even flashed the guys smiles and spoken fluent English while they worked, but others have shown obvious frustration, and the female customer sitting next to Bruce is clicking her tongue in disgust and sighing heavily every ten seconds.

The manager makes her appearance, standing front and center of our seven chairs. She's a tiny Vietnamese woman, dark hair pulled back in a tight ponytail, arms folded in front of her, lips puckered in a scowl.

"Who da boss here?" she asks, her eyes sweep from one end of our group to the other.

Three bodies on each side of me lean forward as three fingers on each side of me point in my direction. Six voices ring out in unison, "She is."

"You need be quiet," she says, flashing me an angry look. "My customers getting upset."

The woman sitting next to Bruce clears her throat and tips her chin, shooting us a haughty glare. "Some of us already are."

My feet are being dried and readied for polish and I see that the six other pairs of feet that accompanied me today are now finished. I stop my pedicurist, letting her know I've changed my mind. I have plenty of polish on the bus; I can do my own.

I rise from my chair, reach for my purse, and pull out the black Amex card.

Shrugging one shoulder and flashing the card, I tell the manager, "Oh well, it's only money, huh?" I lean closer and whisper, "I was just about to talk them into having manicures. It's called laughter. Good for the soul. Have a nice day."

The look on her face is priceless. I just may have been able to talk them into manicures and it would have made a pretty penny for her today. We were having such a good time. The chairs were massaging their backs, the conversation was priceless. My bet was they had never done anything like this before and I know I sure didn't want it to end.

I tip my head towards the door. "Let's roll, guys."

I hear a ghastly noise at the end of the line where Bruce sits next to the woman that's left a bitter taste in my mouth due to her haughtiness. At first, I think it's the sound of his body rubbing on the vinyl of the chair making the typical embarrassing sound no one wants to hear. No…no, no, no. That would be too easy. Too normal.

"Don't worry," Bruce reassures her as he pats her hand and stands. "I'll get up so they'll think I did it."

Mortification fills her eyes as her hand flies to her face. We stop at the register, and I pay for our pedicures with the Amex card. I take a glance back at the woman and see her eyes watering as she holds her shirt over her nose.

"Damn," Bruce says as his face lights up in a grin. "I've been holding that back for the last half hour."

We step outside onto the sidewalk, and I watch as six able-bodied, refreshed men take deep breaths, stretch their arms towards heaven and say, "ah".

Charlie pulls me into a hug and once again kisses me on the top of my head. "Thank you, Millie."

"My pleasure. You get to choose the next thing to do."

He does a little two-step then bounces on the balls of his feet. "I think I want to go for a walk. We'll figure something out on our way."

Colby steps up and wraps his arms around my shoulders from behind. "You don't mind if I take this hand do you, Charlie?"

"She's all yours, Colby."

Our tightknit group starts walking in a direction that will lead us into the downtown area and a nice place for lunch – Google is a wonderful thing to have.

Colby walks with his hand placed over the back of my neck. It feels good, like a massage and protective at the same time. I hook my thumb through the back loop of his jeans. It's comfortable this way. Due to our height difference, it falls exactly where I need it. And if it keeps my hand close to that derriere, well….

He leans down close to my ear and whispers, "You are

incredible. I'd be happy to polish those toes anytime you want."

I giggle. "You have a thing for toes, do you?"

His smile is playful as he winks. "I have a thing for *your* toes, Millicent."

The Concert in Tulsa

Holy crap, it's hot! If the women wore any less clothing, it may as well be a nudist colony out there. It's an outdoor concert tonight and the ice machines with enormous fans are set up in front of the stage as well as on the sides in order to protect the musicians. It simulates air conditioning, so my guys won't pass out from heat prostration.

The sun has gone down, so that helps, but the humidity is a beast. Hydration is key in these conditions so fresh water and Gatorade is replenished every thirty minutes on stage by the roadies delivering them to the designated spots for each musician.

The arguments before the performance were nearly unbearable as I tried to force them to drink.

"Trinket, I'm gonna have to pee every half hour if I drink all this now." Needless to say; Duffy was not amenable.

"Little Bit, you gotta understand the male bladder don't work like a woman's does." Grady was just as resistant as Duffy.

Good old Charlie had his own plan. "I peed in foxholes for years. I'll just twist around on my stool. Nobody's gonna see me relieve myself behind my drums."

"Millie, I'm gonna be floating away from my keyboard," Dave had told me. "And I'd rather wail than sail tonight."

Bruce had simply chuckled and told me, "It's alright, Millie. I'll simply do the back-float when they flood the stage."

Colby had kissed my forehead, held fast to my shoulders as he looked me in the eyes and said, "We'll be fine, baby. Don't worry."

* * *

So here I stand, fretting that one or more of my guys are going to collapse. They wear their usual T-shirts tonight for comfort and coolness, the breeze from the fans moves their hair or over the do-rags. They look like they're doing okay.

The guys from Sticky Whiskers haven't even left from backstage. They stand with me to watch the show.

"Aren't you guys ready to go back to the bus?" I ask Jake. It's unbearably hot where we stand. They've done their show; I should think they want the air conditioning.

He snickers as if holding back a secret. "Nah, we're waiting for the real show."

"What real show?"

We all know the sets; the songs played in order each night so there are no gaps in between. Gaps would be like empty air space on television. It's a no-no.

The band rolls right into Bob Seger's "The Fire Down Below".

"I think you're about to see it now," he says as he points to a group of women in the front row. "They've been gettin' antsy."

Colby's husky, shiver-inducing voice resonates through the night as he sings the song that has a strong tendency to take the crowd to the next level of…shall we say…heat?

I watch as four women drop their tops and shake their nipple-glittered breasts in Colby's direction. One holds up a sign that reads, "Still dreaming about it Shower Guy". I see Colby's eyes close as he continues the song and plays his guitar like a pro. He looks almost angry, maybe frustrated? The security guards move in on the women and instruct them to pull their tops up.

Jake laughs as he stands beside me.

I crinkle my nose. "That's the show you were waiting for?" I'm used to groupies' antics; mind you that was a bit over the top, but….

"It ain't over yet, Millie." He chuckles. "I'll give him 'til the song's over. He's a professional."

"1-2-3---" Colby shouts. They play the final riffs, and the song ends. I see Colby hold up his finger and see Duffy and Grady laugh and nod. He unfastens his guitar strap and sets his treasure on the stand. The guys start the next song as Colby runs offstage toward me. It's not far, only forty or so feet. He grabs the back of my head and pulls me in for a hard kiss. Damn! Colby's only kissed me like this once before – after the shower incident. It doesn't last long, but it's full of passion and heat and literally takes my breath away.

There's a twinkle in his eyes and a giddy grin that blooms as he says, "I love you. Just thought you should know." He drops one more kiss on my mouth and growls in my ear, "Yours are so much prettier."

He's back on stage in a flash, straps his guitar back on, adjusts the volume knob and is playing in no time…with the biggest, brightest smile I've ever seen him wear.

I can honestly say…I am totally blown away. When has Colby ever seen my…*Oh my God! Flashback. I am never drinking margaritas again! Wait a minute, did Colby just say…?*

I feel Jake's fingertip under my chin as he presses my mouth closed.

"Gives a whole new meanin' to no time like the present, huh?" He laughs as he holds a hand on my shoulder. It's now I realize Brody's hand is between my shoulder blades as well. I do believe they've kept me standing, because Colby Jarlsberg just swept me off my feet – metaphorically speaking.

Hold it! Back the train up. That's the shower broad in the audience! The one that saw his tally-whacker. And she just showed him her boobs! Her nipple glittered boobs of all things! That little hussy!

* * *

"Thank you! Good night, Tulsa!" Grady shouts to the crowd at the end of the night. "Drive home safe, sound, and sober."

It's one of their typical sign offs, after two to three encores. Tonight though...

"And remember, folks," Dave adds. "Motel spelled backwards is...let 'om!'"

Good grief. It's always something. Uncle Morty and his dirty friends.

I rush to meet Colby before he can get backstage and jump into his arms. His body is wet with sweat and I feel the moisture transfer from his clothes to my own. The ladies edge as close as they can get to the front of the stage, chanting proposals to the musicians while shaking those boobs. Good God, these men are old enough to be their fathers! Well, the men other than Colby. I hold the flashlight that I obtained from the back and shine it over our heads, so as to be sure they can see us. I hold him in a lip-lock so hard his mouth will probably be bruised. When I pull back from the kiss, I smile brightly and watch as his face lights up.

His eyebrows rise and he laughs. "What's that for?"

"For me." I turn towards the women watching us and nod. "And for them." I yell at the top of my lungs towards the women, "He thinks mine are prettier!" I stick my tongue out and scowl.

Colby groans when he glances towards my target. He squeezes my butt cheeks as he carries me backstage in his arms. "Come on, troublemaker."

"She saw your tally-whacker!"

I feel his chest rumble with laughter. "Your turn's coming."

"You'd better not ever ask me to glitter my nipples," I warn him.

He shoots me a sexy grin that only makes him more kissable. "Not even if I offer to remove it with my tongue?"

Can someone bring me a fire extinguisher, please?

* * *

One more night in the KOA campgrounds before we make our way down the highway to Vegas. Vegas Baby! It's a crapshoot. What happens in Vegas stays in Vegas. Isn't that what they say?

Everybody has gotten a shower; the second one for today. The heat here is only half what it is in hell, I'm sure, but the humidity is killer. No need for warm showers after the concert tonight; the cool water is a welcome reprieve.

The camp is quiet, so we have retreated to the bus for the night – tired and ready for bed.

"Goodnight, guys," I wave to one and all as I head for my room. "I'll see you in the morning."

"'Night, Millie."

"'Night, Trinket."

"'Night, Little Bit." And the list goes on.

I find my way under the sheets and blow out a deep breath as my head hits the pillow. It was another extremely successful concert. No mishaps, none of my guys dropped from heat stroke.

And Colby told me he loves me.

Oh shit! I didn't tell him I love him too. I do though. He's funny and kind, giving and gentle. He's sweet, caring, and when he laughs the whole room lights up. When he gets mad, he doesn't fly off the handle; he takes deep breaths until he gathers his composure and approaches the problem with reason. Well, with the exception of that day I went off the beaten path in Utah, but he was worried, and he didn't know…

There's a tap on my door and Colby lets himself in after I answer.

"Came to say goodnight."

I sit up in bed, tilting my head. "I thought we already had."

"Not my way."

"What way is that Mr. Jarlsberg?"

"Never go to sleep without a proper kiss goodnight."

The bed sinks with his weight as he sits beside me, leans in, and takes me in his arms, delivering a kiss that makes me moan and want him to deliver a whole lot more. It must become obvious because he pulls back and leans his forehead on mine and takes a deep breath.

"We're in Vegas next weekend. A hotel for two nights. Maybe then, okay?"

"Maybe?" I sigh heavily, my frustration growing; though I'm not sure why. Is Colby really going to want to devirginize the virgin? Am I supposed to tell him ahead of time or do we just pop that ol' cherry and let bygones be bygones?

His smile is soft, his eyes shine. "Definitely. I meant what I said. I love you."

"I forgot to say…"

He places a finger over my lips and shakes his head. "Don't force it. You'll say it when you're ready." He leaves one last chaste kiss on my mouth, rises from the bed, and walks to the door.

"But…"

"Goodnight, Millicent. I'll see you in the morning."

"Wait!"

He turns, raising his eyebrows, and drawls, "Yes."

I sit up taller, puffing my chest a little and grin mischievously. "Are mine really prettier?"

His chin drops to his chest, and I hear him groan. "You're killin' me, Mils."

Mils. I like it. I like 'baby' too.

I yank my tank top up so that my breasts are on full display. "Hey, Colby." He looks up and his eyes nearly bug out of his head. "Just wanted to make sure my girls were the last thing you thought of before you close your eyes." I jiggle them a little with a fast shake of my shoulders, wink, and slip my tank top back down. "Goodnight, big guy."

I hear the door slam as I giggle quietly, lie down and pull the sheets back over me. I've waited a long time for this. At nearly thirty years old, I'd better be ready. And Vegas better be ready for me.

Chapter 17

Colby

Sweet Jesus, the woman's going to kill me. And I thought her toes were pretty… Newsflash! They've got nothing on her….

"Helluva concert tonight, Cheddar." Duffy bumps my shoulder on my way through to my cubby and laughs. "Those headlights didn't blind ya, did they?"

Wonderful. I've just come out of Millicent's room; a spectacular view to play like a movie reel to the insides of my eyelids while I sleep, and Duffy goes and reminds me of the mammary exhibit from earlier this evening. A year ago, I might have enjoyed it. Tonight, not so much.

"Not blinded, Duffy, just burned my retinas a little," I reply with a wry grin.

Bruce shudders exaggeratedly. "One of them had a barbell pierced through her nipple. Did you see that? Why would somebody maim themselves on purpose? For God's sake, if you want a little pain, ask your man to add some teeth to the action."

Duffy laughs, flexing his arm as if lifting a hand weight. "I thought about asking her how many men had tried to use it for bicep curls."

"How about the one with the hoop? Can you imagine gettin'

that thing caught on something?" Grady asks, shaking his head. "Reminded me of the ring on a damn hand grenade."

Charlie holds a hooked finger next to a clenched fist. "Pull on that sucker and..." he spreads his hands high and wide "...boom!"

Dave holds a hooked finger up and turns it sideways. "Or... you could twist it and see if she shoots a gumball out of her belly button."

Other than my laughter – face it, these guys are freaking hilarious – I remain speechless because my only comment would be...what fun is a nipple if you can't put the whole thing in your mouth?

Grand Canyon

"Sandy, can you take a picture of all of us together?" Bruce asks our driver as he hands him his camera. "Actually, take a slew of them. I'll find the best out of the bunch later."

"Sure thing," he says. "Line up."

"We need Sandy and John in here for some," Millicent tells us. "They're as much a part of our group as any of us. Grab one of the roadies to come over before we're done." She's right, too. We travel together day in and day out. They watch over us, watch over our belongings when we're not on the bus, keep us safe on the road. And Millicent watches over them; makes sure they've eaten good food, kept up with their exercise, gotten enough sleep. She'd make a damn good mom someday. *Where in the hell did that come from?*

"No donkey rides?" I ask her. I thought for sure she'd want to take a deeper ride into the canyon, exploring the ridges and depths only the donkeys can provide.

"The next ride I plan on taking," she murmurs through a clenched jaw, looking up with narrowed eyes, "holds no risk factor of a fall any farther down than off the edge of the bed."

I hear a couple of the guys snort behind us.

"I think the lady means no, Norway." Grady slaps my shoulder. "Time to get back on the road anyway. It's hotter than Hades out here."

We've been on the road for two days, having stopped last night at another KOA and seeing a few sights along the way. This has not been a typical road trip whatsoever. Morty had scheduled the concerts one to two weeks apart – giving any of us the opportunity to go home in between concerts here and there – or stay together and treat it like a long vacation. So far, no one has left the group for even a day, and it feels more like family with each one we spend together. One would think a 45-foot home for nine people would eventually become cramped but somehow, we've made it work. Here's a little food for thought:

Three months without a fist fight or argument.

Five prostates in their sixties.

One female tolerating eight males in that small space.

That said female willing to share her bathroom when needed.

Dietary and lifestyle changes made by that female – none of which have resulted in her being tossed off the bus in the middle of the desert – but instead resulted in her being virtually adopted as the daughter they never had. See! Family.

* * *

One more night on the road and we hit Vegas. Millicent's birthday is the day after tomorrow. Her 30th birthday. Morty booked us rooms at the Bellagio for two nights; one night for Millicent's party and one night after the concert. Unfortunately, Morty isn't going to be able to join us.

He sent her gift to the hotel and told Duffy where to pick it up. As far as Millicent knows, we're oblivious and she hasn't said a word about it; Morty told us to keep it a surprise. Apparently, he's led her to believe he's either forgotten or let her know he won't be seeing her because she's seemed distant the past couple days. Knowing how close the two of them are, I would imagine it's quite a blow to her.

But it's also the reason I was able to say '*definitely*'. We have two nights in a hotel, totally separated from the rest of the world as well as our bus mates. And I have every intention of helping her celebrate #30 by giving her that many before those two nights are over. Confident much? Why yes, yes I am. Call me an overachiever. Better over than under. My plan is for her to be *both* before the weekend has passed. *Over* me and *under* me that is.

* * *

The bus pulls up in front of one of the fanciest hotels in Vegas and we step out one-by-one, taking a deep breath as our feet hit the concrete. Sandy and John hand down our suitcases before they take the bus to the depot to park it for the next couple days. They'll be taking an Uber back to the hotel as this is a bit of a vacation for them. Not to mention they'll be celebrating Millicent's birthday with us.

Sticky Whiskers' bus pulls in shortly behind us. The guys deboard, laughing and cheering. "We gotta do this more often," Brody says as he admires the surroundings. "Damn, Morty does know how to throw…"

"Unload your stuff," Charlie shouts, throwing him a glare that makes him shrivel. "And don't drink a lick of alcohol before the show tomorrow."

Dumbass almost blew the surprise. They don't drink before the shows…ever. Charlie simply needed something to justify his tone and sudden flare of anger. As Grady makes his way over to their bus – I'm sure to remind them that the birthday party is a surprise – Duffy snatches Millicent's luggage from her hand and I escort her in the door.

* * *

"Reservations under Mortimer Montgomery," Millicent tells the hotel desk clerk. "Should be several of them. There will be more showing up over the next hour or so. In the meantime, this group goes under Fourplay."

"Ah," the desk clerk says with a bright smile. "The concert tomorrow night. I take it you must be Millie."

"I am."

The clerk reaches for multiple key pass cards, all separated into envelopes with names on them, one for each of us.

"There are four presidential suites," the clerk explains, then shrugs. "Guess you guys have run of the top floor for the next two nights. Lucky you, Ms. Trinkett." She winks as she tries to hand one card to Millicent. "You get your own."

Millicent's mouth is agape, and she doesn't reach for the card. "I don't need a suite; I just need a room."

"Little Bit," Grady tries to sway her. "Imagine the soakin' tub. How long's it been since you sat in a tub o' bubbles?"

Oh, where my head goes at that moment.

The desk clerk giggles. "There's a full jacuzzi. You're going to love it."

Oh, where my other head goes…

"Damn!" I rub the back of my head at the sting of Charlie's slap.

He growls in my ear, "We already *know* what you're thinkin'. We don't need to *see* what you're thinkin'. Check your pockets, dumbass."

Changing my stance, I do a quick surreptitious adjustment, and hang my head in shame.

Tiny bubbles…I don't care what anybody says. Don Ho was not singing about wine. Did you see the look in his eyes?

* * *

Using the special elevator keys, we make our way to the top and the presidential suites, despite Millicent's resistance and objections.

The plan is three rooms be divided between six of us; the other to be used by Millicent, and every service provided by the hotel be at her beck and call for the weekend. Thank you, Uncle Morty, and Happy Birthday, Millie.

"I'll take your things to your room," I offer, hoping for a few moments alone with her to lay clear my plans for the rest of the weekend.

"Thanks."

I set my luggage down by the door of my room that I will

be *(cough)* sharing with Uncle Duffy. Duffy, my ass. I'm sharing a bubble bath with Millicent. I grab her suitcase and wrap my arm around her shoulder as we walk down the hall towards her suite.

"What do you say after dinner we excuse ourselves and come back up here?"

She stops walking, turns in my arm, and lays her hand on my chest. "Promise?"

"I promise."

She reaches for my face and runs those fingertips through my scruff, and I feel that familiar rush up my spine again. The one that makes me want to sink into it and relish the sensation until the day I die.

"You did say definitely." She tilts her head and smiles.

I take advantage of the tilt and drop my mouth to hers for a kiss. "I most definitely did."

"If you come in with me now, I'll give you something to look forward to."

"You're killing me, Mils."

She giggles. "Just warming you up."

We rush the rest of the way down the hall, and she passes her card over the sensor. The door opens and….

"Uncle Morty!" she screams.

Well….shit.

He extends his arms as she runs toward him for a hug. His face lights up like a Christmas tree as he pulls her into his arms and kisses the top of her head. He leans his cheek on her head and whispers, "You didn't think I'd miss your birthday, did you?"

I hear her sniff. "I thought you forgot."

He rocks her back and forth in his arms and laughs. "Not a chance, Millie." He tips her chin up. "It's the only day on the calendar that holds any significance for me. Happy birthday, baby girl. Feel any older, any wiser?"

"I just feel good, Uncle Morty. I feel really good." She squeezes him around the waist again.

"These guys aren't making your life too difficult, are they?" He squares his eyes on me.

She looks to me, then to him and back to me again and smiles softly. "No, not at all."

"Good. I told them you'd put them in their place." He takes her hand and leads her over to the sofa. "Got two bedrooms here. You've got your own bath, your privacy, everything you want. I'm staying until Sunday. We've got the whole weekend together. I've got a massage booked for you in an hour, the spa after that for a hairdo and your nails. Then you visit the boutique and pick out a dress for tonight."

"What?" Her eyes fly open as she gasps. "Uncle Morty, we can eat pizza and watch Netflix. I don't need anything fancy."

"Too late, sweetheart," he chuckles. "The room is booked and the whole gang is going to be there. Get your dancing shoes on. It's party time!"

I feel like an idiot standing here, an intruder on a private moment. I should have left five minutes ago. I'm going to murder my uncle Duffy. I'd bet a hundred dollars he knew all about this. I'm happy for Millicent…I really am, sort of. I knew about the party. I knew we were spending the evening with friends and the fact that hours were going to be spent in a room full of people. I had no idea the evening – scratch that – the weekend would end the same way every other has since the tour started; surrounded by people we love, but never alone together.

Morty stands and extends his hand to shake mine. "Thanks for bringing her to the room, Colby. I'll see you at the party tonight."

I see the disappointment in Millicent's eyes as she paints on a forced smile and says, "Thanks, Colby. I'll see you later."

"Save me a dance, Millicent." I study her face for probably too long, but finally tear my gaze away. We both know what this means: cast out into the land of MC Hammer "U Can't Touch This" for who knows how long.

Hey, wait a minute! The buses are parked at the depot and everybody else is going to be here at the hotel and… *oh, pull your head out of your ass, Colby! It ain't happening.*

* * *

The door to the room closes a bit harder than I intend.

"Did Trinket get settled in okay?" Duffy asks as I enter.

"Why didn't you tell me Morty was coming?"

He looks up from the news he's watching on television. "Morty's here?" From the look on his face and the fact his eyebrows would have disappeared under what would be a hairline if he had one, I believe he really didn't know. "That's great!"

"Yeah, he was waiting in the room when we got there," I huff. "Would have been nice to know."

He grins. "You get caught doin' something, did ya Cheddar?"

"No, Duffy," I sneer. "We didn't get caught doin' something. Good God, what is it with you guys? We're not teenagers."

He sits up straighter, arching a brow. "No, you're not. But I'll bet anything you left her with a wave and a see ya later, didn't ya?"

Biting the inside of my bottom lip and staring at the ceiling, I mumble, "Yup."

"Man up, son." He rises off the sofa. "You kissed the woman in front of Tulsa. Morty's only one guy. Besides, he can't run for shit. You'd be miles ahead before he could catch you." He laughs as he opens the mini bar and takes out a soda.

"You think he'll be okay with it?"

He turns slowly to look at me, takes a drink of his soda and belches. "Would it stop you?"

"Hell no." I sigh. "But would it stop Millicent?"

He shrugs. "Only one way to find out. I never let Rita's daddy stand in my way and he hated me. Morty's no fool; he knows you're good for Millie. He'd be an idiot not to. Don't let him get in your way, Cheddar."

"I did ask her to save me a dance."

"Aww, I'm so proud of you." He chuckles and pinches my cheek. "Sounds like you're ready for me to take the training wheels off your bike."

I shove his hand away. "Smartass."

Pounding on the door pulls us out of our glare/grin contest

and Duffy pulls the door open. Outside stand the other members of Fourplay.

Grady pushes the door open, and they make their way into the room. "You ready to go?" he asks. He waves his hand towards me in an up and down sweeping motion. "Apparently not, you're still in street clothes. Get a move on."

"What are you talking about?'

Charlie smiles, tongue in cheek. "We heard Morty's in town."

"So?"

"Thought you might want to hit the gym, Norway," Grady explains. "We'll observe while we toss back a few."

Bruce starts a spiel as if teaching a classroom. "It is common knowledge that strenuous exercise is the next best thing to relieving sexual tension." He shrugs. "Unless there's a good cold shower close."

I roll my eyes and snarl, "Or a good cold beer."

Bruce grins. "Care to join us?"

"You buying?" I ask.

"Oh no, Morty is," he answers with a laugh.

Duffy leads us out of the room. "Let's go tap that keg, boys."

Millicent

"How long has that been going on?" Morty asks me as soon as the door closes. There's a twinkle in his eyes and a gentle smile that increases the lines around them.

"What?"

"You and Colby." His gentle smile grows into a happy grin.

"A couple months." I heave a dreamy sigh. "He's a really good guy, Morty."

"Does he treat you well?"

I nod slowly, over and over. "Yeah, he does."

He wraps his arms around my shoulders and brings me in for a squeeze. "That's all that matters, Millie. I saw the way he looked at you. Don't ever settle for less."

162

Colby

Finding a table in one of the many bars in the Bellagio isn't hard this time of day. The casinos are a whole other matter in Vegas; they are bustling no matter what time of day it is. We each pull out a chair at a round table with plenty of room to spare. The waiter greets us within moments of us taking our seats.

"We'll take beers all the way around," Grady tells him. "Make 'em cold, make 'em good, and make 'em fast."

"Oh," Bruce holds up a hand. "These are billed to the top floor."

The waiter nods as if this is knowledge he was already privy to and scoots away hurriedly. He returns within a couple minutes with a tray of cold mugs of beer and sets them around the table in front of each of us.

Charlie picks his up first and holds it in the air, closely examining the pale ale inside the mug. "What the hell is this?" he asks, glaring at the waiter. "I can see through it."

"It's lite beer, sir," he explains, "by orders of Mr.

Montgomery. Anything ordered before the party tonight is either lite beer or soda. Just following orders.”

Charlie grunts and waves the waiter off. He holds the mug up one more time to examine it before taking a heavy chug, sets the mug down hard and swipes his mouth with the back of his hand.

“Lite beer,” he growls, disgusted with the contents in his glass. “Like makin’ love in a canoe.”

“How’s that?” I ask.

“Fuckin’ close to water.”

Damn! Someday I’ll learn. Never be mid swallow post asking a stupid question. Beer coming up and out your nose burns. Makes a mess on the table too.

“Just keeping you sober, boys.” Morty’s laughter comes from behind us as he makes his way to the table.

“Morty,” Grady threatens. “Either line up shots of tequila right now or have that waiter bring us real beer.”

“Fine, fine,” Morty laughs before he yells to the waiter. “Sonny, bring them two beers each. Cut them off after that.” He shoots a pointed look at the rest of us. “You step on Millie’s toes tonight while dancing, I’ll break your legs.”

“You expect us to dance?” Dave asks, his voice rising an octave.

“You betcha.” Morty grins.

“Uh, Morty,” Dave replies. “We’re musicians. We dance with our instruments. There’s a reason our wives danced together… with each other when we played.”

“Fanny never made you take lessons?” Bruce asks him.

Dave whirls his head towards Bruce and wrinkles his nose. “No! Did Ellie make you take them?”

“Of course,” he tells him.

“So, you know how to dance?”

Bruce snorts and laughs. “Hell no, but it made her feel better.”

“Well apparently,” Dave huffs, “Fanny had no complaints about my sense of rhythm. I knew exactly how to dance where it mattered…be it on the floor or on the bed or…”

"Yeah, yeah, yeah," Morty groans. "Regular mattress monkeys. Now," he points to Dave and Bruce. "You guys go watch a couple of YouTube videos. Figure out some dance steps." He points to Grady, Charlie and Duffy. "And you guys go make friends with the nose trimmers I left in your rooms. There's supposed to be a distinction between what grows on your upper lip and what grows out of your nose."

"What the hell?!" Duffy hollers. "We always fine groom before concerts."

"Fine groom before Millie's party," he instructs them with a stern glare.

"You don't like my nose whiskers?" Charlie teases with a sniff and a crinkled nose.

"It looks like a damn chinchilla crawled up in there." Morty rises from his chair. "In the meantime, I've got something I want to talk to Colby about." He looks to me and then tilts his head toward the bar. I scoot my chair out and stand, feeling nausea rise in the pit of my stomach. The only reason he would need to speak to me alone is Millicent. I'm sure of it.

"Hey Morty," Grady says, a mournful expression enveloping his face as he curls his finger for him to get closer. "Come here a minute."

Come on guys, I don't need you running to my rescue. I can handle my own.

Morty makes his way over to Grady and leans down. Grady grabs Morty's nose and pinches…hard.

"Ow!" Morty screams as he pulls back and rubs his nose. "Sonofabitch!"

Grady holds pinched fingers up as if examining them against the light. "Yup, I got it. Thought I saw a straggler in there. Curly little bugger too. I can see how you may have missed it."

The laughter from all five rings throughout the bar. I fight to keep mine to a small snicker.

"You're welcome to come up and use the trimmer you left for me, Morty," Duffy offers, then smirks. "After I'm done with it."

Morty flips them off with one hand, holding his nose with

the other, as he walks to the bar. "Let's go, Colby."
Thanks, guys. If he wasn't pissed off before, he sure is now.

"What's the plan, Colby?" Morty sits back and folds his arms across his chest and squares me in the eyes after we've settled on the bar stools.

"With what?"

"After this tour. Where to next?"

I open my mouth and close it. I blow out a short breath. I feel my eyebrows bob up then down, furrowing as they fall. I feel my palms start to sweat. Had I even considered it?

"Yeah, that's pretty much what I thought." His face twists in disappointment, and concern.

"No, I'm not gonna let you do this." I don't know if it was a thought spoken aloud or a direct comment aimed at him. I will not let him run interference. I turn in my seat and meet him eye-to-eye. "I'm in love with her, Morty. I'll find a way to make this work."

His eyebrow arches. "And if you can't?"

Determined even more by his lack of faith in me, I answer, "Not an option. I'll figure it out."

"What if I can help?"

Now that I did not expect.

"How?"

"I know how much you love playing, Colby," he says. "I can't imagine you walking away from it, not at your age."

"I'd give it up in a heartbeat," I confess. "If it meant the difference between being with her or without her."

"Colby," he sighs. "I'm trying to keep you playing...and with her."

"What did you have in mind?" My internal grimace stays hidden at the thought of traveling again while backing up the bands. I'm ready to hang it up. Shit! The bands she manages...Millicent will be traveling. It's not just my job; it's hers as well. We'll be on opposite ends of the country forever. Unless...

"Studio musician," he tells me. "Pay is fantastic. You'd be in high demand, and you'd be home every night."

"I'd be home every night," I snort sarcastically. "While Millicent drops in when she's back in town. Is that what you're offering me?"

"Not sure Millie will be too anxious to go back out any time soon," he says, waiting for my reaction.

"What?" My reaction must be exactly what he was anticipating.

He shrugs and grins slyly. "Fob to a new Porsche might have had something to do with it."

Dropping my forehead onto the heel of my palm, I groan, "What color?"

"Silver. Why?"

"Carrera?" I groan again.

"Colby," he draws out my name with warning. "What did you do?"

"I already had one waiting for her."

He narrows his eyes. "You were going to bribe my niece?"

"I call it incentive to have a little fun. She deserves it."

"Great," he scowls. "The driveway will be lined with twins."

"Fraternal twins. I got the red one. I'll bet she drives mine first," I goad him, adding a smirk. I don't bother to tell him it's not his drive I plan on her parking the car in. But then, I'm not in the mood to die today either.

"Where did you get money for something like that?" he asks, eyeing me curiously.

"I went to school for software engineering, Morty. Have you tried the Minxlinx app yet?" I watch him blush and pat him on the shoulder as I rise from my barstool. "Uh huh. Pretty good, isn't it? Popular too. Developed it three years ago. It's only one of three patents I own and apps I have running." I lean close and whisper, "I don't play because I *need* to, I play because I *want* to. I can take care of Millicent. I wouldn't have it any other way, and I know you wouldn't either. I'll see you at the party." I start back for the table to join the others.

"Colby," he calls after me.

I stop and turn slowly. "Yes, Morty?"

His face has turned to stone, his eyes narrowed and cold. "You ever hurt her…"

I don't let him finish his threat and match his steely glare. "It'd be like putting a knife through my own heart."

Chapter 18

Millicent

My body is relaxed due to some beefy chunk-a-hunk kneading every muscle into a limp noodle while I laid on the table and hummed and moaned. I saw the advertisement for couples' massages while I was in the spa and I'm still internally chastising myself for the thoughts that ran through my head. He sees their glittered nipples and she sees his tally-whacker while I spend more than three months on a bus with him, and the most I've ever gotten to see is the damage I left from elbowing him in the ribs when I thought he was a mugger in a state park.

I saw plenty when I was in the military; probably more than I should have. Those guys weren't shy…at all. When I picture penises, I always think of the Eric Burdon and the Animals song "Spill the Wine". Strange I know, because the lyrics were written about ladies, but think about the words:

"There were long ones, tall ones, short ones, brown ones, black ones, round ones, big ones…"

You get my drift. So many penises, so many possibilities.

My nails are done in a pretty dusted mauve color that the technician told me "goes with everything". Toes and fingers "just have to match" you know. Yeah, right. I can't remember the last time my fingernails and toenails have actually coordinated. I go for match the top I'm wearing, leave the toes for next week. I never did let Colby paint my toes after he offered. Would it be as erotic as sharing a potter's wheel like they did in "Ghost"? Would it tickle or would he find a way to caress my arches and give me a foot orgasm? Is there such a thing? Would that be known as a footgasm? According to my romance novels, there are so many erogenous zones yet to be discovered. Maybe I should read more….

"I'll get that for you." Colby's deep timbre echoes in my ears as he reaches from behind me and takes the dress bag from my hands. He takes the bag in one hand and keeps his other arm wrapped around my waist as the elevator doors open.

We step inside and as we turn around…

"Hey Cheddar, you goin' up?" Duffy calls as he heads towards us with Charlie and Grady close behind him.

Colby inserts his card for the top floor, glares at them and says, "*We* are. You're not. Wait for the next one."

Duffy waves a hand and laughs. "No hurry. Have fun kids."

He's silent on the way up, holding the dress bag in one hand. He reaches for the elevator button when we're halfway there and hits stop.

He grins, that twinkle in his eyes that I've grown to love. "Am I going to mess up your makeup if I kiss you senseless?"

"Only one way to find out." I shrug. "I've got more to fix it if I need to."

"And your hair?" he asks, reaching for a tendril and twirling it in his fingers as he backs me up to the wall. "If I run my fingers through it? Are you going to be able to pin it back up again?"

"Meh, I can probably wear it down tonight."

"Is that right?" he whispers, gently stroking my jaw with his thumb as he moves his fingers to the back of my neck and pulls me closer. He brushes his nose against mine. "And the marks I might leave behind?"

"Shut up and kiss me, Colby."

Downstairs on the first floor

"Where the hell is the elevator?" Morty growls, standing at the bank of elevators in the lobby.

"Just a little blip," Duffy tells him. "I'm sure maintenance is on their way. Take a chill pill, Morty. What's your hurry?"

"It's been stuck on the 9th floor for the last ten minutes! What the hell? Is it broken? This is the only one that goes to the penthouse suites."

Duffy, Grady and Charlie chuckle.

"Probably somebody slow with loadin' their luggage," Grady says.

Charlie looks up at the ceiling and mumbles, "Or ditchin' some excess baggage."

"I wanted to make sure Millie's getting ready for the party," Morty explains.

"Pretty sure Millie's got her hands full, Morty." Duffy looks to his two cohorts. "Wouldn't you agree, guys?"

Morty glances around the lobby, then to his friends again. "Where's Colby?"

"Uh, pretty sure Colby's got his hands full right now too," Duffy replies, dipping his chin and offering a challenging stare.

Morty stares at the numbers above the elevator and his cheeks flush with rage. "On the elevator?!" he yells. "Colby's defiling my niece on…"

Grady slaps the back of Morty's head while Charlie places

his hand on Duffy's shoulder to restrain him.

"I oughta punch you right now," Duffy growls. "Cheddar has shown more restraint than a bus full of Mormon schoolteachers over the last three months. He ain't defilin' nothing, you asshole. He's probably stealing a kiss or two, a private conversation maybe, because the fire breathing dragon stepped away long enough."

"Gentlemen, gentlemen, gentlemen," Bruce tsks as he walks to where they stand. "Where is your sense of decorum? One of the swankiest hotels in Vegas and you're trying to start a street fight? Your mothers didn't raise hoodlums."

"What the hell's going on?" Dave asks, eyeing the situation cautiously. "And since when do we resolve anything with arguing and not a beer in sight?"

Grady rolls his eyes and heaves a sigh. "Morty's upset about the kids."

Bruce laughs. "Kids?" He slaps Morty on the back. "Morty! Are congratulations in order? I hadn't heard the good news. Did you bag a wife as well?"

While his comment renders a round of snickers from the others, Morty glowers. "This is about Colby and Millie."

Bruce continues his feigned puzzlement and routine peacekeeping tactic. "I thought I heard someone say kids. You mean those two well-rounded, responsible, mature *adults* we've been traveling with for the last three months?"

Dave slaps his arm around Morty's shoulder and leads him towards the bar. "Those are the only Colby and Millie I know. Damn good people. Fanny and I never lasted as long as they have. We were in the backseat before you could say…"

"Yeah, yeah, yeah," Morty grumbles. "Mattress monkeys. We know."

"Ellie and I wore out our fair share of Sertas too," Bruce says cheerily.

The ding of the elevator doors sounds behind them and Morty hesitates.

Dave pulls harder on his shoulder and murmurs, "Nope. This ain't how we roll, Morty. You fix this with Duffy. We're all we've got."

"You're right," Morty sighs. "You guys go ahead. I'll walk with Duff."

And just like that, four men walk ahead while Morty and Duffy walk together behind them. Within a few minutes, apologies are given without hesitation, forgiveness is easily offered, a man-hug is uninhibitedly shared, and amends are made – all before the beers are poured.

There was a time when all these guys wanted any one of the others to marry their sisters – it didn't matter which one – and it wasn't because they liked their sisters. No, it was because they wanted them as brothers.

ANNIE MICK

174

Millicent

I reach for my dress bag as we get to my room door and smile. "I never thought of the elevator as a kissing booth before today."

My face is flushed, my lips are properly bruised, and my neck is feeling the whisker burn. I may have to wear my hair down now to cover any marks left behind. And yet we remained fully clothed and unsated thanks to the security cameras. Ever the gentleman, Colby was not willing to give security a show.

"I know I'll never step on one again without thinking of today," Colby whispers, his fingers brushing the tendrils of fallen hair away from my face. "Save that dance for me."

"I'm sorry about the way this weekend turned out." I wince, knowing the opportunity to be alone again is in the far-off future.

"Don't be, Millicent. You get to see your uncle; he's thrilled to be able to spend your birthday with you." He presses his lips to my forehead for longer than usual before he leans his on mine. "We'll get there." He chuckles, mumbling, "I may have to throw my bandmates off the bus one of these days, but we'll get there. You get ready, and I'll see you downstairs."

* * *

Morty and I walk through the lobby on our way to the party room reserved for what feels like my 'coming of age' party when we hear a shriek to the left of us.

"Purple nurple!" Trevor screams as he runs toward me, picks me up and twirls me so fast my head spins. He laughs as he turns to the other four former pains in my ass strutting our way and yells, "Check it out, dudes! Damn, she smells good too!"

Devlin approaches, releasing a wolf whistle. "Nice legs, Millie."

Trevor sets me on my feet and eyes me head-to-toe with a devilish grin. "I'd comment on the other *tit*-illating *ass*-etts, but I'm afraid she…*owww!*"

He bends forward as I pinch his nipple and twist. He quickly stands upright, rubbing his future bruise, and shoots me an impish grin. "I haven't had my nipple twisted since the last time you did it. I've missed you, Millie."

"Still calling women broads, Trevor?"

He laughs boisterously. "No, Millie. I learned my lesson." He leans close and whispers, "I don't say tits and ass anymore either. I've learned how to accentuate the positive without being obvious."

I point to his chest. "You still feeling that nipple twist?"

"A little bit." He grimaces and rubs his nipple with the heel of his palm.

I reach out and pat him on the chest, grabbing the other unguarded nipple and pinch lightly. "You're still obvious, Trevor. Work less on accentuating the positive and more on eliminating the negative."

The other four reach us and step in for hugs and I hear a growl as they do.

"Those hands drop any lower than her rib cage and you'll

176

be wearing casts all the way to your shoulders for a month. Got it?" Colby's glare is apparently harsh enough to put the fear of God into each of them because they wrap their arms around my shoulders for a hug.

Morty shakes hands with the boys as they exchange friendly hellos.

"So, you must be the bodyguard?" Trent teasingly asks Colby.

Colby smirks. "Millicent doesn't need a bodyguard. I'm the boyfriend." He narrows his eyes. "We're a whole lot meaner."

"Down boy," Duffy laughs as he lays a hand on Colby's shoulder and looks to the group of rebels. "So, I hear you boys don't walk around barefoot much."

Five sets of shocked wide eyes turn to me, and I shrug. "I didn't show them any videos. Consider yourselves lucky."

Grady steps forward, wearing a shit eating grin that makes him look ten years younger. "I want to know which one is afraid to take his socks off."

Calvin gasps, "Millie!"

"You know," Charlie advises them. "I hear if you take regular old #3 grit sandpaper…" He moves one hand over the other in a back-and-forth motion, "It'll take the polish right off a gorilla's ass."

"Charlie!" I scold.

He holds up his palms in defense. "What? Just helpin' out the youth of America."

I sigh and shake my head. "Would you boys like to join us for dinner and a piece of cake?"

"Already planned to. Morty knew we were in town. Ready, Miss Millie?" Trent asks, grinning and bending his elbow for me to take.

As we make our way towards the room, I hear a slapping sound behind me followed by, "Damn! That hurt." It's hard to discern who it came from.

"Eyes up, dickhead." *Colby.*

"I was looking at the floor." *Devlin.*

"Floor's down there, and I'll be happy to introduce you to it face first if you stare at my girlfriend's ass one more time. Got it?"

I'm kinda enjoying what this dressing like a real lady does. I mean the jealous boyfriend thing, not the teenage hormone reactions. Just ick.

* * *

Four hours, a full dinner, a delicious three-tiered cake, a few drinks – a lot for some – and a ton of gifts later, the party is winding down. My feet are aching from dancing and my cheeks hurt from smiling and laughing so much.

My trust fund is open. What trust fund, you ask? Odd, as that was my question as well. Seems I've had one for years. My parents left it for me, and Uncle Morty has added to it every year since. We had a long talk this afternoon, my uncle and me. He would have opened the funds years ago but feared if he'd given in immediately when I came home from the military that I wouldn't have fought as hard as I did to recuperate; that I wouldn't have had the drive or initiative. He was right, you know. Why bother if you don't have to? Added to that was a brand-new Porsche waiting for me when I get home. A beautiful silver Carrera. At least he didn't buy me "arrest-me red". Me and the speed limit have yet to become the best of friends.

We also talked about Colby, the way we've come to know each other, how he treats me, *the fact that I've fallen in love with him.*

* * *

"Goodnight, Miss Millie," Trent says as he leans in to place a kiss on my cheek. "Should you ever want to manage another tour for us, we'd love to have you."

I giggle as I pat him on the cheek. "I'm still trying to smooth out the wrinkles you gave me from the last one, big guy."

He slides his thumb softly across my forehead, down the

side of face and gently cups my jaw. "There's not a wrinkle in sight. More beautiful than I remember." He smiles impishly. "Tell me, Miss Millie, do you like younger men? I've always preferred my women a little older."

I sigh; this kid's flirting is going to get him shot someday. "You're trying to piss him off, aren't you?"

His eyes flash with mischief. "Is it working?"

"As a matter of fact, it is," Colby growls from behind him. "Say goodnight, loverboy."

Trent holds his hands up in surrender and laughs. "Just testing your observation skills."

"What you're testing is my patience," Colby warns him. "Say. good. night."

* * *

Colby escorts me back to my room, my hand in his, and we walk in comfortable silence. I pass the card over the lock and as the light flashes green, he reaches from behind me, twists the knob and opens the door. I pause at the threshold and turn for one last kiss.

"You're not going to ask me in?"

My shoulders sag in disappointment. "Colby, Uncle Morty will be…"

"With Uncle Duffy tonight," he interrupts, hands on my hips as he walks me backwards into the room slowly.

"Wh-what?" I stutter as the air leaves my lungs. I wasn't ready for this. I'd already placed us in the no-go zone earlier today once I saw Morty in the room.

Having the spa give me "the works" was purely coincidental. I was treating myself to a little extra luxury to counteract the disappointment of remaining the virgin Millie for yet another time span of who knows how long. Oh God, I hope the wax rash is gone. *"Hold still, just a little zip here, a little zip there. Voila!"* the esthetician had reassured me. Holy moly. Little my ass! That shit hurts. She's lucky I didn't kick her into next week like a Tuesday football. It would have been knee jerk reflex but still….

"His message was 'Tell Millie I'll see her at brunch tomorrow'." He smiles playfully, but his eyes darken a shade when he whispers, "Which means, I get you to myself all night." He drops his mouth to mine and I'm suddenly getting a replay of the elevator antics from this afternoon. Only this time there are no cameras, no doors to unexpectedly slide open, no one to interrupt us, and most importantly…no stop buttons.

He takes my face in his hands and palms my cheeks, tilting my head up to hold my gaze. "You okay with this?"

No second thoughts enter my mind regarding what I want. I know there's pain the first time, but if I can take shrapnel and last for two days in a burned-out building, I can handle a broken hymen, can't I? If I can tolerate an esthetician ripping hair off my lady bits, I can handle losing my virginity without screaming, can't I? We don't have to discuss it, do we? I can fake it 'til I make it, right?

Suck it up, buttercup. You don't have to tell him, Millie.

"I'm more than okay with it." I run my fingers through his beard the way he likes and watch as he closes his eyes and relishes my touch.

"I wish I could describe what you do to me, Millicent," he whispers, his nose gently brushing the side of mine. "There are no words."

His kisses are painstakingly slow and gentle, warming me up for what I know he's capable of. My clothes are being removed in such a way I'm not even aware it's being done. It's a one zipper off-the-shoulder dress – that is now on the floor at my feet – and I'm left in a lacy bra and panties.

Smooth, Colby.

His tie is off, his shirt buttons undone, the hem pulled out of his pants.

Did I do that?

Smooth, Millicent.

"God, you're beautiful," he murmurs, taking in the sight before him. Now, I know I didn't help him out of his pants…unless I'm experiencing blackouts? Standing before me is a nearly naked

Colby in black jersey briefs and the outline of what's underneath them is giving me palpitations.

Just once, Millie. After that, it's homeward bound.

He lifts me off my feet and I wrap my legs around his waist as he carries me to the bed where he gently lays me down – following right on top of me – burdening his weight on his elbows.

Is this sounding like a romance novel? It ought to because it sure feels like one. Screw you, Fabio. If this were you, I'd be picking your hair out of my teeth right now, puffing my cheeks and blowing it out of my face. I'll bet you wear a man bun in real life unless you're on your back.

He kisses me again, deeper and harder this time. His mouth moves to my ear, then to my neck, my collarbone. I writhe and wiggle underneath him, trying to gather more friction.

I hear him chuckle. "We'll get there, Millicent. Patience."

"Colby," I whine.

His mouth clamps on a nipple through the material of my bra and I swear I'm going to come undone. He moves lower onto my belly and swirls his tongue into my button. He hooks his thumbs into my panties and slides them down and off. When he doesn't return to his original position – on top of me – I raise my head and look to where he takes his position.

"Are you coming back up?"

His grin is near devilish as he winks and dips his head. "In a bit."

Total bliss.

* * *

And here we are – the moment of truth – in a manner of speaking. I know the truth; it won't matter after tonight. Actually, it won't matter about thirty seconds from now.

"No reservations?" Colby asks as he hovers above me, his lips brushing mine in a whisper soft kiss. He's right there, inches away from taking what I'm willing to give.

"None," I whisper, determined to keep the shakiness out of

181

my voice, the fear from showing in my eyes.

"I love you, Millicent," he murmurs.

And for the first time, I say it too. "I love you, Colby."

And he thrusts.

"Oohh…" I gasp. *Shit! Shit, shit, shit!*

Ever had anyone tell you size doesn't matter? They lied!!! Those commercials for exercise that encourage you to feel the burn? Ha! Try sex, you assholes.

I feel the burn alright. Unfortunately, it's in two places currently. The one between my legs is calming, but the one behind my eyes is not being cooperative.

"Millicent." I hear the desperation in his soft murmur. I see the shock and anguish in his eyes, and I feel the tears spill from my own as they run down the sides of my face.

Where's that soldier I used to be? Where is that façade I've mastered for years and why has it escaped me when I need it most?

"I'm sorry," I whimper. "I should have told you." They're the only words I can manage through the tears; the tears that he slowly wipes away with his thumbs and kisses softly before he leans his forehead on mine.

"Thank you," he whispers.

"For what," I sniffle.

"For trusting me."

"Thank you," I whisper back.

"For what?"

"For thrusting me."

He's speechless as he gazes into my eyes, his eyebrows raised in wonder.

My shoulder lifts in a slight shrug. "Made it easier. Now comes the fun part."

He smiles…so Colby. "God, I love you."

That soldier I used to be? Tonight, she became a woman.

That façade I mastered so many years ago? It was a shield protecting my heart. And tonight, Colby helped me remove it.

Turns out I don't need it anymore.

Chapter 19

Colby

Her uneven breathing discloses the fact that she's not sleeping, but she doesn't move a muscle underneath the arm I have wrapped around her from behind. The light creeps in from the small opening in the curtains. It's morning – not sure what time – doesn't matter. If I move, I know she will too, and the night will be over.

The day will begin, we'll spend it with the others, preparations for tonight's concert will be in motion as soon as brunch is through, we'll be lucky to get a moment alone until well after midnight.

She surprised me – my Millicent – in more ways than one. One moment of shock turned into two more episodes of awe before we finally fell asleep. I didn't think more than one round after her first time was wise, but Mils can be persistent. And who was I to say no?

If she walks crooked today, shows signs of a little limp, lets out a groan when she bends, her Uncle Morty is going to castrate me…and use a rusty dull knife while he's at it I'm sure. Was it worth it? You bet your ass it was.

"Good morning." My throat is dry, making my voice sound like I ate gravel for dinner, and it's still stuck in my throat.

"Morning," she replies, her voice even raspier than usual. She finally shifts her body slightly to reposition herself. I wonder how long she's been lying here awake.

"Sleep well?" I ask.

Before she can reply, there's a knock on the door in the main room. *Shit!* Millicent shoots up as if her ass is on fire and I catch her by the shoulder, gently pulling her back down. I throw the blankets off and walk to the bathroom for a robe.

"I'll get it." I point to her before heeding a warning. "Stay."

Outside in the hallway stands one of the staff members with a rolling cart; a little guy who jumps when I open the door.

"Room service, sir."

"I didn't order any," I snap harshly. "You sure you got the right room?"

"Y-yes sir," he stammers. "It's right here. With a note." He rolls the cart into the room.

"Hang on, let me get my wallet," I tell him as I start for the bedroom.

"No need, sir. It's been taken care of," he says as he heads for the door. "Have a good day."

I take the note off the cart and open it.

Hey you crazy kids,
Just a few munchies to start your day before brunch.
Call it energy food.
Wanted to make sure you were up on time in case, you know,
morning nookie.
Brunch is at 10:00.
You know how AR Morty is.
Love,
Uncle Duffy

AR: anal retentive. Yeah, Duff, we do know.

On the cart, there's a pot of coffee, two cups, cream and sugar. I open the silver dome on the tray. Inside I find two packages of warmed Pop Tarts, blueberry and strawberry.

God, I love my uncle Duffy.

"Who was it?" Millicent asks as she enters the front room. She wraps her robe tighter with the belt and sniffs the air. "Coffee?"

"Coffee," I confirm with a smile. "Compliments of Duffy." I hold a Pop Tart to her mouth for her to take a bite and watch as she takes a nibble and chews. There's a crumb at the corner of her lips that needs tending. It's not there for me to wipe off. No, it's there for my tongue. It's calling my name…so I answer it.

* * *

Everyone is seated at the table by the time we make it to the dining room for brunch. The buffet is lined with people loading plates with a variety of choices anywhere from fresh fruits to bacon, scrambled eggs, biscuits and gravy, as well as personal chefs to make your waffles or pancakes while you wait.

"Hey, hey!" Grady calls out as we approach. "Time to eat." He gives a command akin to a court officer announcing the judge, "All rise."

The whole lot of them stand and head towards the buffet, not giving anyone a chance to throw awkward glances, toss in smartass remarks, or give Morty an opportunity to shoot a menacing glare our way.

At Duffy's place at the table sits a package of unopened Pop Tarts. The man is obsessed. There is a veritable feast that awaits him, and he insists on his Pop Tarts. He never misses. We've replenished the supply on the bus once already.

We load our plates at the buffet and head back to our seats. The server brings a tray of mimosas and sets one at each of our places. Morty is the first to hold up his glass in a toast.

"To another year for Millie, the best friends a guy could have, a damn fine backup guitar player, and a concert tonight that'll knock them on their asses."

"Hear, hear," the agreement comes from all spots at the table in unison.

"To young love and the lust that follows," Bruce chants and

winks at both of us.

Morty lets out a low throaty growl and Duffy nudges him.

"To all the kisses we've snatched," starts Charlie as he holds up his glass.

"And vice versa," Dave finishes with a bob of his eyebrows before he tips the glass to his mouth.

Poor Millicent's cheeks flush the prettiest pink. On any other given day, she would have been laughing with the rest of them. The only one looking at her is me. All other eyes at the table are concentrated on the food on their plates while they exchange dirty jokes. They're not aimed at her; it's the way they roll.

I place my hand on her thigh, give it a squeeze, and lean in to whisper in her ear, "I'd give you a sausage joke to tell but your uncle Morty is still here."

She giggles and the air is suddenly lighter.

"I have plenty of my own I could use," she says.

We look to each other, laugh, and in unison whisper, "But Uncle Morty is still here."

The Vegas Stage

This is probably the biggest show – at least the most extravagant – we'll be playing the entire tour. The light show is phenomenal, the stage is enormous, the crowd is already pumped due to Sticky Whiskers revving them up, and here we stand in blue jeans and T-shirts. The one thing Fourplay has never done – and will never do – is dress for success.

"I don't care if the Queen of England is out there. I'm playin' in jeans," Duffy told us.

"I'll put a hole in the crotch if you make me wear that shit, and I won't wear no underwear," Charlie groused. Keep in mind he's the drummer; sits with his legs apart.

"Dress attire makes me itchy. What if I have to scratch myself? They might think I have critters," Bruce whined.

"I ain't wearin' no damn funeral suit. You'll have to wait 'til you bury me," Grady growled.

"We could do what the Pope does and wear dresses," Dave joked.

"Shut up, Dave," all of them demanded, in unison, except Dave of course.

It was Morty's idea that we might want to dress up a little for this particular show. Millicent shrugged, agreed it was up to us, and openly stated that comfort was of utmost importance for a performer to "perform" their best. Bruce then of course suggested nudity, none of whom were amenable to the idea.

So here we stand, guitars in hand, dressed in T-shirts and blue jeans, entertaining a crowd of ten thousand people who couldn't care less how we're dressed – only how we sound. And I must admit, we sound freaking fantastic! We can do no wrong.

Even Morty wears a smile so big it swallows his entire face. He stands backstage next to Millicent, beer in hand, cheering us on.

Two hours in and it's Seger time, my turn…and that's when I see it. My biggest hope is that Millicent doesn't. It's glitter nipples and her sign:

> Still dreaming
> Shower guy

What the hell is she doing here and in the front row again – one of only two rows that hold faces that we can actually see? The lights are so blinding up here, the crowd is always otherwise nondescript. It's not her face – nor the nipples – that give her away. No, it's that damn sign. I know about stalkers; we've had to deal with them before on various tours. Not me personally, mind you, but the stars did.

I squeeze my eyes closed and concentrate on playing my guitar and singing the lyrics. I realize I can't continue this way; I can't keep my eyes closed, sing and play. I'll lose my balance and suffer the embarrassment, all complements of one crazy loon in the audience. I don't dare glance in Millicent's direction. If I pretend I haven't noticed, continue to play and sing as if nothing has distracted me, no one will be the wiser. I glance toward Duffy and Grady and see the amused grins they both wear.

What am I doing? It's one crazy fan. I've got Mils. Millicent Trinkett…and she's mine.

When the song ends, Charlie starts the next one with a drum solo while Duffy and Grady get their final digs in as they holler my name and do some quick bicep curls when I look their way. I don't know if this crazy is the one with the barbell through her nipple – I didn't pay attention the first time in Tulsa – but apparently they did. Flipping them off would be the preferred route but not the professional one, so I simply scowl and start my guitar part.

Three encores and we finally take our leave to the red room. *No, I'm not joking.* Glitter nipples is screaming louder than most and she throws her sign at my feet before I make it off stage. I don't think the date standing next to her appreciates it very much, but hey, that's his problem. You can't fix stupid, and horny will beat out gullible any day of the week. Just don't break any teeth on that barbell, pal.

I'm not much in the mood to sit around, eat from the platter of healthy food ordered in by Millicent, and shoot the shit with everyone else, but out of obligation to the woman I love who puts it all together after every concert, I'll do it. I'd much rather call it a night, take her upstairs, and spend it doing the same thing we did last night.

Upon entering the room, I find Millicent sitting quietly on a sofa against the wall. The room has a full spread of prime rib, potatoes, gravy, rolls, salads, etc.

"Whoa, Trinket!" Duffy laughs. "Where's the health food? Never mind, I didn't ask that. Never look a gift horse in the mouth."

"Dig in, guys," she says. "Uncle Morty's treat."

"I misspoke," Duffy says, grinning at Morty. "Never look a gift horse's ass in the mouth."

Morty flips him off.

I take a seat next to her, ignoring the food. "You okay?" I brush her hair away from her face, tucking it behind her ear. She feels warm, her cheeks are flushed.

"Yeah, I'm just tired."

"Can I fix you a plate?"

"No." She shakes her head. "I'm not hungry."

"You're not upset, are you? This doesn't have anything to do with the park ranger from Tulsa, does it?"

She looks at me as if I've placed something sour on her tongue. "The what?"

Okay, so she didn't see her.

"Do you want to go upstairs? You do look pretty tired."

"Go get something to eat first." She waves her hand toward the table where everyone else is serving themselves. "I'm fine. We'll go up when everyone's done."

I fix a quick plate, an extra for Millicent with blander foods like potatoes and gravy and a roll; and take a seat next to her on the sofa. I hand her the plate with some silverware as well.

"You need to eat something. You haven't eaten since brunch."

She lets out a sigh, but it's stuttered and carries a hum of something else I can't decipher.

Morty glances our way and concern washes over his face. "You okay, Millie?"

"Yeah," she answers, her voice a little too cheery, a little too pitched to be sincere.

Morty's brow furrows and we exchange a nod of concern before we both study Millicent. I place the backs of my fingers on her forehead and look to Morty.

"She feels warm."

"A little pale, too," he adds.

"I'm right here," she snaps.

This captures the attention of everyone in the room and the eating stops, all eyes are on us.

"You okay, Little Bit?" Grady asks, making his way across the room to where we sit.

She grasps my wrist and lowers my hand from her forehead. She lets out a frustrated groan, "I'm fine. Eat. It's been a long day."

She picks at the potatoes and gravy and nibbles at the roll that I brought her while the rest eat the feast that Morty ordered in. Every eye in the room flits from Millicent back and forth between the others intermittently, silently questioning her health status. The room is quieter than usual, the adrenaline slowly shutting down after a night on stage.

"Guys finish your meal. I'm fine, really. I'll just rest here until you're done." She lays her head down on the arm of the sofa and gets comfortable.

Morty frowns when he realizes she's fallen asleep. "It has been a long day." He arches and brow and looks to me. "How long did you keep her up last night?"

Bruce laughs. Keeping his voice light, he says, "Technically, the question would be how long he kept *it* up, Morty." He casts him a scolding glare. "Knock it off. They're adults."

I set my plate on the table, ignoring Morty and the sexual innuendo that floated its way around the room, and turn to where Millicent lies on the sofa. I bend down and brush my fingers against her cheek, waking her up gently. "Hey," I whisper. "Let's get you upstairs."

She wakes easily, releasing a hushed grunt. "Okay."

We all leave the room together as a united group and make our way down the hall to where the elevators are. What greets us is quite unexpected and extremely unwelcome. Glitter tits and her date stand near the bank of elevators – seemingly awaiting our arrival – where he paces – and she chews on her fingernails.

I have one arm around Millicent's waist, holding her close to me, my only concern being getting her upstairs and laid down so she can rest. The last thing I need is a confrontation right now. He approaches us as we near the area, scowling as if ready for battle; hotshot in cowboy boots and hat, not enough scruff on his face to contend with pubic hair.

"You been messin' with my girlfriend?" he asks accusingly.

I hear chuckles behind me. The guy must be nuts – given the situation – not to mention being outnumbered by half a dozen or so.

"Judging from her behavior, I'd say she's *everybody's* girlfriend." I shake my head as I walk past him. "Hate to tell you, pal, I doubt you're exclusive. And I wouldn't touch that."

He grabs my arm as I walk past, and I yank it away. "Back off," I warn him.

"Tough guy," he says as he reaches for me again. "Gonna hide behind that bitch?"

I remove my arm from Millicent's waist. "Morty, you got

Millicent?"

"Got her," I hear him say as I feel the absence of her body next to mine.

I stand my ground as the jerk comes at me again. One punch…one crack of bone – could be his nose, could be his jaw – and the stupid ass is laid flat on the floor, out cold. I'd shake my hand out if I weren't standing in front of a crowd of people. Damn, that did sting a bit. I'm a lover, not a fighter, but if the occasion warrants itself…….

I turn to where Morty stands with Millicent, his arm around her shoulder, both looking a bit shellshocked and awed. "You ready?"

Morty nods and pushes the button for the elevator. "Yup."

I look to Duffy and tip my head toward the body lying on the floor. "Check on him, please. Make sure he leaves, will you?"

Duffy grins. "I'm on it, Cheddar. Need some ice?"

I flex my fingers once to ensure they're intact. "Nah, but he probably does."

In the Lobby

As soon as the doors to the elevator close the guys step to the body lying on the floor and stand over him in a circle, smiling at one another.

"Think he's dead?" Duffy chuckles as he taps the body with the toe of his boot.

Glitter nipples gasps and whimpers at the same time, sounding like a wounded animal; or a bitch in heat – hard to tell.

They watch as one eye blinks open from the body on the floor, sheepishly scanning the surroundings. "Is he gone yet?" the guy asks.

Duffy pets his beard as if contemplating. "Whaddya think, boys? Shall we take him out back to the woodshed?"

Both eyes shoot open wide, and the body is suddenly on two feet, holding out both hands defensively as blood drips from his nose.

"I'll go, I'll go. I promise!" he whines, holding his nose as he tries to move out of the inner circle toward the elevator and looks to glitter nipples to follow.

"Oh no, you don't," Charlie says, pressing his hand on his chest. "There's a Motel 6 out there somewhere with your name on it. I've heard they'll leave the light on for ya."

"But we've already paid for this!" he protests, leaning his head back, sniffling.

"That's the price of being a smartass," Grady tells him.

"But our stuff is up in the room!" Glitter nipples whines.

"We'll be happy to escort you and help you pack," Dave tells her.

"Just do it, Jolene," the boyfriend huffs, pushing the elevator button. "I shoulda never brought you here."

After watching them pack, assuring they check out and are escorted out the front doors, the guys make their way back up to the 18th floor.

"Ah," Bruce says wistfully on the way up in the elevator. "Once again proof that youth is wasted on the young."

Eye rolls and headshakes all turn in his direction, once again waiting for the usual philosophical reasoning.

Bruce indulges them, as always. "Genetic disposition when we're young. You know it's the hormones."

Grady groans, "And we all know how to make a hormone."

In unison, they voice agreement, "Don't pay her."

Chapter 20

Colby

I knew something was off when we got back to the room. Millicent was so tired, she felt warm to the touch, seemed weak. I helped her into pajamas and got her laid down. She took a couple Tylenol, drank a bit of water, took a fetal position on the bed, and stayed that way until she fell asleep.

I curled up behind her, sharing my body heat and comfort, and laid awake with worry. Did she eat something that didn't agree with her? Was she exposed to someone who was ill? Is the stress of managing the tour too much for her?

I'm just drifting off to sleep when I hear her groan and feel her shift on the bed.

"You okay?" I lift my head and reach for her shoulder to turn her towards me.

"It hurts," she whimpers. "It hurts, Colby."

I shoot up quickly and lean over her. "What hurts, where?"

"My side."

She holds her stomach, her breathing becoming increasingly rapid. Everything that happens after is a rushed blur. I call Duffy to wake Morty, throw on some clothes, and I carry Millicent in my arms to the door – reaching it as Morty is inserting his pass from the other side; fully dressed and ready to go.

"I need to get her to the emergency room," I tell him. "She's in pain. Said her side hurts."

"She needs her ID and insurance card," he says calmly. "Where's her purse?"

"Inside," I say, my mind racing as I try to recall where she would have set it. "Probably on the sofa."

We're met in the hallway by every member of the band – half asleep but seemingly alert – dressed and ready to assist in any way they can. The doors to the elevator are already open and being held by hands belonging to one of them – no idea whose – and we're soon on our way down.

"Already called for a car. Highest ranking hospital is three miles away. Let's go," Charlie rasps.

"Does she need to use a VA hospital?" I don't know why I ask, have no idea where it came from. I'm nervous, scared; trying to cover all bases.

Three sets of eyes land on mine with a scowl embedded in each.

"Sorry," I mumble.

Duffy pats my shoulder. "It's okay, Cheddar."

"She has insurance through my company," Morty says. "We don't ever mention military. Got it?"

I simply nod and hold her closer as she moans once again. I feel Morty reach for her, knowing he longs to take her from my arms and carry her himself. I see Dave grip his shoulder, reminding him he's not her only option anymore.

She doesn't feel weighty in my arms, I'll carry her for as long as it takes.

We disembark the elevator as soon as the doors open and find Jake and Brody from Sticky Whiskers standing just outside, obviously coming back from one of the bars.

"Whoa, what's going on?" Jake asks.

"I'm guessing appendicitis," Bruce says as we continue our march toward the front doors of the hotel.

Appendicitis? She already has a scar on the right side. I

just assumed...

"What hospital?" Brody yells.

I don't catch the rest of their exchange because I see the car waiting in the drive and my only goal is to get Millicent in the seat and on our way.

"Colby," she whimpers. "Don't run. You're bouncing. It hurts too much."

"I'm sorry," I whisper, slowing my pace. "I want to get you there as fast as I can."

"We'll get there, Colby," she mewls. "We'll get there."

"We'll get there". How many times did I say that to her?

* * *

"It's her appendix," the ER doc tells us. "The surgeon on-call is already here and scrubbing in. Her medical records have come through the system. Anything else we need to know?"

It's only Morty and me in here at the moment; the others are in the waiting room. Morty clears his throat and looks to me. *Is he expecting me to leave? Screw that!*

My eyebrows rise, urging him to answer. "Well?"

"You need to tell me now," the doc says. "We're taking her up."

Morty heaves a sigh. "There's scar tissue built up in that area. Is it going to cause a problem?"

The doc shakes his head. "It shouldn't. We saw that on the ultrasound and CT. The surgeon uses a laparoscope. He can work his way around it."

"Okay," Morty replies, sounding less than confident in the doctor's reassurance.

The sound of a bed being wheeled close by distracts us.

"That's her coming back from the CT. They're taking her up." The doc waves his hand toward the curtain. "Better go see her now."

Morty's on one side of the gurney and I'm on the other as we walk down the hall towards the doors that will take her away from us. The shots they gave her for pain are working well, but they've also made her extremely drowsy.

The attendant presses the button on the wall to open the heavy double doors. Morty leans in to kiss her on the forehead and tells her he'll be waiting.

I lean down and kiss her on the mouth. "I love you."

She mumbles softly – totally indecipherable – but I tell myself it was 'I love you too'.

We walk to the waiting area in silence. Once there, I find a waiting room full of people – not one empty seat available – and anxious musicians, standing or sitting, all awaiting word on Millicent. Sticky Whiskers apparently decided to join us at the hospital instead of waiting at the hotel. John and Sandy both sit with coffees in their hands, heads down. I would do a head count, but I don't have the energy. They all love her, how could they not?

"What's the word?" Grady asks.

"What are they doing?" Dave follows.

"How's she doing?" Duffy adds.

"Colby, come take my chair," Bruce offers, holding out a disposable container filled with coffee.

Charlie stands, holding out an identical container. "Morty, take mine."

I feel like I'm drowning. The air I'm trying to suck into my lungs gets caught somewhere in my throat and I can't get a breath. I feel hands grab my biceps and lead me to chair and plop my ass into it. There's a hand on the back of my neck, shoving my head between my knees.

A low voice in my ear whispers, "Breathe, Cheddar. Slow, deep breaths."

"I gotta get out of here," I choke through scattered breaths.

"You're hyperventilating," he murmurs as he leans close to the back of my head. "You'd drop like a brick right now. Breathe, then we'll walk."

A few minutes later, Duffy and I step outside the room into the hall but stay close by, so we won't miss the surgeon when he comes back.

"Why does she have a scar on her belly?" I ask him. "I took for granted it was from an appendectomy."

He shakes his head, frowning. "Not my story to tell, Cheddar. We've all got our demons."

"What the hell, Duffy?" I sneer. "You know but I don't? That's classic. I felt like a damn idiot in there with the ER doc. Morty knows all the answers and I couldn't tell them anything!"

"Morty's her uncle, come on!" he growls. "He's had her for years."

"And I'm her boyfriend!" I jam a finger to my chest. "I should know these things."

He arches his brow, dips his chin and calmly replies, "Maybe. Gonna need to be a little closer than a boyfriend though. And someday maybe you will be. These things take time."

"Screw you, Duffy." I turn to walk away when he grabs my arm and pulls me back.

"Don't you get cocky with me," he growls. "Some things take years to surface. You're pissed at Morty when what you ought to be is respectful. The guy would give his life for Millie a hundred times over. She became his everything the day her folks died and backing off to make room for you has been one of the hardest things he's ever had to do. I've never seen a guy so damn broken as when he nearly lost her."

The air leaves my lungs. I had no idea. "He nearly lost her?"

"The scar on her belly, it's from shrapnel she took in Afghanistan. Ended up with sepsis." He studies the floor and shakes his head. "You didn't hear that from me."

"She was wounded?" This is all news to me.

"She was wounded on the outside, Cheddar." He squares me a look I've never seen from Duffy before; severe, pained. "She was scarred on the inside."

I feel like I've been punched. Millicent could have died; almost did.

"I'm sorry, Duffy. I didn't mean it."

He slaps his arm over my shoulder and leads us towards the

waiting room. "I know. I've been a dumbass a time or two myself. I forgive you. Don't worry, I won't tell your mama."

* * *

Two hours later – much longer than anticipated – a nurse comes to the entrance of the waiting room. "Millicent Trinkett?" she calls, announcing the surgeon is ready to speak to family.

Everyone in the room stands and in unison says, "Yes."

The nurse nearly jumps, her eyes wide as she scans the room and the dozen or so people eyeing her.

"Uh, it's a small conference room." She scrunches her nose and finishes, "I don't think you're all going to fit."

Morty looks to me. "Colby, let's go."

She leads us to a small room, three chairs and a makeshift desk, where the surgeon meets with us. He's probably mid-fifties, graying at the temples, pleasant.

"She did fine with the surgery," he says. "Appendix was still intact, inflamed but intact. No rupture."

"Good, good." Morty blows out a deep, relieved breath, nodding.

"We did, however, find two fine pieces of shrapnel; one slightly embedded in the small intestine and one in the large. It was by sheer chance we found them, probably worked themselves loose recently."

The implications of what he's said don't dawn on me until I see the side-eye Morty shoots me. *Worked themselves loose recently. Shit....*

"She should be out of recovery in about an hour. The nurse will come and get you when you can see her. Any questions?"

Yeah, I have questions but I'm not about to ask in front of her uncle.

"Not right now," Morty replies. "Thank you, doctor."

The doctor stands first, as if in a hurry, but waits until Morty and I rise and then walks out behind us. Once in the hall, Morty walks toward the waiting room without hesitation, leaving me behind as if I'm not even an afterthought.

I rush in the direction the doctor headed to try and catch him before he disappears.

"Doctor," I call, glancing back over my shoulder to ensure Morty hasn't heard. He didn't. The doc stops, turning around, surprised to see me following.

"Can I have a moment, please?" I ask.

"Sure. What can I help you with?"

I fumble for words. How do I approach this? My mind is racing. Excuse me, doc, should I have not had sex with my boss's niece? Maybe missionary only and not let her take the top? Should I have not pinned her against the wall? Words, Colby, words!

"H-how do you get appendicitis?" *Good start.*

"There are a variety of ways," he explains. "A virus, infection, blockage…"

"Blockage?" I ask, my fear rising.

"Pathology report usually reveals the cause," he explains further. "We'll know when it comes back."

"Could certain, uh, activity cause it?"

His brow furrows. "Ac-*tivity*." He repeats my word, as if dissecting it, while rubbing his chin.

"Could it have worked something loose and caused her to…"

He gets a twinkle in his eyes and grins knowingly. He places his hand on my shoulder and says, "The shrapnel was on the outside of the intestines. One has nothing to do with the other. Foreign bodies are a time bomb waiting to blow up. We took care of it while we were in there. Two birds…one stone."

"That's…that's good, right?" My head bobs – perfect rear windshield decoration.

He chuckles. "That's good."

I grimace. "You wouldn't want to explain that to her uncle, would you?"

He belly laughs. "Son, a little advice. I've got two daughters of my own. You are never gonna be good enough for her. Take what you can get. She'll be out soon. Better be there waiting."

"Thanks." I extend my hand to shake his.

He catches my attention when I make it halfway down the hall, calling my name.

"Oh, and Colby, is it?" I turn back to see him pointing a finger in warning. "Don't plan on any of those ac-*tivities* for a few weeks. Got it?"

My face flushes in embarrassment as I answer, "Got it."

"Good." He laughs. "I'll leave the instruction sheet with her. Read it carefully."

"Morty," Grady sighs as I walk into the waiting room. "We can stay on the buses. They're plenty comfortable. Just set us up in a KOA. We don't need to stay in the damn hotel."

"Already done." Morty pockets his phone and, as usual, doesn't give an alternative. "You aren't getting the presidential suites, but you'll be comfortable. Two queens in each room. Snore and fart all you want."

"For how long?" Bruce inquires.

"The next week. You don't have to be in Denver until the weekend after next. You'll have plenty of time," Morty says. "I'm taking Millie home for a few weeks. She's not going to be able to travel at all for probably another week anyway. We might as well stick together and enjoy each other's company."

What?!?

"Why are you taking Millicent home?" My voice is harsher than I meant it to be, and it comes out more an accusation than a question.

Morty turns his head slowly, narrowing his eyes. "Because she just had surgery."

"I'm well aware," I spit, provoked by his condescending attitude. "How about we wait and see how she feels in a week and then we can ask her what she wants to do?"

He rises from his chair and slowly walks to where I stand. Morty and I are about the same height; give or take half an inch. "Don't try to tell me what's best for Millie," he growls.

"I don't believe I did. It's not my decision what's best for her." I turn to go wait in the hall, and toss back over my shoulder, "But it might not be yours either."

I can take care of Millicent. The bus rides like a luxury home on wheels. We eat healthy food, I can cook, we exercise. Her bed is more comfortable than what a lot of people have in their homes. I'll help her with paperwork, arrangements, anything else that needs to be done. I'll have Tammy, the roadie from Sticky Whiskers, stay with her while we play the concert in Denver.

Am I being a selfish ass? Possibly. Am I afraid Morty will talk her into not coming back? Definitely.

After Millicent has been released from recovery and placed in a room, seven of us file down the hallway together. The guys from Sticky Whiskers had asked us to extend their best wishes and headed back to the hotel.

The nurse hurries out from behind her station – flustered – hands waving when she sees us coming. "Too many people."

Duffy and Grady flash her a look that would curl Satan's toes.

Charlie halts his footsteps when he reaches her, standing so close he casts a shadow over her from the fluorescent lights above. He crosses his arms over his chest and stands a little taller, increasing his already giant stature of six foot-three, his voice so low it sounds like thunder. "We're a support group. Do you limit the number of members in AA meetings?"

Her cheeks flush crimson, eyes nearly bulging, her mouth parted in astonishment. Bruce reaches for her face, wiping the corner of her mouth with his thumb, then swipes it on her shoulder. "He is droolworthy isn't he? But we don't want you dripping on the patients."

"But...but..." she stutters.

He winks at her. "He's complimented on it quite often. It's the squats; he swears by them. We're going to head into the room now. Feel free to watch him from behind as we do." He slaps Charlie's ass before heading towards Millicent's room.

I glance back at the nurse and see her staring – stunned –

eyes glued to Charlie's ass as we walk down the hall.

Charlie shoots Bruce a seething glare and growls, "You ever do that again and I'm gonna break your arm."

"Watching you clench while you walk?" Bruce laughs. "So worth it."

* * *

Millicent looks so tiny and pale in the hospital bed. She has an oxygen tube in her nose, the machines beep as they monitor her heart rate, blood pressure, etc. She seems to be sleeping peacefully but rouses when we enter.

"Hey," I whisper, brushing her cheek with the backs of my fingers.

"Colby," she murmurs, the corners of her mouth tipping slightly. "We got there."

"We did," I tell her. "And we'll get there again."

She grimaces as she shifts slightly and groans, "Promises, promises."

I smile at our inside joke. "You've got a lot of people here to check on you."

Her eyes open wider as she tries to lift her head off the bed to look around but she's weak and it falls back on the pillow quickly.

"We'll come to you, Trinket," Duffy says as he edges closer. He leans over and kisses her forehead, holding his beard in his hand so it doesn't get tangled in her oxygen tube. "You rest, honey. I'll bring you a Pop Tart tomorrow."

Grady squeezes through when Duffy is done. "Little Bit, don't scare me like that again. Rest up, sweetheart. I'll be back later."

Charlie steps up and leans down close to her ear. I'm the only other one who can hear what he says, and I don't think he wanted me to. "I need my pedicure partner. Hurry up and get better, darlin'."

Bruce finds his way to her side when Charlie steps away.

"Eighty years, Millie. We had a deal." He leans in and kisses her forehead. "We need you back on the bus."

As he steps away, Dave steps forward and bends as he says, "Haven't pulled an all-nighter in years, Millie. However, next time I expect you to join the party. Heal quickly; somebody has to keep these old codgers in line." He kisses her forehead as well.

Morty stands back as he watches his friends show their love for his niece. His smile is forced but his eyes tell all. She really is his everything and taking her home for a few weeks to recuperate is probably the best thing for her.

She'll be back.

And I'll survive.

206

Red Rocks

"Is that the crack o' dawn or the crack o' doom?" Charlie asks the saggy-pantsed roadie as he passes by him. "Pull your pants up. Nobody needs to see your ass while we work."

We're getting the stage set for tonight's performance and the roadies trek back and forth wheeling equipment, stretching cords, propping speakers.

"Unless it's mine," Bruce announces, holding up a finger in correction. "It doubles as emergency equipment when the lights go out."

The roadie saunters over to Bruce, stopping to whisper. Bruce laughs loudly and smacks him on the back of the head. "Very creative, but it's not how it works, moron. Pull them up or I'll make you wear suspenders."

"What was that about?" I inquire as the roadie walks away, fingers in his belt loops to hold up his jeans. Curiosity gets the best of me no matter how hard I try to tell myself it's best not to ask.

"His *master plan*," Bruce says, using air quotes. "Flashing his ass cheeks at Tammy and telling her he's a lesbian in a man's body."

I laugh. "Aren't all heterosexual males?"

He tilts his head from side to side, seeming perplexed. "Never thought about it that way."

A short pudgy guy approaches us from backstage, carrying a clipboard. "Is there a Millicent Trinkett here?"

"What can I help you with?" Duffy says, stepping forth without hesitation.

"There's been a food delivery in the dressing room, and I need her signature."

"I can handle that," Duffy says, reaching for the clipboard.

The little guy pushes his glasses up on his nose and eyes Duffy curiously. "And who would you be?"

Duffy grabs the clipboard before the runt can pull it away, holding his other hand out, snapping his fingers, demanding the pen.

As he scratches a signature on the paper, he grunts, "I'm Millie Trinkett." He hands him the clipboard and pen back, and grins. "And now, I'm Darwin Duncan. Pleased to meet ya."

Little guy shakes his head and rolls his eyes. "I didn't see a thing."

Grady looks over his shoulder at us, smiling. "You know what awaits us in there, don't ya?"

Dave heaves a heavy sigh. "Health food."

"You damn betcha," Grady replies. "And we're gonna eat every bit of it."

Bruce grins. "And love it."

Charlie harumphs and rolls his eyes. "Even the prunes."

Dave's face lights in a smile. "Especially the prunes."

Packed stadium, rowdy crowd, dry heat, high altitude. Yet, the concert goes off without a hitch. We laugh and joke in the room reserved for us to relax when we're done. The food is arranged just as Millicent would have done, as per her instructions given to Tammy.

My phone chimes with a text: *Eat first. We'll talk when you get back on the bus.*

"She givin' you orders?" Duffy asks when he sees the smile on my face as he plops down on the sofa next to me.

"Suggestions," I reply, pocketing my phone.

"Of course they are." He laughs. "That's what Rita used to call them too."

"Do you miss her?"

"Trinket? Sure I do," he says.

I shake my head. "No. Aunt Rita."

"Every minute of every day," he whispers in his low raspy voice. "But I don't wallow. I'd rather she hug me than kick my ass when she sees me again. I made her a promise."

"Why have you never remarried?"

He chuckles. "When you've had perfection, why would you make anyone try to live up to that?"

"You really think Aunt Rita was perfect?"

He smiles and his eyes shine with a trace of tears. "She was perfect for me."

"Do you miss her, Cheddar?" he asks me. I know he's asking about Millicent. Rita's been gone for over ten years.

"I feel like a part of me is missing, Duffy." I rake a hand through my hair, pulling at the roots. "I didn't think it would be this bad."

"No," he says, standing to place his plate in the trashcan. "You didn't realize yet it could be this good. Grab the moments while you got them, Cheddar. You never know when you might not get anymore."

210

Chapter 21

Millicent

Omaha - Eppley Airfield

Three weeks since I've seen him and when I do, my heart nearly leaps out of my chest. He's had a haircut, his facial hair is finely trimmed, and his smile is nearly as big as my own. I think. It's pretty big, but my face is stretched so tight I feel as if my lips might crack.

"Whoa," he warns as I jump into his arms. "Slow down there, tiger. You're only a month out of surgery."

I pull my head back to look him in the eyes, a hint of playfulness in mine that I cannot hide. "And I've been given the green light to go back to my regular activities."

He arches a brow, questioning, "And what about irregular activities?"

"All activities approved." I wink.

He chuckles. I tingle. "Good thing I booked a hotel room for the night."

"I knew you had a good head on your shoulders." I giggle and shiver at the same time. "It's been a while since I've seen your other…"

"Millicent," he growls against my ear. "Be a good girl. You can hide your excitement better than I can."

I laugh before I nip his earlobe, squeeze my thighs a little tighter and whisper, "You mean that's not a gun in your pocket?"

He bends to grab the handle of my wheeled carry-on while keeping one arm tightly wrapped around my back. "Let's go," he snaps. "I'm carrying you out. Somebody has to hide the damn thing."

I giggle again. "I'll hide it now if you let me ride it later."

He halts his footsteps, apparently stunned at my forwardness. I pull my head back to look at him once more.

"What?" I tip my chin, smiling mischievously.

The way he looks at me takes my breath away. "God, I missed you."

"I missed you too," I reply, thrusting a hand in the air. "Now, to the car, Mr. Jarlsberg."

After a night to ourselves as well as a proper and fun reunion, we find ourselves back amongst the real world. After three weeks away *resting,* I was antsy to get back. I missed these guys.

"Trinket!" Duffy shouts as we climb out of the Uber. The buses are once again parked at the campsite in a KOA campground near Lincoln, Nebraska. We're soon joined by the others as well as numerous roadies and the members of Sticky Whiskers, and they each take their turn welcoming me back into the fold.

The concert is tomorrow night – another crowd of ten thousand – and the real work doesn't start until tomorrow morning. The guys tell me they've utilized the last three weeks well; practicing and tossing together a couple new songs. They'll only be used as encores – their sets are written in stone – but it gives them a new challenge and it gave them something to do while I was gone.

"So," I say as I look around at the circle of people surrounding me. "Mexican tonight?" My question is met with open stares and gaping jaws.

Bruce and Grady are the first to break the silence with a burst of laughter. "You really did miss us, didn't you, Little Bit?"

"So much," I reply, tears rimming my eyes as I sniff.

"Come here," Bruce lovingly says as he opens his arms for another hug. "We had Mexican three nights ago and these guys' farts damn near killed me. We had to have the bus fumigated and the cleaning ladies left not minutes before you got here."

Dave adds, "Morty's gonna have a shit fit over that cleaning bill. Do you know what it costs for a mobile maid service?"

My eyes wander from Dave to Bruce to Grady, then to Charlie and Duffy, and on to Colby. "Do we still need to go do laundry?"

"Nope," Charlie answers. "Got that all done yesterday while the playboy…" he nods at Colby "…was out playin'."

Colby's cheeks flush, his chin dipping, and he toes a rock on the ground. "Uh, thanks for that, guys. I appreciate it."

Grady slaps his shoulder and laughs. "I wouldn't thank us just yet, Norway. Your underwear and T-shirts came out pink."

"What?!" Colby shrieks.

"No," Bruce corrects Grady, tsking. "It was his T-shirts and socks. We turned his underwear inside out so he could wear them for another week, remember? You refused to wash them."

"Duffy refused to wash them," Charlie corrects him, throwing a thumb towards Duffy.

Duffy shrugs, wincing. "Sorry, Cheddar. I wasn't sure if the softener would make the boys itch. Figured it was safer flippin' them inside out."

Colby glares, his eyes flit from one guy to another as he restrains his anger. I fight to keep my giggle back. Colby doesn't wear white underwear – that I know of – he should have caught on immediately. Admittedly the team of sorrowful faces they wear might be convincing to even the most seasoned judge, but I'm well aware of what they're doing.

My poor boyfriend. It's group hazing. He's one of them; just doesn't know it yet.

"You've gotta be kidding me," Colby grumbles, hands clenched while he takes a deep breath.

Dave only adds fuel to Colby's already sour disposition

when he shrugs and suggests, "You could always go commando. Lotion helps with chafing."

Colby palms my cheeks and kisses my forehead quickly. "Sorry, seems I've got laundry to do."

We watch him storm off toward the bus, look back once and flip off the other band members.

"That boy is just too damn easy," Charlie says, laughing.

"Just wait 'til he can't find them," Bruce adds.

Duffy grins. "He's just a pup."

"Can't teach a new dog ol' tricks," Dave says.

Grady smiles and moves his hands like an orchestra conductor. "And a one, and a two…"

They all look towards the bus where Colby stands, red-faced and fuming. He screams, "Where the hell are my clothes?"

"Alright, guys," I groan. "Enough. Where did you put his clothes?"

Duffy shakes his head, laughing. "We kinda figured you'd be sharing the back room now. We moved them in there."

"Oh!" My brows furrow, my mouth twists and I feel myself bite the inside of my flushing cheek. "We were going to continue things as they were."

Five foreheads crease as eyes open wide with surprise.

My fingers twist together as I wring my hands, embarrassed. "Out of respect for you guys," I shrug. "On the bus it's still business as usual, you know?"

Duffy places his hands on my shoulders gently. "Trinket, business is what we do to survive. Love is what we're meant to enjoy in order to live life to the fullest. Take every moment you're given." He winks and gives me a hug. "If it helps to know, we all bought noise canceling headphones yesterday."

* * *

We barbecue this evening, sit around the campfire, drink a few beers, and enjoy conversation. I had missed this so much more than I realized. Twenty-five people traveling together in four buses across the country. Four months into this tour and no major mishaps, no injuries, sans one set of injured testicles – well deserved mind you – and the most fun I've ever had in my life. The injured testicles did apologize, verbally and on paper, and we've gotten along ever since. The fact that he keeps his distance – a good 30 feet or more – probably helps, but that's neither here nor there.

As usual, it's our bus mates who sit at a table together, our close-knit group; Colby one on side of me, Duffy on the other.

"What's your favorite thing to barbecue?" I ask Colby. Tonight we did bratwurst. We've run the gamut of burgers, dogs, ribs, etc.

He finishes chewing and smiles. "Steak, without a doubt. Medium rare."

My nose scrunches automatically. The thought of something bleeding when I cut into it is anything but appetizing. "Medium rare? As in still red in the middle?"

He nods. "Yeah. How do you take yours?"

"At least medium," I tell him. "I don't want it to moo when I slice into it."

A round of laughter ensues as Dave mimics a cow and Bruce oinks.

"That's pork, you idiot." Charlie rolls his eyes at Bruce.

"Are you sure?" Bruce asks, feigning puzzlement as he grins. "We are crossing into Iowa this week. Let's not get caught looking foolish. It's the state fair. They serve pigs wings, bacon ice cream, butter cows. They fry Twinkies, for crying out loud."

"They what?!" I can't have heard that correctly. That sounds like fat on fat on fat. "Why on earth would you fry a Twinkie?"

Bruce shrugs. "For the same reason you would fry a Snickers, I guess?"

I visibly shudder. My teeth hurt just thinking about it.

"You've never had a fried Twinkie?" Colby asks, wrapping his arm around my shoulder. "No fried Snickers?"

"You are joking, aren't you?"

He chuckles softly and kisses my temple. "Oh baby, you're in for a treat."

Duffy tips his chin, inquiring. "What's your favorite food, Trinket?"

Without hesitation I answer, "Fresh fruit, any kind." He winks and nods slightly. He knows. Fresh fruit was the one thing we didn't get a lot of in the service. There were days I would have sold my soul to bite into a fresh crisp apple. Fruit was always canned, preserved. I imagine Duffy, Grady and Charlie never got it. I could live on fresh fruit for days on end. I nearly gagged on the applesauce they brought me after surgery in the hospital.

"What's yours, Duffy?" I ask.

Not hesitating either, he grins. "Pop Tarts."

Cue my eye roll. That package of foil wrapped sheets of cardboard is on the table every morning regardless of whatever else is fixed. I watched him eat from a smorgasbord at the hotel and still consume those godawful rectangles of jelly filled wafers. The man is obsessed. To top it off, he always takes half of the last one and feeds birds with it, crumb by crumb.

I giggle, thinking of his habitual breakfast food. "What is your obsession with Pop Tarts?"

He looks slightly forlorn, a bit wistful, as he whispers, "I have breakfast with my Rita every morning each time I open that package. It was the only thing I had in my lunchbox the day I finally met her. We shared it while we argued about her giving me a ticket for parking my Harley in an illegal spot. Couldn't talk her out of that damn ticket, but I got her to go out with me."

I laugh at the justice of his ticket, and the chance meeting of Duffy and his wife. "You got lucky."

"Lucky, hell," he says with a chuckle. "I parked in that spot every day for three weeks, hoping to catch her in the act. I used to walk three blocks to get to the construction site, so I could park in her district. It cost me two days of a paycheck in tickets. Finally figured out it was cheaper to take a day off and wait in hiding until I could catch her." He winks. "I had to get the timing right."

I eye him curiously. "Why did you have a lunchbox if you took the day off?"

He snorts and shakes his head. "I didn't want her to think I was stalking her."

"So you knew who she was."

He smiles so sweetly, reminiscing. "I knew she made that meter maid's uniform look like a prom dress. Prettiest smile I'd ever seen. Put a song in my heart, a pep in my step, and took me outta of my head."

"How do the Pop Tarts play a role?" I ask.

His eyes twinkle as he grins. "Told her she wasn't a real cop, so she didn't qualify for a donut." We all laugh. "Snapped off a bite of Pop Tart, stuffed it in her mouth and kissed off the crumbs. The rest is history."

The Beatles: "Lovely Rita, Meter Maid"

Not so fast, Darwin. The story he tells is hilarious, I'll admit, but something's missing; something significant. I can feel it.

"Why do you feed the birds half of one every morning?"

He stares out into the darkness and then his eyes turn toward the sky as if he's searching. He shrugs slightly. "Thinking maybe one of them will fly high enough to take her a nibble. Let her know I haven't forgotten."

I lean my head on his shoulder and feel his arm wrap around mine and squeeze. The tears spill from my eyes, dampening his shirt. That has to be the sweetest thing I've ever heard.

"Take every moment you're given, Trinket," he whispers into my hair before he kisses the top of my head. "Live life to its fullest."

Climbing under the sheets after a shower to rid myself of the campfire smoke smell, and slipping into PJs, I slowly release a deep breath and stretch. I'm back, in my element, amongst friends. The conversation around the campfire was deep and emotional, once again giving me insight into these friends of my uncle Morty's. I've finally figured out four of the songs that seemed to be odd choices. I've never asked why they do them; it's not my job. I wonder what Grady's story is. Less than six weeks left on this tour.

I wonder if he'll ever tell me.

There's a soft tap on my door before Colby lets himself in. He makes his way to the bed and taps my butt lightly.

"Scootch over roomie," he says playfully.

Oh boy! I'd forgotten all about it. He and I are now cohabitating…on the bus…with approximately 25 feet between us and everyone else.

I slide over to the other side of the queen size bed, my heart racing – not for the reasons you're thinking, I'm sure. This is to the beat of a different drum. We had already discussed how to handle the ins and outs – no pun intended – of traveling with our companions while maintaining respect and comfort for all parties involved, myself included. You see, Millicent has a little problem with volume. As in, she doesn't need speakers…or megaphones… or amplifiers. Seems I have a lot of bottled-up repression that has a tendency to surface in the act of, well, you understand. In other words, I'm a bit of a screamer. Colby growls, sometimes he even cusses; it's sexy as hell, but he definitely has better control.

"Colby," I whine, sitting ramrod straight up in the bed, the beginning of protestations that he silences with a stern look and an utterance of his own.

"Millicent." He grasps my chin gently with one hand, kisses me chastely and releases his grip. He fluffs his pillow, lays on his side, holds one arm in the air to invite me in and says, "Are you going to let me hold you?"

My mouth twists as I sigh. "You know what that's going to lead to."

He squeezes his eyes closed tightly and takes a deep breath. "What I know is that if you don't shut up and go to sleep, I'll have to silence you with a kiss." He opens his eyes, arches a brow and growls, "And we both know what *that* is going to lead to."

He curves his finger to beckon me closer and I curl into his arms, my head on his chest. "Three weeks I couldn't touch you, Mils. I'll take what I can get." He kisses my forehead and settles his chin above my head.

"Thank you for understanding," I whisper, sinking deeper

as I relax more.

His chest vibrates as he chuckles low.

"What's so funny?"

"Just wondering how long your resolve is going to last. If memory serves, it was you who made us late for brunch with your uncle Morty, and we were ten minutes late for checkout at the hotel today." He lifts his chin off my head and gently tips mine up between his thumb and forefinger. His smile is cocky as he winks. "You do love mornings, don't you, sweetheart."

Rolling over onto my other side, slightly frustrated and now a little turned on – he's not lying – I punch the pillow, pretending to fluff it, and grunt, "Goodnight, Mr. Jarlsberg."

He scoots closer, spoons me from behind and kisses my shoulder. "God, I love it when you get formal. Sounds sexy as hell."

"That had better be a gun in your pocket," I warn, feeling him hard against me.

"Ready to fire when you pull the trigger." He laughs. "See you at sunrise, baby."

I wake to an empty bed, the sound of laughter and voices coming from the kitchen area, and the smell of coffee permeating my nostrils.

Are you kidding me? So much for promises in the dark.

Tossing the blankets back, I rise out of bed, brush my teeth, slip on some running clothes, and open the door. Straight ahead of me stands Colby, at the counter, pouring a cup of coffee. He looks my way, smiles brightly, and holds up a cup.

"Good morning, Ms. Trinkett," he says cheerily. "Coffee?"

I step up beside him, firmly grasping the cup in my hand. "A little *formal* this morning, aren't we?" I growl softly, arching a brow. "And it's not so sexy when you do it."

He chuckles, a slow rumble that makes goosebumps break out on my arms and sends a shiver through my spine. He's entertaining himself at my expense and I'm failing to find the humor in it…at all. Millicent is going to be suffering blue… What do women suffer? Men suffer blue balls but what do women suffer?

There has to be a name for it. Blue bits?

"I'm going for a run," I tell him.

"You need breakfast first." He scowls, lifting a plate full of French toast. "Don't run when you're hungry."

"I'm not hungry." I flash a wry smile and whisper, "Never got the chance to work up an appetite." I wiggle my fingers to wave goodbye. "Toodles."

He grasps my elbow and glares. "Seems I didn't either. Sit. down. and. eat. Now."

This bus thing is really going to take some getting used to.

Des Moines, Iowa-State Fair

Hot, humid, dusty, sticky. And let's not forget…stinky. Livestock…everywhere. A butter cow. Actually, it's a cow carved out of butter. They weren't kidding. Fried Twinkies, fried Snickers. Bacon flavored ice cream.

You've heard the age-old answer to ludicrous requests "When pigs fly"? They must be putting effort into getting those porcine bodies off the ground here; they're serving pigs wings. I have no idea what they're made of; I avoided that booth, as well as all the others. I also avoided the rides. Remember? The only "Raindrops Keep Falling on My Head" reference I want to think about is the one BJ Thomas sang about. And I prefer they be raindrops instead of stomach contents due to a carnival ride that should not have been ventured.

I also had no idea I would be meeting Colby's family. Nice heads-up, *boyfriend*. His mother, grandmother, and two sisters. Duffy is Colby's mother's brother. They share the same smile, same eyes, but Duffy has a playful side that Mrs. Jarlsberg seems to be lacking. She's very friendly; even hugged me when we met. I will admit, it caught me by surprise. His grandmother is spunky, funny, and appears younger than her obvious age. His sisters are crazy… just plain crazy. But the one thing they all have in common is they love Colby. His mother and grandmother cried when they saw him. His sisters jumped in his arms, pinched his cheeks, mussed his hair, and one even kicked him for not telling her all about his girlfriend.

The first night here we visit the beer tent. Not wanting to show a side of me that could be misconstrued as improper – aka drunken Millicent – I had decided ahead of time to limit myself to two beers. It takes all of a half hour for Colby's mother and grandmother to drink that much and his sisters order two just to get started. I nurse my first one over the first half hour and by the time I finish it, due to the heat, it's warm and flat.

Two hours later, Grandma is obviously buzzed, mom is two sheets to the wind, and his sisters are dancing sans music. My decision to limit myself to two beers? Yeah, goes right out the window when Grandma eyes me and asks, "So, tell me, Millicent, does my grandson keep you happy under the sheets?"

Mrs. Jarlsberg bumps her shoulder and waves at me. "Mama, just look at the girl's smile. She is the owner of one happy hoohoo."

Alrighty then, maybe she does have a playful side. But referencing my vagina as a hoohoo? Is that midwestern slang?

My jaw is agape as the ladies giggle. I'm too embarrassed to look to Colby so my eyes dance between the two women as I wait for a deep timbred voice to come to my rescue. It doesn't happen.

"Oh darlin'," Grandma says, patting my hand as if to soothe me. "Sex is nothing new. It amazes me sometimes how the young ones these days think they invented it. Let me tell you something.

"In days of old
When knights were bold
And women weren't too particular,
They'd line them up in single file
And screw them perpendicular."

Her mouth flattens in a straight line, and she nods once as if to prove a point. The entire group at our table snorts with laughter and lifts their beers in a cheer.

And Colby? He simply drops his chin to his chest and rocks with laughter. He doesn't get upset with his grandma or his mom.

He takes everything in stride. He blushes, shakes his head, and groans a bit. But not once does he gasp, shush them, or stomp away in embarrassment. He laughs and therefore…so do I.

"Is it always like this?" I mutter to Colby as the table swallows another drink from their glasses.

"No, no," he chuckles. "Liquor usually plays a part, and she always takes Sundays off." He leans closer and whispers, "It's the day of rest and she's afraid God might be sleeping when she says her last 'forgive me', so she has to be a good girl."

This is family. They're crazy, fun, warm, loving – most definitely entertaining – and they think the world of my Colby.

Mrs. Jarlsberg makes me wonder what it would be like if I still had my mom. But I have my uncle Morty and I can't picture my life without him. I've had Morty longer than I had my mom, and I don't remember a time when I wished someone else were there instead of him. It was more a wish that my parents were there with him. Does that make sense?

Duffy and the rest of the team soak up the banter, share dirty jokes, make bets on the livestock contests, and we finish the evening with the women being virtually carried out to the waiting shuttles where the guys will see them back to their hotel and tuck them in for the night. Safe, sound, comfortable in an air-conditioned room, with water and Tylenol on the nightstand next to the bed. Duffy is staying on the couch in the room with his "mama and sister to make sure they don't puke on themselves". The sisters are in the adjoining room and know that their uncle is on-call if they need him.

The one thing I do know is Grandma and Colby's mom are going to be backstage from the grandstands where it's cooler tomorrow night. The dry ice and enormous fans will send some of that air in their direction. There is no way I will have them sitting amongst 11,000 people in this heat.

We stand backstage the next evening, the air from the fans extending into our little space. Grandma is sitting in a chair that gives her the best view of Colby. He flashes us smiles off and on, turning our way when given the opportunity. He's so happy...so Colby.

"You're good for him, you know," Mrs. Jarlsberg says, swaying her hips to the music. "I've never seen him smile like that."

"He's good for me, Mrs. Jarlsberg," I tell her.

She places a hand on my shoulder and turns me toward her. "Colby would be good for anybody, Millicent. Not just anybody would be good for him. But you are. And call me Linda, please." She pulls me into a hug. "Take care of my boy."

"You have my word," I promise her.

"Something tells me that's as good as gold." She tilts her head and smiles. "It's all I'll ever ask." She looks back towards the band and sighs. "A couple of grandkids would be nice though."

Where the hell did we put that defibrillator?

Chapter 22

Colby

Memphis, Tennessee

One month left on this tour. Atlanta, Georgia after we're done here and then on to Moline, Illinois. For the life of me, I'll never know why Morty chose Moline as our last stop. It's a big venue, but why Illinois? Why Moline? Why not Chicago?

And then one hella long bus ride back to LA after.

If I thought the southern accent in Arkansas was difficult, it's got nothing on Tennessee.

Three syllable words? Nonexistent.

The th sound? Good luck with that…I mean dat.

Anything ending with ing? Forget it.

We're not in Tennessee. We're in "Tensee".

I heard a customer tell a clerk they were feeling 'puny'. Now by all accounts, I've always thought puny meant small. When you hear someone that has to stand six foot-two, weigh close to 300 pounds say they feel puny? Well, I learned today it means sickly. Not that I will add it to my personal dictionary, but somewhere deep in my brain is a new wrinkle. A very useless wrinkle, but a wrinkle just the same.

The Great Smoky Mountains though? They will take your breath away. And amongst them is where we are spending the next two days while we await the third to last concert of this tour. We have four days before the concert but for some reason – I've learned not to ask anymore – the guys wanted to park the buses and stay at the KOA in Pigeon Forge for two nights before trekking the remaining 400 miles into Memphis.

The heat is overbearing this time of year in the south and the pool is calling our names, one by one. The kids are back in school, so the campground is inhabited by mostly adults – give or take a few young children – and the pool is devoid of anything but water at the current time.

"Dippin' time," Charlie announces, throwing a towel over his shoulder as he steps down off the bus. "You guys comin'?"

"Last one in is a rotten egg!" Bruce shouts as he rushes ahead of him once off the bus. We all walk behind him, watching him virtually skip to the pool.

"I swear that boy never did grow up," Dave grumbles, shaking his head. "Just keep him off the playground. He's bound to break a hip."

Grady grins slyly. "Which one of us gets to dunk him first?"

Charlie's eyes light up, his white teeth show with his beaming smile. "Hold him under 'til he blows bubbles?"

Millicent huffs as she glares at them, "That's dangerous!"

Duffy laughs and waves his hand in dismissal. "He'll be fine, Trinket. It ain't his mouth he's blowin' bubbles from." He shrugs and proffers, "We can wait if you want to use him as a flotation device first. Once that gas has gone though, the guy sinks like a brick."

* * *

We sweat our asses off for 7000 people four nights later. The dry ice and fans provide no relief. The guys from Sticky Whiskers are back on their bus within minutes after their performance to gain relief with the air conditioning. Millicent hadn't even ordered a post-performance meal for us out of fear of it spoiling and causing food poisoning. *Yeah, my balls are sweating.* And sweet relief is going to come in the form of a cold shower and gym shorts for the next few days. Probably a shitload of Gold Bond powder as well.

They're calling it a heatwave. I'm calling it one degree short of hell. It's hard to smile, laugh, look like you're having the time of your life when you're drenched head-to-toe. Then I look over to my bandmates who seem unfazed by the climate and conditions. They're more than twice my age, been through two lifetimes and ravages more than I could ever imagine and every single one of them are smiling, playing their hearts out, and giving it their all.

Yes, I'd love it if it were 30 degrees cooler, my clothes were dry, and if I didn't feel like I smell like last week's dirty laundry and ass crack.

I watch as Duffy takes lead on a Lynyrd Skynyrd song. He closes his eyes, leans back, and lets his fingers take control on Rita. The bandana tied around his head is soaked and I see sweat seep through on the sides and down his neck. Still doesn't faze him. He plays through it perfectly – just like always. The man isn't a rock – he's a fucking boulder. Unmoved, strong, solid…and everything I would love to be someday.

Suck it up, Jarlsberg. Sweat, smile, and play your ass off. Be here for your role model; he's been there for you and your family at every turn.

And just like that, the rest of the night falls into total comfort doing what we do best. Can't say my balls don't sweat anymore. Oh no…they're soaked, as is the crack of my ass by the time we finish. The showers at the KOA are going to be busy as soon as those buses pull in. I'll be starting with my clothes on just to rinse the sweat out of them, and strip while I'm in there to end with soaping off. I have never sweated so much in my life, but damn it feels good. Who would have thought a bus full of old farts – Millicent's words – could teach such invaluable lessons?

"Grab the moments while you can, Cheddar."

228

Atlanta, Georgia

Imagine Music Festival

I knew the conditions of this next to last concert would be different than anything else we had done so far – it's a music festival – but different doesn't come close to what I may have been expecting. There seems to be a strong military population in the Georgia area; lots of camouflage clothing, young soldiers and their families, a virtual walkway of three shades of green.

When I think of music festivals, I picture crowds in everything from blue jeans to T-shirts, shorts, boots, and cowboy hats. Looking around, I see all of that as well as everything from white T-shirts with camouflage pants topped with standard camo caps and combat boots to full uniforms.

I think of Millicent in her combat boots in the hotel lobby months ago and it makes me smile. I much prefer the sandals she wears now – those dainty painted toenails. Everything has changed over the last few months; the feminine side she portrays versus the tough little woman she fought to represent with clothing, heavy footsteps, and a near saunter that made one want to clear a pathway for her to walk. She's still tough as nails – make no mistake – but getting to see and know the soft side of my Mils has been the ride of my lifetime. A ride I don't ever want to get off.

We're here two days early. Good thing too because the arrangements are excruciating. Multiple stages, multiple groups, timelines, deadlines, hours of waiting for the right people and instructions. Millicent has worked her ass off to ensure everything is in order. We have another day before anything moves for us. The roadies will do the setup, we'll do sound checks, carry our own instruments tightly in our hands as always with the exception of the keyboards and drums, and Millicent will worry herself into a stupor.

Morty is here for this; not sure why. He reserved hotel rooms for all of us months ago. Hope he plans on sharing with Duffy again because I plan on sharing with Millicent. He can't be so daft as to think we won't be staying together.

He hovers over Millicent like a watchdog, though it's not her work he's observing. No, it's her reactions to her surroundings. Is it the military garb? The place? The people?

She and I have yet to speak of her experiences in the military. I want her to tell me when she's ready. Duffy talked of inside scars. I can't explore those with her until she's ready to share, until she's ready to open up and let me in.

I've been keeping her close, trying my best to be a support system and help with the overwhelming amount of work she's had to do, but I've noticed the small changes. She's uneasy. She gets lost in thought sometimes, and they're not good thoughts. Her brow will furrow, and her eyes are void of any happiness. She's a million miles away in her own head. I've seen her grasp both sides of her head and shake it slightly as if to empty it of whatever is inside.

Oh, Mils. I'll take those thoughts and burn them if you'll let me.

* * *

She sits at the desk in our hotel room studying papers in front of her, as if they hold new information or instructions. Her mouth is twisted to the side and her eyebrows are furrowed once again. She's deep in thought…again.

She jumps in surprise when I place my hands on her shoulders.

"You ready for dinner?" I ask, gently squeezing. "The guys thought we should walk the grounds a little bit, get a feel for the area and grab a bite while we're out."

"Uh, yeah." She nods and stands. "That sounds good."

We make our way downstairs where the guys stand in the lobby waiting for us. Morty gives me a questioning look and I meet his gaze with a glare. He's hiding something and to say I'm pissed would be an understatement. He either wants me to push her into divulging her secrets or he's doing his best to drive a wedge between us.

Duffy walks towards us and throws an arm over Millicent's shoulder. "I say we go for Mexican, Trinket. Morty and I are sharing a room. Death by farts sound good to you?"

She bursts into a fit of giggles. Leave it to Duffy to lighten the mood and change the entire atmosphere with one joke.

"Good thing it's an outdoor concert, huh?" Millicent shakes her head and tucks herself under his arm as we head for the door.

I watch as Duffy bends close and whispers in her ear. I can't hear it, but she nods. He squeezes her tighter, kisses the top of her head and says, "That's my girl."

No, Duffy. That's my girl and I want into all parts of her world.

We have dinner at a restaurant two blocks from the hotel; yes it's Mexican, and the guys have their fill of burritos and beer. Millicent stops at one margarita tonight. Her appetite is diminished but her mood is good. The guys from Sticky Whiskers have joined us so our tables have been placed together to accommodate twelve. The roadies join each other at tables in various places throughout the restaurant and Morty pays the bill for everyone.

The uniforms make their appearance in the restaurant as well; groups of soldiers in military garb – both male and female – dads with their wives and kids.

As we near the end of the meal and see patrons in the entrance waiting for seats as well as standing outside in a line, we take our leave.

Standing on the sidewalk away from the crowd, Sticky

Whiskers and the rest of us make plans to meet up the next day as a black SUV pulls up in front of the restaurant. We watch as the driver runs around to the passenger side and opens the door for an older officer in dress uniform who exits the vehicle. He stands tall, squares his shoulders, and adjusts the cuffs of the uniform that instantly commands respect. The soldiers standing in line immediately stand at attention and salute him as he walks past them without a return salute or acknowledgement.

Apparently the uniform deserves the respect more than the man wearing it.

"Asshole," Grady grumbles. "Probably never seen a day of actual duty in his life."

"I'll shove the water tube up his ass myself," Charlie growls.

"Ah gentlemen," Duffy chuckles. "Take pity on the poor bastard. If his life is anything like Miller's was, he has his own misery to suffer."

Millicent eyes them with curiosity. "Who's Miller?"

"High-falutin' Navy jackass we had to deal with a long time ago," Grady replies.

Charlie laughs and bobs his eyebrows. "Yeah, but his daughter sure was friendly."

"She was only an admiral's daughter," Duffy chants, "but her naval base was filled with discharged seamen." His shoulders bounce with laughter until he shrivels from Morty's glower. "What?" He sheepishly shrugs. "We were Marines. We never took advantage. My mama would have killed me for catchin' syphilis."

It's the first time all night I've heard Millicent laugh raucously, as does everyone else. Everyone but Morty that is, who simply rolls his eyes and shudders.

* * *

The streets are full of festival goers, primed for the music to come and pursuing chaos of their own before it starts, so we walk the grounds along the outskirts. It's as organized as it can be — before tens of thousands show up to literally party for days on end.

Our work starts in the morning and will continue until the day after tomorrow. Two weeks after that it's Moline and the tour is over. And then back to. . .

"Millie!" The shriek comes from somewhere on the field. "Millie!" The voice rings out again, sounding frantic, nearly desperate. . .and closer.

Millicent gasps and freezes, her breath stutters before she places her hand over her heart. Her eyelids flutter, her knees start to buckle, and I grab her waist and hold her up. She's not looking in the direction of the shout to try and find the source. I pull her close and hear what sounds to me like a terrified mutter, "No, no."

"Millie!" he shouts again. I look to where the voice is coming from and see a man running towards us. He's wearing shorts which reveal he's running on one leg and one prosthetic replacement for the other that's missing. He limps as he runs, but the man has speed and he's putting full effort into his strides.

He reaches us and without hesitation he pulls her out of my arms and lifts her into his – feet off the ground – holding her tight as he buries his face in her hair.

"Millie." He says her name like a prayer. I watch Millicent visibly shake in his arms as she wraps hers around his shoulders, and I hear her sob, "Jordy."

Morty steps up behind me, his voice laden with shock, "Did she just say Jordy?"

"Yeah," I answer.

"I'll be damned," he mutters. "He made it."

I feel two strong hands on my shoulders pull me back and away before I can step between them.

"Norway." Grady's low rumble echoes through my head as he pulls me back farther away. "There's a story here. Might want to hear it before you go jumpin' to conclusions."

"Cheddar," Duffy warns low and soft from my other side. "Breathe."

"I just lost her, didn't I?" I hear myself whisper.

I feel a thump on the back of my head. "What the hell are you talking about? She's right there, idiot," Dave chides.

I watch as he holds her in the air, their arms still locked around each other's bodies; his neck, her waist. I'm frozen as I observe them, my heart racing so fast it feels like it's going to burst through my rib cage. I can't swallow my throat is so tight. She doesn't even remember I'm here.

I feel a hand grasp the back of my neck and squeeze tightly. "If it were romantic, dumbass, she'd be wrapped around him like a boa constrictor," Charlie growls. "Pull your head outta your ass."

They finally pull back from each other, just enough to make eye contact. "You look great, Millie."

"Y…you look…not dead," she says through tears. "They said you died, Jordy." She breaks down once more, burying her head in his shoulder.

He gasps. "They told you I was dead?" He laughs, hugging her tighter. "Well, I'd make a helluva ghost, sweetheart. I'm here in the flesh."

He sets her on her feet and takes her cheeks in his palms. "Millie, you did it." He kisses her forehead, holding his lips there far too long for my liking. "We made it, baby girl."

And my stomach takes a dive for rock bottom. 'We made it, baby girl'.

"Your leg," Millicent says, looking down at the prosthetic and back up to him.

"Still got two." He smiles brightly and winks. "It's the one in the middle that I would have missed most. And it's working just fine."

She giggles through her tears and slaps his chest. "Still a pervert."

He grins impishly and winks again. "Still seeing your boobies in my dreams."

She slaps his arm playfully and narrows her eyes as more tears spill. "I knew I should have made you close your eyes."

He pulls her into another hug, and I see his eyes water. "Oh, Millie," he says lovingly. "I never thought I'd see you again."

A woman walks through the field in our direction carrying a child in her arms; a toddler who fights to get down. She relents when they're about twenty feet away and the child runs to the man next to Millicent. Jordy lifts him high in the air and settles him in his arms proudly.

He turns and waits for the woman and when she reaches them, he wraps his arm around her shoulder. "Millie, this is my wife, Jennifer. Jen, this is the famous Millie Trinkett."

Millicent extends her hand, but Jennifer pulls her into a hug. "He talks about you all the time. I've always wanted to meet you," she says, her voice cracking. "Thank you."

"And this little monster," he announces proudly, bouncing the little boy on his hip, "is Miles." He looks to Millicent and smiles. "It's a masculine form of Millicent, don't you agree? Jen wanted it."

Bruce whispers in my ear, "I think you can release that breath you've been holding now. As far as your head being up your ass?" He pats me on the shoulder. "Well, we ate Mexican earlier. Give it time, it all comes out in the end."

Millicent looks toward our group and her eyes land on Morty. "You were there. You heard them." Morty is by her side before the last word leaves her mouth. He wraps her in his arms and props his chin on the top of her head.

"I was there, sweetheart," he tells her, then sniffs. "They screwed up."

"Six years, Morty," she sobs. "I've wasted so much."

He takes her shoulders and patiently waits for her to look up at him. "Millicent Trinkett, you and the word wasted don't belong in the same dictionary." He firms his brow and stiffens his upper lip. "Nothing and no one in my whole life has given me more purpose…or joy. Onward and upward, okay?"

She nods slowly, unsure as a small whimper escapes.

"Millie." Jordy steps forward and lays a hand on her shoulder. "Six years of what? Feeling guilty because you thought I was dead?"

"I thought," she hiccups, "I'd let you down."

He pulls her to him again, one arm around her waist, his hand cradling her head to his chest. "Mighty Millie," he groans despairingly. "I would have searched the ends of the earth to find you if I'd known. So many of us just wanted to forget."

"So did I," she mumbles.

"Maybe now you can," he says.

She nods against his chest. "Yeah."

He tips her chin up. "Not all of it. I'll never forget you, sweet Millie." He taps her on the nose and grins cockily. "With or without your T-shirt on."

"Jordy!" his wife yells. "Stop teasing that poor woman!" She looks to Millicent and rolls her eyes. "Always a boob man."

Millicent's cheeks flush with embarrassment. "I can't believe he…"

Jennifer waves a hand to stop her. "Millie, you probably gave his heart the extra kick it needed. Be proud of your girls."

"And on that note…" Millicent's voice rises an octave as she changes the subject. "Colby," she calls as she waves me over. "Could you come here?"

I waste no time joining them and nearly trip over my own feet on the way.

"Guys, this is my boyfriend, Colby Jarlsberg. Colby, this is Jordy Medford, his wife, Jennifer and their son, Miles." I extend my hand to shakes theirs, taking an extra moment to pay attention to the little boy who grips one finger and pulls.

No, I didn't fart. Thank you grandpas everywhere.

"Jordy and I served together in Afghanistan for a year before…" she pauses, "…we were discharged." I place my arm around her shoulder and squeeze gently. Gut instinct tells me she needs it right now.

"So, you're the lucky guy who finally won her over," Jordy says, smiling softly. "She's the best. Right next to my Jen." He winks at his wife.

"I know," I reply, dropping a kiss on Mils' head.

"She saved my life," he says, brows pinched, his lips pressed together. "I doubt she likes to talk about it, but I'll sing her praises any day. Take good care of her."

"My favorite thing to do," I say.

Millicent introduces the rest of our group and we bid each other farewell after the exchange of phone numbers with the promise of staying in better touch and a plan to meet up next year with a vacation; either us on the east coast or them on the west.

As we walk back to the hotel, Millicent walks with Morty the Bulldog's arm over her shoulder while I walk with the group behind them. I realize taking care of her is my favorite thing to do. I love to see her happy, watch her smile, hear her laugh. I love it when she hums with the first sip of coffee in the morning or when she moans over her first bite of a pancake, or when she moans with….yeah, that's my favorite sound. Better yet? Knowing I'm the only one who's ever made her moan like that is…

Wait a minute! Still seeing her boobies in his dreams? Back the train up.

"Wondered how long it was going to take you," Duffy mumbles next to me, slapping me on the back. "Boy, you are slow as mud some days."

"What?" I snap, glaring at him.

"He only saw them," he whispers. "Never said nothin' about playing with 'em. Cheddar, don't ever play poker again. You just don't have the face for it."

"How in the hell would you know what I'm thinking?" I hiss.

"Because you're scowling and puckering at the same time," he answers. He glances around us to ensure no one else is paying attention. "Now you're either practicing for when you get back to your room, suckin' on a lemon drop, or overthinking a conversation that took place half an hour ago. Let it go, Cheddar. She'll explain when she's ready."

"So you know what that was all about?" I whisper.

"Not a damn clue about the boobies," he says with a laugh. Then he flashes me a stern look of warning. "That ought to be the least of your concerns at the moment. Keep your eye on the things that matter. Emotions are high right now and she's fragile. Don't push. Let her come to you."

He's right, I know it. He's worked with vets and PTSD

victims for years. If anyone knows what scars of war can do, it's Duffy. He carries a few of his own.

I nod and assure him, "Got it."

"I know," he utters and pats my shoulder. "A little reminder never hurt though."

* * *

"I suppose you want an explanation." Millicent tosses the covers back on the bed before climbing in and lying on her side. She's been quiet while we get ready for bed, deep in thought.

I crawl in on the other side and settle next to her, my front to her back. "What I want is for you to tell me what you need from me. That's all."

She rolls over to face me and places her palm on my cheek, running her fingers through my beard the way she always does. That way that makes my knees weak if I'm standing, my spine tingle if I'm sitting, and makes my blood hot if I'm lying next to her.

"How are you so perfect?" she whispers softly, her eyes filling with tears.

"Hardly perfect, Millicent," I return. "Patient. You'll share when you're ready."

She lays her head on my chest and snuggles in. "I was supposed to keep him alive. I promised him he wouldn't die. I made him swear he'd fight, and I swore to him I'd get him through." She hiccups and sniffles, and I feel a tear fall onto my chest. "I wanted to see him before I left Germany, but they told me he didn't make it.

"We spent two days holed up in a mud-crusted, filthy building waiting for our guys to show up. Our vehicle ran over an IED when we were on patrol and pieces went flying everywhere. Jordy got hit and went down. I dragged him into that building to get him away from any further active danger. He had a hole in his leg that went through the bone in his calf. He was in agony." She stops to catch a sob. "I tied his leg off with my belt to stop the bleeding and tamped the wound with my shirt to plug it, but the conditions were so filthy. I knew infection was inevitable, but I didn't think he would die." I hold her tighter in my arms as she cries.

"He didn't die, Mils," I murmur. "They gave you the wrong information."

"But this whole time, I thought I'd let him down. That I didn't deliver the one thing I'd promised; that we would both make it home."

"What did you mean when you said you'd wasted so much?"

"Time," she says softly. "Time spent in therapy dealing with survivor's guilt, anger, PTSD, nightmares," she hesitates and shrugs, "feeling like I wasn't enough."

"Why did you continue to wear the boots?"

"Self-inflicted punishment," she snorts. "My constant reminder to try to do better. Uncle Morty told me to take them off before this tour because of Duffy, Grady and Charlie." She tips her head up to look at me and grins. "You were the reason I bought the cute sandals though."

The air in the room shifts and suddenly becomes lighter and with it the mood lightens as well.

She giggles and rolls her eyes. "Colby, the only reason he saw my *boobies*," she uses air quotes, "is because I didn't wear a bra that day due to heat rash and I had to strip off my T-shirt to tamp the wound. I put my flak jacket back on immediately."

I roll her onto her back, and she gasps as my hand gently squeezes one of my favorite body parts. "Can't say as I blame the man. They certainly are what my dreams are made of."

* * *

The next morning the equipment bus pulls up to the hotel, fully loaded with roadies, a cold lunch, snacks, and a full day's supply of chilled water and Gatorade – complements of Millicent's planning ahead.

I swear the woman is like a mother hen on steroids.

The roadies will be out there until the concert ends this

evening; we'll be there long enough to do sound checks and inspect anything we feel necessary. Then we come back, shower, eat, get ready to go, and entertain our asses off. One long, arduous, hellish night. One night none of us would trade.

"You coming with us?" Jake asks, passing us on his way to the door of the bus.

"Got a Lyft van on its way," Morty answers, glancing at his watch.

"Of course you do," Jake replies, smirking.

Morty lifts a brow. "Who works for who, Jake?"

"See you there, Morty," Jake snorts, stepping up into the bus.

It's hot, humid, and the day is only getting started. When it's just us, we all travel together, under the same conditions, and we do it as a unit. But when Mortimer Montgomery is around, there is air of arrogance that follows him. He's in charge and everyone knows it. Millicent's in charge otherwise and no one ever questions it. She can shrink a man in his shoes with one glare and make him go all wobbly in the knees with one smile. I should know; I'm one of those men. However, on any given day, you will never find anyone to make you feel more comfortable than Millicent does. She's like a human care package. And therein lies the difference between her and her uncle.

"Where's Millie?" Morty asks, frowning.

"She's going to hang back for this one," I answer. "We're just doing equipment checks."

A quizzical furrow forms on his brow. "She okay?"

I nod and smile. "She's fine."

* * *

"Uh, I want to stop by the room and see if Millie has time to do somethin' with me before the show tonight," Charlie says once back in the lobby of the hotel.

We basically worked in the shade today; no heavy lifting as that is the reason we have roadies, and with Morty around you'd think he had the magic asshole that they couldn't shove their noses up far enough. The work was finished so fast we're back hours before we anticipated, therefore leaving us with most of the afternoon before go-time.

"If it's what I think it is," Duffy side-eyes him and says, "I'll join you. That massage felt pretty damn good on my back."

"Count me in," Bruce chimes.

"Me too," Dave and Grady say in unison.

Ah, toenail time.

"What are you guys talkin' about?" Morty asks, eyeing them suspiciously. "You had Millie massaging you?"

"Hmmm," Bruce hums. "That girl is the best. A glass of wine with a massage and a toe job sounds pretty good right now."

Morty stops short and whirls on them. *"A what?!"*

"Always were too easy, Morty." Grady laughs, slapping him on the back.

I slip my card key in the slot and wait for the green light to shine before pulling it out and pushing the door open slightly. I want to give her a heads up before we all walk in, but Morty grasps my shoulder when we hear the sweetest melodic sound coming from the bedroom.

He presses his finger to his lips to quiet us and pushes the door farther open and pokes his head through to listen. The guys gather closer in order to hear as well and we stand frozen; seven of us squeezed in the doorway of our hotel room, listening to Millicent sing.

My God, she's got a beautiful voice. Airy but clear, crisp, strong.

I look to Morty and have to turn away due to the tears falling from closed eyes down cheeks on a pain filled face. I see Duffy's hand reach out for Morty's shoulder and hold it firmly.

"She's singing again," Morty whispers, scrubbing his hand over his face to wipe the tears. "I haven't heard her sing in years."

Just then Millicent steps into the living room, startled when she sees us standing in the doorway. She has earphones in and stops singing the moment she sees us, pulling the earphones from her ears.

"I...I didn't hear you come in," she sputters, seemingly embarrassed.

"We heard you," Grady says, grinning. "Don't stop on our account, Little Bit."

"Millie," Morty breathes in astonishment. "You're singing."

She shrugs casually and makes a squirrely face. "I found my voice."

"You sure did," I tell her. I stare at her in amazement. So many facets to this woman, and I want to know every one of them.

She points her finger at Morty, raising her eyebrows and shaking her head, her face lined with worry. "Don't even think it, Uncle Morty. It's just for me, okay?"

He wraps his arms around her shoulders and kisses the top of her head. "As long as you found it again, Millie. It's been way too long."

Turns out Millie was the star of the stage in high school as well as a popular backup singer in Morty's studio with a promising future. Morty was extremely encouraging – and so hopeful – he could talk her out of the military, but it never happened. Her father was a serviceman, and she was determined to follow in his footsteps. She exceled in school and money was never in question – she could have gone to college anywhere – but she could not be deterred and stars on a uniform drove her more than stars in her eyes.

* * *

She studies the faces before her, narrowing her eyes, deep in thought. "You were all at my going away party, weren't you?"

"Well," Duffy grimaces, "my gallbladder prevented me from showing up, but Cheddar took my place. These guys," he points to the others, "were all there."

She looks to me and her mouth twitches in enlightenment. "That's what you meant by wanting to kiss me goodbye eleven years ago."

"Uh," I clear my throat and look down, toeing the rug. "Can

we talk about this later?"

"Uh," Morty mocks, "or we can talk about it now."

"Still got that stick up your ass, don't ya, Morty?" Charlie slaps him on the back. "Millie, you up for a toe job?"

Millicent's face lights up and she gets absolutely giddy as she claps her hands and bounces on her toes. "Oohh, tootsie time. I'd love to. Let me grab my purse." She runs for the bedroom and shouts, "Give me just a minute, I'll call the salon!"

Morty glares before he squeezes his eyes closed and growls, "Toe job, salon." He shakes his head slowly. "Pedicures. Do you guys have *any* balls left?"

"We're good," Charlie laughs. "It's poor Colby that lost his the minute he laid eyes on your niece."

Morty lets out a throaty groan as he glowers at me and then heads toward the door.

"Oh no you don't," Bruce says, grabbing his arm. "These little piggies go to market together. You can go wee, wee, wee all the way home when we're done, tough guy. We do this for Millie. Suck it up, buttercup."

Morty heaves a sigh in resignation. He knows he's not going anywhere. They'd probably tackle him, give him noogies, drag him down the hallway and out the door, into the salon and tie him to the chair and order colored nail polish if he doesn't go willingly.

Ha! No Morty, that would be Millicent. Just ask the boy band you made her manage.

ANNIE MICK

Chapter 23

Millicent

"You guys ready?" I ask as I exit the bedroom. I called the salon downstairs in the hotel to make arrangements for all of us to get pedicures. Unfortunately, they didn't have enough chairs to accommodate us, but they were nice enough to find me one that did. It's within walking distance of the hotel and our appointments are in a half hour. Eight pairs of feet, one that needs polish. Here goes.

I'll be sure to get Uncle Morty a seat on the end, but I need to figure out who to seat next to him or he'll never live it down. You see, Morty has unbearably ticklish feet. If you'll remember, I also explained Morty has OCD. He'll be wiping down that chair before he sits in it, I'm sure. The thought of putting his feet in a tub that other feet have been in might not be in his comfort zone either. So, I'll sit next to Morty, Charlie will be on my other side, and so on and so forth, putting more distance between him and the others. I'm making seating arrangements in my head as we walk to the salon.

The sign for "Pretty Digits" comes into view when Morty bends close and whispers, "Are you ever going to tell me how this whole thing started?" He arches a brow. "How you got five old hippies to get pedicures?"

I gasp. "Uncle Morty they're your age! They're not old," I hesitate, "and young at heart does count for something."

He glares for a moment. "Hey! I'm years younger than these guys." He smiles and nods before he pulls me to him. "But I'm glad you finally figured that out, Millie."

He pulls the door open, and we walk inside. The salon is clean, large, nicely decorated, with seats open for all of us.

"Morty!" a woman behind the counter says breathlessly as she runs towards us and jumps into Morty's arms. She's blonde, stands about 5'6", slim, quite beautiful actually, and near tears as she hugs my uncle quite affectionately. Morty returns her hug hesitantly, but eventually wraps his arms around her waist and squeezes.

"Hello, Maggie," he says softly, closing his eyes as if savoring a memory.

I look to the men surrounding us for answers – they obviously aren't coming from the couple entangled on the floor in front of me at the present time – and wait. Grady clears his throat first and Uncle Morty is driven from his Maggie stupor, or, I don't know, maybe vapor lock.

"Uh…uh, Maggie this is my niece, Millie Trinkett," he fumbles. "Millie this is Maggie Jensen. An old friend of mine."

I hear soft chuckles from the group before Duffy murmurs, "Think I just lost my roommate for the night."

Morty shoots him a glare and they all quiet quickly and glance away to break eye contact as they hum or clear their throats.

Maggie cups my cheeks as she studies my face. "So this is Millie. Oh, Morty, she's beautiful."

My eyebrows crease and I scrunch my nose. "And right here."

She giggles. "I'm sorry, sweetheart. I've heard so much about you. I'm just surprised is all." She has a slight Georgia accent, beautiful warm brown eyes, and a slightly tilted smile that seems sincere.

"Well," I say clumsily, glancing at my watch and clapping

my hands once, folding them together. "I don't want to be rude, but we are here to gets pedis and time is of the essence so…we should probably get started."

"Oh!" she says surprised as if being brought back to the here and now. "Let's get the ball rolling then." She walks back to the counter and assigns us all a pedicurist and leads us to chairs.

"Maggie," Morty leans towards her, gently placing his hand around her elbow before he takes a seat. "Are you really busy or can you take a break?"

"No, I have time," she tells him, obviously pleased with his question. "We can talk in the back room, if you don't mind?"

Morty smiles and nods. "That would be perfect." He looks to me. "Millie, I'm going to pass on the pedicure. You all have fun. I'll see you when you're done."

My eyes flit between the two of them, but neither notice as theirs seem to be glued to one another. Well, well, well. What have we here?

Colby stands from his chair, walks to mine and leans down, taking my mouth in a delicious kiss. He chuckles as he stands back up.

"Oh yeah," he murmurs. "He's hooked."

"What are you talking about?"

"If he didn't punch me after that," he says, laughing, "he didn't even see it."

"We did," Charlie grumbles.

"Hey Charlie," Colby calls to him. When all heads turn to look at him he says, "I checked my pockets. Found 'em." He smirks and takes his seat.

I have no idea what that was about but I'm sure there's a story somewhere.

* * *

I've never seen my uncle Morty look so rumpled, flushed, and calm at the same time as when he exits the backroom after being notified that our pedicures are completed. Is that a smudge of lipstick? By golly, it is. And it just so happens to match the shade Maggie was wearing when we entered the salon. Mind you, I said *was* as she is no longer wearing it. Seems she either removed it or had assistance in doing so. Due to the fact her lips are nearly twice the size they were when I first met her, my bet is she's been in a lip-lock with my uncle since entering that backroom – possibly more – but *ewww.* Nope, not going there. I've just begun to explore my own sexual experience; I'll be dipped if I think about someone else's. But Uncle Morty…did he just have up against the wall sex in the back of a nail salon? Even I wouldn't be that daring at this point. Uncle Morty…you dog!

No, Millicent. That's when you're on your hands and knees and… Oh God, I've got to get out of here.

"Oh no! These are on me," Maggie says, gently pushing my hand back when I try to hand her the black Amex to pay for the pedicures. "And Morty already took care of the tips."

Bruce snorts loudly and exits the salon in a rush. Dave follows quickly and I watch through the window as the two of them bend in laughter and slap each other on the back. Duffy gives a quick wave and says, "See ya, Maggie," on his way out the door with Grady and Charlie doing the same and following him.

Colby steps up behind me and wraps his arms around my shoulders, leaning in to whisper in my ear, "Let Morty take care of this. We'll step outside to babysit the boys and give him a few minutes."

"Okay," I say awkwardly, accepting Maggie's offer of generosity, and tuck the card back into my wallet.

"Millie," she says, stepping out from behind the counter, stretching her arms out to me. "Can I give you a hug?"

Her arms are around me before I can answer…or decline. I reciprocate because, well, she is a friend of Morty's. Smelling my uncle's cologne all over her as she pulls me in indicates she's more than a friend; at the very least more than friendly.

When Colby and I step out into the Georgia heat, we see the guys have moved away from the storefront and stand together in front of another one two doors down. Apparently they haven't seen us.

"Oh come on," Bruce laughs. "Morty already took care of the tips? I can only hold a straight face for so long. I'm sure Morty did a pretty good job on those *tips.*"

They all chuckle, but Duffy still reprimands him. "You keep your shit together around Trinket, Bruce. She has no idea."

"Pretty sure she's getting one," I say as we walk up behind them. "Somebody want to explain?"

They startle at the sound of my voice and spin towards me.

"Millie," Charlie says cheerily. "My toes feel great. I think you got me hooked on these things."

"Cut the crap," I snap. I tilt my head back towards the salon. "What's the story?"

Duffy tucks his hands in his pockets and steels his eyes on mine. "No more ours to tell than yours was, Trinket. Ask Morty."

I feel Colby's grip over my shoulder tighten protectively. He chuckles and kisses my temple. "Baby, this could be a really good thing. Gives him something to concentrate on besides planning my demise."

I slap his chest and giggle. "He's not planning your demise. His bark is much worse than his bite." I look to the guys and ask, "Is he happy?"

Dave breaks into spastic laughter. "I'd say right about now he's really happy."

Bruce nearly giggles and adds, "Downright giddy."

Grady holds out his hand, tilting it back and forth. "I'd go with more relaxed."

Charlie says, "I'd say probably less uptight."

Duffy twists his mouth and closes one eye as he ponders. "Stick's halfway out of his ass."

"You morons ready to go?" Morty yells from two storefronts down. "You've barely got time to wash the stink off before showtime!"

Duffy shakes his head and rolls his eyes. He looks at Morty and a sly grin appears before he turns to the rest of the group. "You ready to go shove the stick back up his ass?"

They all take off at a dead run towards Morty, leaving Colby and me behind. We watch as they pick him up off the ground and carry him down the street; four of them, each holding a hand or a leg while Morty hollers obscenities, Duffy leading the pack. There's a fountain not far ahead and I get the feeling that is exactly where Morty is going to land.

Colby and I follow them…well, I don't know why. For the show, I guess.

"We'll get showers, Morty," Grady yells. "You get the bath." And then my poor uncle Morty meets the water as they toss him in the fountain. He sputters and clambers to get to his feet, soaked to the skin.

"You assholes!" Morty screams as he begins to make his way to the edge of the fountain.

Duffy holds up Morty's dry cell phone and wallet, which he apparently removed from his pockets before they tossed him in. "Who's the moron now?" He holds the phone and wallet in a threatening manner as if they're about to be thrown in the fountain to join their owner. "Say you're sorry, Morty or the phone and wallet get it."

Morty stands with his hands on his hips, glaring and grumbling obscenities before conceding. "Sorry," he growls as Charlie and Dave reach for his hands to help him out of the fountain. He slaps their hands away and steps out on his own. We turn and head down the sidewalk to return to the hotel, Uncle Morty sloshing in his shoes and leaving small puddles with every step.

"You're still a bunch of assholes," he grunts, running his hands through his hair.

Duffy shrugs and laughs. "Never denied it."

"So how is Maggie?" Bruce asks. "She looks good."

Morty's eyes flash to mine and then he looks ahead again. "Let's concentrate on work, shall we?"

We walk in silence the remaining block back to the hotel. As we reach the front door, Morty sighs and looks to Bruce. "She's good."

Bruce chuckles and flicks at his collar. "I'd say with the

lipstick stain she left on your shirt, she's really good."

Morty slaps his shoulder so hard the sound can be heard across the lobby. "Asshole."

Bruce only laughs harder. "Never denied it."

The sweat literally pours off of them as they play their hearts out. The crowd is rowdy, but appreciative and controlled. Sticky Whiskers doesn't run back to the bus when they're finished; they stay by our sides, enjoy a few beers and chat with one another while the guys finish. One more job to go and this tour is over. Here come the special songs:

Elenore – The Turtles for Bruce's Ellie.
The Weight – The Band for Dave's Fanny.
Lovely Rita Meter Maid – The Beatles for Duffy's Rita.
Mustang Sally – Wilson Pickett for Charlie's Sally.
Susie Q. – Creedence Clearwater Revival for…

That's it! There has to be – or must have been – a Susie somewhere. These are the odd songs, all fit as a medley. Who is Grady's Susie? And why has it taken me six months to put it together? But then, who is Morty's Maggie? And how have I never known anything about her at all, ever?

It's not like they could do a song for her. Those weren't exactly complimentary lyrics, were they? Rod Stewart didn't sing highly of that woman.

* * *

After three encores, they're able to leave the stage. They're exhausted, running on adrenaline, and in severe need of cold showers and sustenance in the form of healthy food and a couple of beers. After a substantial amount of water and Gatorade.

"You wanna hug me sweaty?" Colby bobs his eyebrows and grins as he holds his arms out, his shirt soaked with perspiration.

I pierce him with a warning glare. "I'll hug you *wet*, later. After you shower."

His eyes flash with a playful look. "That could be taken two ways."

Grady slaps him upside the head. "I'm givin' you two words, Norway. *Cold shower.* Move it. I'm hungry."

* * *

Once back at the hotel and showered, we all gather together in a small banquet room on the first floor that Morty had reserved months ago. The roadies, Sticky Whiskers, and the rest of us file in group by group. Sandy and John along with the drivers from the other buses join us as well. This is as close to a farewell dinner as we will get. One more concert to go. The thought tugs at my heart and makes my stomach roll a bit. I'm really going to miss these guys. We've spent the last six months together with no major mishaps. We've camped out at KOAs across the country together, barbecuing and sitting around campfires, telling stories and laughing; none of us going home during the travel times because none of us felt the need to get away from each other. No drugs, no groupies on the buses, no unruly teenagers to babysit. And the music…oh the music.

And this is where I met Colby. Oh God, Colby. What happens when this is over? We haven't discussed the *end.* But there is an end, isn't there? There always is. In two weeks. Unless you count the bus ride back to LA. He'll pick up with another band and leave the country to tour and I'll be . . . Alone. Again. Naturally.

Oh, screw you Gilbert O'Sullivan.

How had this not occurred to me before? I watch him as he stands with a few of the guys laughing and talking, probably about tonight's concert. Maybe even about upcoming ones on the roster. He's beautiful. So talented. So…Colby. An original.

I feel the burn as the water gathers behind these betraying orbs of mine that had been trained not to release the tears for so many years. I was guarded, steeled, a soldier. And now? Now, I'm a mess of emotions that needs to get the hell out of this room before anyone sees me fall apart over my first – and only – love I've ever known. Because in two weeks he will be a memory and it will be

Just. Like. Starting. Over.

Oh, screw you John Lennon. Damnit! Why does everything lead to lyrics?

I head for the door and make a fast exit to the elevators. I turn around as the doors are closing and see Colby as he yells my name. Silence surrounds me as the elevator ascends, and as soon as the doors open I rush down the hall, open the door to the suite, lock myself in the bathroom, and sit down on the floor and cry; remembering the night this soldier surrendered and became a woman.

Stupid, stupid Millie.

"Millicent!" Colby calls out as he enters the room. He taps on the bathroom door seconds later, his voice softer this time. "Mils? You okay?"

Masking my voice as best I can through a stuffed nose and clogged throat due to sobs and tears I answer, "I'm fine."

"You don't sound fine," he says softly. "Talk to me."

"Please go back downstairs," I beg, reminding myself this too shall pass.

Oh good, no lyrics to match that line to. Well, there are but no one artist to blame so there's always that.

I hear his back slide down the bathroom door on the other side and feel his head thump lightly against it once he's seated. He's mere inches away, only the thickness of the door separating us.

"I'm not going anywhere," he says, then finishes with a heartbreaking statement, "Millicent, I hate it when you're mad at me."

I'm not mad at him, am I? This is just the way things have to be, isn't it? It's the nature of the business.

I muster all the strength my voice has and tell him, "I'm not mad at you, Colby."

"I'll wait," he says patiently. "When you're ready, I'll be right here."

This makes me cry harder. He is here, now. But where will he be two weeks from now?

Colby's phone rings but once. I've never heard him sound so mad as he does when he answers. No hello, nothing other than… "I swear to God if anybody knocks on this door or shows up to this room, I will murder you myself. Got it?" That's it. Other than a heaved sigh and another head thump on the other side of the door.

After agonizing minutes of draining myself of tears and accepting what was once wishful thinking is now cruel reality, I rise from the floor. Taking a moment to look in the mirror before making my appearance, I'm abhorred by what I see. I'm a mess. Swollen, red rimmed eyes, runny mascara. I can't bring myself to care. The emptiness has already started, the voids that won't be filled ever again. Just one more hole in my heart that bleeds a little bit more. Grab that shield and put it up, Millie. It's not the first time – probably won't be the last either.

I turn the knob and open the door slowly. Colby catches himself before he falls backwards and gets up quickly.

His face is filled with worry as he reaches out to me. "Tell me what you need."

I fall into his arms and break down all over again, sobbing. "It's over. I didn't think about the end and now that it's here, I…I…"

He holds me and gently rubs my back. "You're going to miss them, aren't you?"

This starts another flood within me. Miss *them*? He doesn't even get it.

"Come over here," he whispers and leads me to the sofa where we both take a seat. "We still have two more weeks, and they are going to miss you just as much."

I let out a soft sarcastic chuckle and sniffle. "*They* are."

"What?" His eyes open wide as his forehead creases. "Millicent, what did you just say?"

"Simply repeating what you said." Shrugging, I turn away and swipe another tear. "You said *they* are going to miss me. What about you, Colby?"

"Me? Why would I miss you?"

Whirling back around, I swear I pull a muscle in my neck. Something within me snaps and my pain is suddenly overtaken by ire. I'm not going to need Uncle Morty to plan his demise; he won't make it to the room fast enough.

"Gee, I don't know, Colby. Maybe because I slept with you!" I scream, incredulous at his cold ignorance. "Because it's over!"

He stares as if I've slapped him. If his mouth weren't hanging open, it wouldn't put me in the difficult position of deciding whether I want to shove my tongue in it or slap it shut. Damn you, Colby! He grasps the nape of my neck and pulls me to him. His kiss is firm and demanding. He breaks it suddenly and pulls back just slightly, studying my face as if trying to solve a puzzle.

"Stay here," he growls. "Do. not. move." He stands up and glares at me. "Give me five minutes. Ten tops." Then he rushes out of the room slamming the door behind him.

Chapter 24

Colby

I probably should have tied her to a chair. Who knows if she's going to be there when I get back? Someday they're going to come up with a cure for 'foot in mouth disease', and I will be their test subject. *"Why would I miss you?"* Way to go, Colby. She thinks we're over? Ha! Over my dead body.

The elevator ride will take too long so I choose the stairs – three at a time. If I fall and break my neck on the way down, I can only hope they bury me in something classier than a cardboard box. Oh hell, I won't care. I'll be dead and it won't matter because I won't get to do the one thing that matters most.

I step into the banquet room and all eyes turn on me. Great. They don't have to ask; I already know what they're thinking. They want to know where Millicent is. Well, I want to know where Morty is and that trumps their question.

Apparently I don't have to look too far because he's headed for me right now, and he doesn't look happy. Welcome to my world, Mr. Montgomery. But that's about to change – if you'd hurry your ass up. I see Duffy stalking close behind him and I shake my head to ward him off. This one is on me. He slows down and keeps a farther distance, but still within range to jump in if need be. I also see the blonde from the salon this morning following as well.

"Where's Millie?" Morty demands. "And where the hell do you get off talking to me like that on the phone?"

"I can take care of Millicent," I grind through a clenched jaw. "If I had needed your help, I would have called you."

"Where is she?" he demands again, taking a deep breath and puffing his chest in a show of challenge.

"Can we step out into the hall?" I ask him.

He leads the way as always, claiming his usual place of authority; heels of his Ferragamo's clicking with every step. For God's sake, Morty, buy a pair of tennis shoes. Apparently they did shove that stick back up your ass.

"What is it?" He crosses his arms over his chest, legs spread wide; commanding stature and all. You know, Uncle Morty style.

I match his stance and his folded arms. "I'm gonna marry her, Morty."

He chokes, "You what?"

"You heard me," I say. "I came down to get your blessing. I understand it's the proper thing to do."

He manages a snarky laugh. "You want my blessing."

"It would be nice," I reply, shrugging one shoulder. "I don't need it, but I know how important it is to Millicent because she loves you just that much. And because she's just that important to me, her happiness means everything. So tell me, Morty, how much does Millicent's happiness mean to you?"

He lifts a brow, curious. "Has she said yes?"

I roll my eyes and huff, "Would I be here asking for your blessing if I'd already asked her?" I look at my watch and see I have approximately three minutes left. "Would you hurry up, please? I'm in a bit of a rush here."

"Do you love her?" he asks, his eyes studying mine as he waits.

Without hesitation I answer, "So much it's almost painful."

He tilts his head toward the elevators. "Go on, get out of here. You've got my permission. Get her down here for the party."

"I didn't ask for your permission," I sneer. "I asked for your blessing. Just once, Morty, quit being an ass."

He snickers and slaps my shoulder. "Just checking for balls, Colby. You got it."

I reach out to shake his hand and squeeze a bit harder than necessary. "Thank you," I breathe and run for the elevators, hoping I don't have to take the stairs again. Down is one thing, up is a whole other animal.

"Colby!" Morty shouts before I step into the elevator. "You ever hurt…"

"We've had this conversation, Morty," I interrupt him. "Never gonna happen."

"She lives in the gatehouse until the ceremony's over," he hollers. "You are not shacking up with my niece!"

Before the doors start to close I holler back, "Better get moving on the venue then, Morty. I don't believe in long engagements."

Upon entering the room I see Millicent, surprisingly, sitting right where I left her.

"You're two minutes late," she says. Still sassy, but I hate the lack of confidence I hear, the loss of teasing in her voice. I know she hasn't moved from the sofa; her makeup is still smudged from crying and it looks like she may have even shed a few more tears since I've been gone.

"Where did you go?"

"Had to go see Morty for a minute," I reply casually.

I walk to the bedroom, open my suitcase, and collect what I'm looking for, stuff it in my pocket, and make my way back to the living room. I plop down on the sofa next to her.

"Over, huh?" I lift a brow and study her face. "Is that how you see us?"

She swipes at her cheeks again and sniffles. Her mascara is gone from her lashes; having been washed to underneath her eyes and upper cheekbones by tears. Her lip gloss has vanished; either chewed away by her biting her lips or my kissing them. She's still the most beautiful thing I've ever seen. Millicent doesn't need makeup; she only needs a smile.

I turn my body towards her – propping one bent leg up on the sofa – and touch her cheek softly. "Millicent Trinkett, nearly twelve years ago I met the most beautiful girl I'd ever seen – for all of a nanosecond – before being interrupted by another partygoer who wanted her all to themselves. I didn't know her, I'd only heard about her, and I had to watch her walk away out of my life for what I thought would be forever that day. But the one thing I never did was get *over* her. She popped into my thoughts on a random basis over the years and put a smile on my face. I'd play slow songs and wish she was there to hear them. A blue sky always reminded me of her eyes. I always wondered what it would have been like to kiss this girl, just once." I stop and sigh through my nose. "And then fate stepped in. Or, I don't know, maybe it was Uncle Duffy. I got to see this girl again, and I fell head over heels in love with her. Best part? She fell in love with me too."

I watch as a tear slowly rolls down her cheek and I wipe it away with my thumb. "There is no over with us, Millicent. I let you go once, I'm not stupid enough to let it happen again. I want your pain, I want your sad, I want your happy. I want you."

I move forward on the sofa and drop to my knee onto the floor and reach into my pocket. Opening the box, I hold it in front of her. "Millicent Trinkett, make me whole and give me a better half. Will you marry me?"

Her nod is slow and shaky, but she doesn't say anything. I need to hear the word.

"Talk to me, Mils," I whisper.

"Yeah," she whimpers. "Yeah," she says again as she flies off the sofa and tackles me to the floor. I hold her as her body trembles, and she works her way through another round of crying. Then I hear her giggle. "You propose when my makeup is smeared and I'm a slobbery mess?" she says through tears, but her laugh that accompanies them is all I need.

"Those raccoon eyes, be it from tears or waking up in the morning, will be my reminder of the day you said yes," I tell her, tucking back the curtain of hair that falls forward. "Best day ever." I bring her mouth to mine and seal the deal.

Millicent Trinkett agreed to marry me. And Morty better get his ass moving on a venue because I really don't believe in long engagements, at least not ours. I may have to reconsider that someday when it involves one of my little sisters or, God forbid, my own mother, but not us.

We enter the banquet room half an hour later and as expected, all conversation halts and every head turns our way. I take Millicent's hand and hold it high in the air. "She said yes!"

The entire room erupts in cheers. It is a surprise to most, I'm sure. Anyone with half a brain or a romantic bone in their body should have known it was coming eventually. Uncle Duffy and Morty already knew. Duffy went with me to choose the ring when we were in Denver while Millicent was recuperating after surgery back home in LA. *Yes, I knew that long ago I was going to marry this woman and while I didn't want to rush her, I didn't want to miss my opportunity or ever risk the chance of losing her again.*

Morty's the first to reach her – what a surprise. "You're sure about this?" he whispers, as if questioning her decision. I roll my eyes and take a deep breath, letting it out slowly as I silently count to ten.

"Make it twenty, Cheddar," Duffy murmurs in my ear. "This is Morty we're talking about."

Ah, my lips must have been moving.

"I'm sure, Uncle Morty," she says, then looks to me and smiles.

"Don't smirk," Duffy warns quietly. "He can still make your life a living hell. The guy's got more tricks up his ass than a team of Barnum and Bailey's circus clowns."

"Do we have your blessing?" Millicent earnestly asks him, her eyes studying his.

"Wholeheartedly, sweetheart," he tells her, then kisses her forehead while he arches a brow at me.

"Told ya," Duffy mumbles. "Take the good with the bad. Morty's the ugly. T'ain't no way gettin' around him." He slaps my shoulder and laughs.

"Morty," Grady says as he pulls him away from my fiancé, "I do believe you're preventing the rest of us from extending our congratulations for the best news we've heard since the beginning of this trip." He picks Millicent up off her feet and into his arms. "Little Bit, I knew from the moment I saw the bruise you left on his ribs, you were a match made in heaven."

Morty's brow creases in confusion.

"Uh, uh," Dave says, "I think it was the naked shower incident that got the ball rolling. The tally-whacker that dreams are made of."

"No," Bruce quips, "I truly believe it started with a flash of butt cheeks."

"Nope," Charlie argues. "It was the glitter on the nipples that drove him crazy."

Duffy holds up his finger and adds the final card that brings the tower down, "Lest we forget the romance novels and BDSM."

Morty glares at me and screams, "What the hell have you been doing on that bus?!"

Oh Morty... if you only knew.

Now if I were a betting man, the sound of silverware behind us is the knives on the tables being collected by the captive audience in the room, doing their best to either prevent my death or keep Morty out of jail. It's a toss up right now, so I'm going to keep my wallet in my pocket and not make a wager. I hope they're collecting the forks as well. Those little pricks can leave some pretty nasty holes in their wake.

The guys are on Morty before he's on me. His face is a nasty shade of red and his eyes flare with heated rage. I laugh. He's restrained. This may be the one time in my life I can laugh at Morty and not die within two minutes of it.

"Uncle Morty," Millicent chides. "Settle down. It wasn't me that saw Colby's penis, it wasn't my nipples decorated with glitter, and it was a mishap with Bruce's butt cheeks for which he profusely apologized." She frowns as she looks to the men restraining her uncle. "Why do you do this to him?"

Duffy smiles, his eyes shining with mischief. "Sport."

Grady shrugs and grins impishly. "Because it's fun."

"Morty," a soft voice sounds behind us, and the guys let go of him. She steps between us and stands in front of Morty, reaching out to touch his cheek and I see him nearly melt with her touch. "You raised her so well. She knows what she's doing. She's grown up." Maggie shoots a wry look to each and every one of the guys and they nearly cower. "Which is more than I can say for some other people."

"Come on, Maggie," Duffy protests. "He's just so damned easy."

Morty shoots him a glare and I hear his throaty growl to match it.

Duffy holds his hands out, palm side up, and his eyes widen as he shouts, "Well, ya are!"

"I thought that dunk in the fountain might wash off some of the uppity," Charlie grunts.

"That's yuppity," Bruce hums. "He's younger than us, you know."

"Which would explain why he's so damned easy," Dave chimes as he fixes his eyes on Morty. "With age comes wisdom."

Morty narrows his eyes. "Or a shit ton of nose hair and joint replacements."

Growls in unison come from a few of them, "Watch it."

"Come on," Morty says, throwing his arms around Maggie and Millicent. "Whiskey shots are on me." Keeping his voice loud and clear, he looks to Millicent. "So you had to bear the brunt of seeing Bruce's butt cheeks, huh? Blinding, isn't it?"

"You asshole!" Bruce yells.

Morty laughs. "Never denied it."

ANNIE MICK

264

Chapter 25

Millicent

"You gave up the woman you loved to raise me, didn't you?" And I thought I didn't have any tears left after last night. I had cornered Uncle Morty after brunch this morning and told him we needed to talk about Maggie. He's leaving this evening to go back home, and we hit the road tonight to head north for a slow trip to Moline. Turns out they have an extensive history and he's given the lamest story I've ever heard. Differences, geography, incompatibility, etc.

But I recalled Maggie's reaction to me in the salon yesterday. I also recalled Morty's reaction to Maggie when he saw her. They were hardly old friends and seemingly anything but incompatible. He also hadn't introduced the guys to her – they were all familiar with one another. On top of that, she was at brunch this morning, obviously having stayed with him last night at the hotel.

And in the end, just like always, the truth prevailed. My uncle had rearranged his entire life to take me in and raise me like his own. Not that he would ever say that; I'm intuitive enough to figure it out. I just never thought it involved a woman.

"Why would you do that, Morty?" I ask, studying the face of the man I had prodded for the last six years to date, to get a social life; anything other than babysit me.

He sighs so deeply I wait for him to take air back into his lungs just to make sure he's still breathing. "I didn't give up anything, Millie. It was a mutual decision that my full efforts would be put into my highest priority, and that was you. I wouldn't change a thing."

"You put your life on hold for me," I cry, wiping my eyes and feeling the rawness underneath from so much rubbing.

"Nope," he says cheerily, "just gave it a better direction. Millie, you're my twin sister's daughter. You were a high priority *before* I lost her, and you became top priority *when* I lost her. Maggie understood that. Being your guardian was never a job. It was an honor, a privilege." He pulls me into his arms and lays his cheek on the top of my head. "My God, I'm so proud of you."

I look up at him with teary, hopeful eyes. "So are you two going to get together?"

He smiles and winks. "She'd love to help you with wedding plans." He rolls his eyes. "And yes, I know Colby's in a hurry. I'll have the venue set by the time you get home. I'll even call in some favors to make it soon. How fast do you want it done?"

"As soon as possible?"

He frowns. "You're not pregnant, are you?"

"Uncle Morty!" I gasp. "No!"

"So it really is because you love him?"

"I really do, Morty. He's a lot like you, you know."

He arches his brows. "Really?"

"Yeah. He cares, he's gentle, loving." I shrug. "Of course, he doesn't have your OCD and he doesn't have a stick up his butt so there's always that…"

"You little shit!" he growls, narrowing his eyes.

"But those are good qualities," I laugh, patting his chest. "Sort of."

"Let's go," he orders, gently wrapping an arm over my shoulder. "By the way, I've already told your fiancé there will be no shacking up before the wedding."

I smirk before asking, "And just where is Maggie going to

live?”

Silence.

“I have an idea,” I offer happily. “She can stay with me in the gatehouse.”

He side-eyes me with a warning glare. “Millie,” he drawls.

“Uncle Morty,” I mock his drawl.

“We’ll talk about this when you get home,” he mumbles.

“I’m sure we will.” I giggle and hug his middle. “I’m sure we will.”

ANNIE MICK

On the Road Again

The last gig…ever. This was a reunion tour for Fourplay and Sticky Whiskers. Excuse me: Fourplay *with* Sticky Whiskers. Now that's something you'll want to tell your grandchildren about, isn't it?

"Did you know, I got to see Fourplay perform with Sticky Whiskers?"

"That's nothin' Grandpa. I performed foreplay and got sticky whiskers."

Smack!

Yeah, probably not good dinner conversation.

Colby is done with the road; he said so. I am done with road; I know so. The roadies will go on – it's what they do. It doesn't matter who they work for as long as they work.

Eleven thousand tickets sold for this concert. The Quad Cities area is going to be one enormous party. The Mississippi will probably flow with more than river water. Along the banks will be plenty of beer drinkers adding their overflow of liquid waste to wash downstream to join the Missouri somewhere around the city of St. Louis.

The trip here has been leisurely and slow; stopping at KOA campgrounds along the way, avoiding tourist traps, barbecuing nearly every day so as to include everyone around the campfires and conversation; not to mention the necessary showers taken in bulk form.

We're at our last campground, our last BBQ, our last night under the stars before the last performance. It's just the seven of us tonight in our own little circle; the others are spread throughout the campground, rowdy and celebrating early. Maybe this will be the night I hear Grady's story.

"How did you and Bruce end up not getting drafted?" I ask Dave as we sit around the campfire drinking beers and chatting.

"Only sons," he explains with a grim look. "Our dads had already passed." Using air quotes, one hand clumsily holding two fingers up while the others hold his bottle he says, "It deemed us *un-expendable.*"

Bruce shakes his head, disgusted. "Unlike these three," he nods at Grady, Charlie and Duffy, "and nearly 60,000 others they sent that never came home."

"Don't forget the ones that did," Charlie grunts. "Some have never gotten over it. Some ended the pain after they got home."

"Some came back to less than they had when they left," Grady mumbles so softly I barely hear him before he gets up and walks toward the bus. "I need whiskey," he calls back over his shoulder. "Anybody else?"

"Bring the bottle," Duffy shouts. "We'll pass it around."

Silence befalls our group as we wait for Grady to return with the bottle of Jack, and we pass it between us.

"You ever been to the Wall, Trinket?"

I watch the fire burn before me, the flames dance and the wood crackles and pops as it burns. *The Wall.* My greatest fear. The place where I would see all those names etched into the marble, reminding me of my biggest failure. But Jordy is alive and well in Georgia.

"Never been," I reply, studying the flames, a sudden wave of guilt passing through me. *The Wall isn't about me. It's about those who served and didn't come home.*

I look up to see them glancing at one another. "Have you guys been there?"

Duffy nods before taking a chug from the bottle and releasing a long sigh. "A few times. Helluva sight."

We finish out the evening, douse the campfire, and enter the bus for a night of travel from south Missouri to Illinois. The end of the road.

Damnit! Still no Grady story.

272

Concert Night

"You guys ready for this?" I ask Duffy as we make our way out of the backroom and out to the side stage to wait for Sticky Whiskers to finish the opening act.

He grins his trademark leprechaun smile above a long white beard and under bright blue eyes highlighted with laugh lines, a handkerchief do-rag tied around his scalp with an eighteen-inch white braid hanging below. "Have you ever known us not to be ready, Trinket?" He looks like the typical, yet very special, early 70s throwback hippie.

Charlie follows him. Snow white hair, white goatee and mustache, all finely trimmed. Hazel eyes that can pierce with one glare if necessary but get on his good side and you'll see the kindness beneath that harsh exterior. A few wrinkles that only define him as distinguished and slightly weathered. A voice that sounds like he eats gravel at every meal, but when he sings, it comes straight from his soul.

Dave is next in line. Still mostly pepper in his hair mixed with a little salt at the temples. I was almost convinced he colored it due to the contrasting white in his goatee and mustache, but it turns out he's a lovable mutt with beautiful blue eyes who's kept his silky brown hair over the years. And just like a lovable mutt, it matches his gentle spirit, the way his fingers move over the keys – playing 88 from one end to the other without missing a lick.

Bruce nearly dances as he falls in behind his bandmate.

He is never without a smile. Still has a bit of curl to his thinning, but carefully cut to make it look thicker dark brown hair with the beginnings of silver strands here and there. Brown eyes surrounded by thick lashes and deep-set wrinkles that only show more when he smiles. He's the only one in the group sans facial hair. Clean shaven every day that has a tendency to give him a boy-next-door appearance.

Looking a bit stoic, hands in his pockets, Grady stands behind him. His mix of blonde and gray hair is pulled back in a ponytail, his beard trimmed to a handsome length. Striking silver eyes that hold more than he displays openly. He's ready to play, but is it more to get it over with or the dread of it ending…here, tonight, for the last time?

Then there's my Colby, bringing up the rear. Mussy blonde hair; finely trimmed facial beard and mustache just a few shades darker, that I love to run my fingers through. Blue eyes that sparkle, though slightly hidden behind those adorable glasses. He reminds me of the naughty professors in the romance books, but he's all mine. The ring on my finger proves it. I've always been his too, I just hadn't found him yet.

* * *

Sticky Whiskers ends their set, and the crowd is warmed up and ready.

"This is it!" Grady shouts as they enter the stage. "Do or die!"

Grady, you're not going off to war. I knew something felt different.

No one else seems offput by what he says, and they grab their instruments and wow the crowd for the next two and a half hours, extending the usual time by half an hour. I'm not surprised as this is the end. It's over. But they've never played better than they did tonight.

The auditorium begins to empty as the crowd disperses. Backstage it's amped up, loud and busy. The roadies are onstage immediately, packing up equipment, wrapping cords, tearing down the drums and placing everything in cases. The guitar players are the last ones to walk off stage as those personal treasures are placed in those cases by their own hands. Duffy carries Rita in her case like always; never letting anyone else handle her. I wait for Grady, Bruce and Colby to do the same with theirs – as is usual – but then I see Colby carrying a guitar case in each hand as he walks behind Bruce.

"Where's Grady?" I ask, looking past him to scout for our missing bandmember.

"Had something to do," Colby informs me. "Asked me to grab it."

"Where did he go? I don't see him."

"Said he was hitting the head on the other side of the stadium." He shrugs, the weight of both guitar cases impeding the lift of his shoulders.

I huff, "There's a bathroom right over here."

In the green room, I arrange the table of food from the coolers and set out the cutlery while we wait for Grady. It's been nearly half an hour and still no sign of him.

"Where is Grady?" I inquire, looking to the others. "Was he not feeling well, Colby?"

Charlie glances up, eyes narrowed. "What do you mean, not feelin' well?"

"He asked Colby to take his guitar and said he was going to the bathroom."

"He looked fine, Millicent," Colby says, puzzled.

Charlie and Duffy exchange glances.

"Cheddar, what exactly did Grady say?"

Dave and Bruce suddenly perk up, looking as if they're ready to bolt from the room.

Colby frowns. "Asked me to take his guitar and said he had to hit the head on the other side of the stadium."

Duffy's eyes roll as he groans, "Aww shit. Let's go."

All four stand at once and head for the door in a rush. I grab my purse; Colby by my side and we try to follow.

"Stay," Charlie orders us. "If you hear anything, call us, pronto."

* * *

An hour later Sticky Whiskers and the roadies file into the green room; the job finished, the equipment packed up and on the buses.

"Hey!" Jake greets us. "Where's the stars? Thought we'd be celebrating together."

"Yeah," I answer solemnly, "us too." I turn to Colby. "I'm going to go wait on the bus. If you hear anything, let me know."

"I'll come with you." He's out of his chair and by my side before I can object.

"You guys know anything about the fight in the parking lot?" Brody asks, grabbing a plate and piling it high with food. "Cops were all over the place."

"When?" I ask, my stomach dropping.

"Right after the concert," he says.

I run for the door, leaving Colby either behind or left to catch up. His choice.

"Millicent wait!" he yells. "You don't even know if it involved him. You don't know where to go."

Reaching for my cell phone in my purse, I growl, "I'll figure it out on my way."

Duffy's phone rings four times before he answers.

"Trinket," he answers cautiously, but it's not a worried tone. It's more relief mixed with *you ain't gonna believe this*.

"Where is he?" I demand.

"Well," he drawls, his voice pitching an octave higher than usual. I picture his one eye closing as he ponders an unbelievable explanation of the words he's about to spew from his mouth. "You got Morty's black Amex with you?"

"Of course I do."

He clears his throat and chuckles. "Good. Grab my nephew and get a Lyft. Have them bring you to the Rock Island County Jail."

"The what?!"

"See you soon, Trinket." The call ends after I hear him release a deep sigh.

* * *

I insisted Grady go to the hospital and have his hand x-rayed. It's a boxer's break. From my understanding, well worth it to him. It's been a longtime coming...over 40 years. He smiled the entire time they put the splint on and wrapped it up.

Turns out the former sheriff, Tommy Graham, an old friend and fellow vet, felt the same way and his influence over the current department carries a lot of weight. These Iowa boys are one of a kind. Tommy is originally from Davenport, as is Grady, and Duffy called in a favor. Seems all those at the scene of the *incident* described the antagonist to be the one who is now the hospitalized recipient of a broken jaw, nose, and a few ribs.

It also turns out we didn't need the black Amex. Grady was released without arrest. Thank you, Tommy Graham.

"What made you do it?" I ask Grady as we sip our coffee around the table on the bus. We haven't started moving yet. No one seems to have the desire to start the trek back to LA. It'll all be over, and we're not ready for it to be over. The other three buses have left already; they pulled out early this morning.

"Because he was there, walking around free and easy. And because if I'd done it when I really wanted to, I'd have killed him." He studies the coffee cup in front of him. "I got more restraint now." He turns towards me, lifts his eyebrows as he inclines his chin. "Just not enough to let it go."

"Who is he? What did he do?"

"Took the only thing that ever mattered to me," he says, his voice low and broken, just like the man housing it.

"Your Susie," I whisper.

"My Susie," he confirms. "As well as my baby she was carrying."

"Oh God," I whimper, holding my hand to my mouth. I feel

Colby's hand gently squeeze my thigh, offering comfort.

"Offered his sister and my Susie a ride in his new car one day. Rolled it by showin' off. Killed both of them." He snorts softly. "My last letter to her was askin' her to marry me. My next letter was from my mama tellin' me she was gone."

I lean on his shoulder, clinging to his arm. "I'm sorry, Grady."

"It's okay, Little Bit. It was a lifetime ago." He leans in, wraps an arm around my shoulder and kisses the top of my head. He holds up his broken hand. "And this was a long time comin'. I'd do it daily if I thought it'd help."

"Did it help?"

He shakes his head and snorts softly. "Band-Aid."

"Good thing you waited until after the last concert. At least you were able to play."

"Ha!" Bruce laughs. "He's played with full casts on; arms and legs."

My eyebrows shoot skyward as my jaw hangs agape. "You're kidding."

Charlie explains, "Broken arms, ribs, legs, nose. Sounded a little nasally when he sang, but the women didn't much care."

Duffy gives Grady a stern look and adds softly, "Grady used to have a bad habit of beating himself up for something that wasn't his fault."

"Good to see you dish it out this time, Grady." Dave casts a knowing glance and smiles.

Grady slaps his good hand on the table. "And…" he sings loudly, "that will be enough of that. Let's get this bus moving. We still have a trip to make."

"Ah yes," Bruce holds up a finger as he flips through a travel brochure. "There's a big ass ball of twine calling our name in Kansas. Anybody up for it?"

Charlie squares him with a steely glare. "Only if I can cut some off, tie you up and stuff you in the back of the bus to shut you up."

"Alrighty then," Bruce chirps. "No ball of twine. How

about the corn palace in South Dakota? Ooh look! Different colors of cor… Ouch!" he says as he rubs the back of his head. "Damnit, Charlie was that necessary?"

"You done yet, dumbass?" Charlie growls.

Bruce studies the brochure further. "Not really. Oh look here. A hair museum in Missouri." His mouth twists in discouragement. "That's probably more for Duffy though as he's the only bald… ouch!" He rubs the back of his head again. "Stop slapping my head!"

Duffy smiles slyly as he eyes his friends at the table. "He ain't had a swirly yet."

"Duffy!" Bruce screeches. "I swear to God, I will date your sister."

Duffy looks unconcerned as he leans back in his chair, pops a bite of Pop Tart in his mouth and smiles. "Did I tell you she puked in my shoes after the fair? Ruined my best Reeboks." He leans forward, placing his elbows on the table. "She's on my shit list. Be sure to take her to Taco Bell."

Just so you know, they didn't dunk him in the toilet. They used the kitchen sink, utilizing the sprayer, pretty much like a Bidet.

280

The Trip Home

We wanted a leisurely trip home. What's a day or two extra when you have all the time in the world…not to mention Uncle Morty's black Amex?

John and Sandy had worked hard, driving us all over the country for the last six months. They deserved a couple nights in a posh hotel, a room of their own, dinner and drinks on the house; well, technically Uncle Morty. Sounded like a good excuse for us.

We decided to go over the rivers and through the woods – despite the fact we weren't going to grandmother's house – and took the northern route home. Upward and onward, so to speak. Across the northern states and straight south along the west coast once we hit Washington.

"Millie," Morty huffs as I explain our trip back will be extended by approximately 72 hours. We're crossing Montana at the present time, and I've procrastinated in finding the appropriate moment to inform Morty of our route changes. I'm not sure seven o'clock in the morning is his favorite time of day either. "What about the wedding plans you were so anxious to get started with?"

"We'll get started as soon as I get back."

"You'd better hurry up, young lady," he warns. "You've got one month to be fitted for a dress, choose your flowers, and be ready to say 'I do'."

The phone drops from my hand and lands on the floor of the bus. One month?

"Colby!" I shriek from where I sit in the bedroom at the back of the bus.

I hear Duffy's voice from the kitchen area, "I think he told her."

Told me? They knew?

"Hey, what's up?" Colby asks casually as he leans on the frame of the door. I screamed for the man and he's acting as if I just asked him to pass me the salt.

"A month?" I yell. "You knew?"

He nods as if it's no big revelation. "Morty and I have been in touch."

"Out!" I shout, pointing to the door and jumping off the bed. I push on his chest and shove him towards the kitchen. "Out, now!"

"Milli…" I slam the door shut. "…cent," he finishes with a sigh. I hear his head lightly thump on the door. "Open the door, Mils."

I growl in frustration, "Sorry, I'm busy. I have a wedding to plan."

"I'm more worried about the bride," he says. "I would have married you yesterday, last week, last month. Hell, I would have married you twelve years ago." He groans in frustration. "Open the door, Millicent. I hate it when you're mad at me."

Damnit, he had to say that didn't he?

I throw open the door and glare at him. "What?"

He smiles…that irresistible charming Jarlsberg smile, closing the door behind him. He takes two steps forward; I take two steps back.

"Marry me?"

"Can I think about it?" I sass, not that I would ever change my mind.

Two more steps forward; two more steps back and my legs hit the bed.

"Nope."

"Why in one month?" I ask. "Did you guys already choose the date too?"

"Morty did," he says softly. "It's the anniversary of the day he brought you back from Germany. Said he clung so tight he thought he'd never be able to let go. Wants to mark it as the same date he finally felt he was able to."

My heart literally breaks. I'll wear pajamas and carry dandelions if it makes Morty happy.

"So, Ms. Trinkett are you going to marry me?"

I sniffle and shrug. "I suppose I have to since nobody else has asked me."

He tosses me on the bed, laughing as he lands on his knees over me. "Always a smartass."

* * *

"Okay," I say, eyeing the group as I arrive in the main area of the bus, "I get the choice of dinner since you all held out on me. Tonight, we have sushi. I'll check for restaurants in the area after I get the schedule from Sandy."

Five groans in unison, in harmony no less, reach my ears as the protests start.

"I ain't eatin' raw fish, Millie," Charlie starts. "I may sound like a grizzly, but that don't mean I eat like one. Clean it, *cook* it, then eat it."

"I eat Mexican food for you guys all the time."

"At least it's cooked," Duffy retorts.

"Twice," I grumble, "by the time it gets through your bellies."

"Hey!" Dave scolds. "We've been good with the Beano."

Grady plays with his phone until he jumps up from the table and goes to the front of the bus where he carries a conversation with John and Sandy.

"Solved," he says confidently when he returns. "If Little Bit wants it raw she can have it. We want it cooked so we'll cook it." His grin is so big it lights up his eyes. "But boys, we gotta catch 'em first."

45 minutes later the bus pulls into a sporting goods store

parking lot. An hour after that, we are fully loaded up on bait, tackle, fishing licenses, and new rods for everyone. Clarification: *Poles, fishing poles.*

Now we are on our way to White Lake, where the trees are tall, the air is clean, the water is clear, and the fish are enormous… supposedly. I've never been fishing, but before this tour I'd never been a lot of things and look how that turned out.

* * *

Turns out I prefer my trout cooked. It also turns out I prefer to not watch it be cleaned beforehand.

We don't cook it inside in the skillets on the stove in the bus. It's not fried in a pan on a cooktop. No, it's done in a skillet over a fire at the campsite, outdoorsman style. It also means no forks, no spoons, no knives. A day of fishing, an afternoon in the sun, and a few beers throws etiquette out the window. *And brain cells.*

"Trinket, use your fingers," Duffy instructs me as he snatches another bite of fish off his plate. "Just pinch it and put it in your mouth."

"That's what Colby always says!" I declare with a giggle and…zero forethought. I feel the heat of Colby's glare from my left. *It was just a joke!*

After the sputtered laughter from around the circle has calmed, I hear Dave ask, "Rock, paper, scissors?" His question is obviously aimed at the other famous four as they all roll their eyes and nod.

"For what?" I gasp.

Grady snorts, then laughs. "To determine who bails Morty out of jail and who guards his…" he points a finger at Colby, "… hospital room to keep Morty from gettin' at him a second time."

"I have an easier solution," Colby proffers as he scowls at me. "Abstinence from alcohol for Millicent until after the ceremony."

I scoot close to him, lean my head on his shoulder, tilt my

mouth up to his ear and whisper, "I hate it when you're mad at me."

He wraps his arm around my shoulder, pulls me in a tight hug, drops his chin on my head, and murmurs, "But I always love you."

"Oh good," Bruce says cheerily. "The honeymoon's back on."

"Speaking of which," I eye Colby curiously. "Where are we going?"

His eyes light up as his brows rise and his gaze travels the circuit of our travel companions before it lands back on me. "It's a surprise."

"So we are taking one?"

He chuckles softly and I feel the rumble of his chest against my shoulder. "Baby, we are taking the honeymoon of a lifetime."

ANNIE MICK

Chapter 26

Colby

It's been a month of chaos; cake tasting, tux fittings, flower choices, etc. – all of which I was more than happy to participate in. However, I would have been more than happy to sweep Millicent off to Vegas, find a phony Elvis in a chapel and get it over with.

I've participated in the honeymoon plans as much as possible, though the guys have done most of the work. The perfect time of year for it. The leaves will be in full color, the weather couldn't be more conducive if we'd planned it. More on that later.

I've met with my business partners, spent a dizzying amount of hours going over the numbers, spreadsheets, programs, new ideas, and upcoming advertising campaigns. Yes, you can be a musician and a businessman at the same time, but it's going to make my life so much easier now that I've found what I was looking for. *One step ahead of Bono.*

Maggie, my mother, and my grandmother have been at Millicent's side for the past week, putting the final touches on preparations. It seems Maggie has moved to California and in with Morty – her partner having bought out her share of the nail salon. Shocker!

My sisters have been here soaking up the sun, invading my

condo and personal space to the point where I feel like they've moved in and taken over. I love my sisters – don't get me wrong – but like all little sisters, they're much more lovable when you don't occupy the same space under the same roof. I finally started locking my bedroom door and banned them from the master bath because – just like when we were teenagers at home – they're still the typical adolescent slobs they always were and hang their bras and underwear over the shower door. The perks of using a soaker jacuzzi tub comes with a price of cleaning up after yourself. Apparently they ignored that memo. The only lingerie I want to see for the rest of my life is my wife's.

My mother and grandmother are staying with Millicent in the gatehouse. I've talked with my future bride multiple times a day. I've seen her twice in the past week; long enough to participate in a family meal and the rehearsal dinner last night. The week prior to that she was booked everyday with gown fittings, a bachelorette party scheduled for a different night than my bachelor party, I had meetings for work, and Uncle Morty managed to schedule all sorts of odds and ends that kept us apart. All done with a gleam in his eye and a smirk on his mouth. Seriously, how many massages, facials, hair appointments and mani/pedis does a woman need?

The point I'm getting at is…I have literally not *been with* Millicent since we arrived back home.

My other point? Morty is a dick.

* * *

As she walks toward me down the path in Morty's backyard – on the arm of her uncle – all fleeting thoughts of time away from her leave me as does the breath from my lungs. The last month is nothing. I've waited the last twelve years for her. If I'd known back then what I know now. I'm glad I didn't kiss her goodbye. No, that first kiss on the bus was the right one, the perfect one. The one that brought us to where we are now.

* * *

The ceremony went off without a hitch. I didn't have to punch Morty for objecting. The guys didn't have to muzzle him. I swear I saw tears in his eyes, the good kind. I am now married to Millicent Trinkett-Jarlsberg. I asked her to hyphenate. Where do you find a name like that? Duffy's trinket, my jewel.

And now we're here at the hotel for the reception; guests ranging from big shots in fancy suits to musicians in blue jeans and boots. My kind of crowd.

The champagne pours, the cake gets cut, the music plays, the people dance. My sisters giggle as two guys grind…

You've gotta be kidding me.

I cross the room in seconds flat and grasp the backs of their necks gently – *total lie* – pulling them away from my giggling sisters. "Didn't know you boys were going to be here."

"Mr. Millie!" Trent greets me with a cocky grin. "Congratulations! Now that you got her locked down, you won't mind if I lay one last sloppy on her, will ya?"

"Think I can get her to give me one last purple nurple?" the other asks. If memory serves, his name is Trevor. "I'm kinda getting into pain lately. Must be a 50 shades phase that I…"

"Shut up," I spit, squeezing my eyes closed, exasperated with only seconds spent with these two. How in the hell Millicent spent months with them, I'll never know.

I glare at my two sisters. "Stay away from these guys. They're trouble overload." I look back to the two grinning idiots consisting of skin, bones, and raging hormones. "And you two, stay away from my sisters!"

Trent's hands fly up in front of him, palms out. "Whoa, whoa. Sisters?" He shakes his head vehemently. "That's bro code violation number one." He puffs his lips in a deep pout as he eyes them once more. "And they're so pretty."

I glance at his partner, narrowing my eyes. "Still into pain?"

"Uh…I think I'll go see Millie about that purple nurple," he mumbles as he walks backwards away from us. "Good seeing ya again. Congrats."

"Colby," Cassie whines. "Do you know who that was?"

Corrine sneers, "You're no fun."

"You're older than both of them," I snap.

Their faces light up as they playfully ask in unison, "We are?"

"They're not even legal in all 50 states."

I know I shouldn't, but I really want to get back to my wife and enjoy the rest of this party, and these two aren't easily deterred. I lean in close as if sharing gossip and whisper, "Their best kept secret is wearing toenail polish. Need I say more?"

What? It isn't a lie!

"Ohhh," they hum, again in unison, enlightenment showing in their matching wide eyes and lifted brows.

"Appearances can be very deceiving. Sorry to disappoint." I give them my best big brother face. "Best to not look for something that isn't there. Got it?"

They both nod, though disappointed.

My job here is done.

Now to get them out of LA and back to Iowa.

Tomorrow cannot come too soon.

* * *

The crowd is thinning out and the reception is nearing the end. All clearing has been done by the catering staff, the top tier of the cake has been packaged and is ready to go – whatever that means. Mom and my grandmother are staying at the gatehouse with my sisters as their flight takes off early morning back to Iowa. Morty and Maggie are tending to all the arrangements for them, so our goodbyes take place tonight. We're staying here at the hotel… honeymoon suite no less. Checkout time of noon, brunch served in the room at ten o'clock. Thank you, Uncle Morty.

"You're so perfect for each other," mom says, hugging me again.

"I know," I return with all sincerity.

"You won't be a stranger," my grandma orders as I bend

290

down to hug her goodbye. "Now that you're not traveling, you'll have to start traveling. Come see me." She sniffles and laughs, then wipes at her eyes. *Little does she know. It'll be soon. Might as well make it one of the stops.*

"Hey, bro," Cassie sniffles. "We had fun. Same time next year?"

Grumbling with our hug I tell her, "Keep your undies off my shower rack, you got a deal."

Poor Millicent is being squeezed with each hug I'm getting, but seems to be enjoying and relishing them as much as I am.

"Hey!" Corrine shouts. "Where are you guys going for your honeymoon?"

"It's a surprise," I answer before Millicent can.

"You can tell us," Corrine whines.

I shoot her a wry smile. "Fat chance. Then it wouldn't be a surprise."

She looks to mom. "Do you know?"

Mom shakes her head. "He hasn't told anybody anything."

Meh...I wouldn't say "anybody".

"Including me," Millicent grumbles.

"Especially you," I say, kissing her temple. "Trust me?"

She casts me a knowing glance and smiles. Our first night together. It might have hurt, but only a little. God, I hope this is the right decision.

"It worked the first time," she answers softly.

"Sure did," I whisper, tipping her chin up and placing a gentle kiss on her mouth.

"I think we need to go," mom says with a giggle. "We could say goodbye all night long, and it's not our night to have."

Understatement of the year, mom.

Chapter 27

Millicent

"Rise and shine, Mrs. Jarlsberg," Colby murmurs in my ear before kissing that sweet spot under my ear.

I bury my head deeper into the lush pillow and whine, "No, I want to stay right here. I'm not ready to leave yet."

"You don't want a honeymoon?" he teases.

That gets my attention and I'm suddenly on full alert. As I try to sit up, Colby pulls me back to the mattress. "First things first, Millicent. I didn't say we were leaving…yet."

* * *

Two hours later we are showered and dressed – Colby specified wardrobe of blue jeans, tennis shoes, and long sleeve T-shirt. Where he got it, I don't know. Now we sit at the table in our room eating breakfast where I drill him about the day's agenda.

"Patience, Millicent. We'll get there."

I eye him skeptically. "The last time you used those words with me, it took a long time, Colby."

He laughs. "Was it worth the wait?"

"Can I get back to you on that?"

There's a knock on the door and Colby rises to answer. A hotel employee stands outside holding an envelope in his hand.

"For Mrs. Millicent Trinkett-Jarlsberg."

Colby takes the envelope and tells him, "Thank you. I'll be sure she gets it."

Colby hands me the envelope and offers and slight bow. "For you, madam. And you can get back to me on that whenever you're ready."

I open the envelope and unfold the note inside:

"Your chariot awaits. Bring your old man with you. He's the driver."

Colby has both of our bags in his hands as I look up. "What does this mean?"

He shrugs. "Only one way to find out. Let's go, baby."

Down the hall to the elevator and into the lobby. My mind races and my heart skips a few beats as I anticipate the surprise. A horse-drawn chariot? Well, that wouldn't be any fun if Colby is the driver. That would make it a buggy. Or one with buckboards and… *Oh stop it, Millicent.*

As we near the center of the lobby, I see a large group of people gathering at the front doors as they take in whatever is happening out front.

A bellhop runs to meet us and takes our bags from Colby's hands. Colby wraps his arm around my shoulder and uses his other hand to cover my eyes. "I won't let you fall. Get ready."

We walk slowly and steadily to the front doors, Colby's strong arms guiding my way, and I hear the whoosh as they open. We take a few more slow steps before we come to a complete stop.

"Last step in the healing process, Millicent," he whispers in my ear. I literally hear his heart breaking as his voice cracks. I feel his strength pour into me as he holds me tighter. "I told you I want your pain, and your sad, and your happy. It's the step I want to take with you, and so do they."

He removes his hand from over my eyes and turns me so

I can see what he's talking about. In front of me is seven Harleys, five of them fully dressed with saddle bags and road trip gear, each partnered with a familiar musician leaning on it. The other two are trikes. Uncle Morty stands next to one with a smiling Maggie at his side, the other waiting for, well, apparently us.

"You ready to go see The Wall, Trinket?" Duffy asks, his soft, understanding smile melting my heart.

Grady walks to where we stand and holds out a helmet for me to put on. "Brain buckets are mandatory, Little Bit. There's a headset in there so you can talk with your hubby while you ride."

Charlie follows him, carrying a leather jacket. "This is for after we get out on the highway." He turns it to show me the letters on the back: MTJ. *Millicent Trinkett-Jarlsberg.* "We figured if it didn't work out with Colby," he grins, "we'd find ya somebody with the last name of Johnson or Jones."

"Very funny, Charlie," Colby growls.

"What do you say we get this show on the road?" Morty shouts.

I'm stunned. I've never traveled by motorcycle, much less across the country on one. "What about clothes and things I'll need for travel?"

Maggie quells my concerns immediately. "I packed your things days ago, sweetie. Hope you don't mind me going through your drawers, but…" She scrunches her nose and shrugs. "It's not like I had much choice. Anything you need, we can buy on the way."

"So," I say as I throw my hands out in the air and laugh. "You're all sharing my honeymoon with me?"

"You okay with that, Trinket?"

My smile is so big I'm afraid my face may split. I've never grown to love so many people in so little time in my life.

"You've all got your meds?"

"Yup," they answer in unison.

"You've all seen your doctors and had your checkups?"

I hear a combination of groaning "yes, Millie and yups".

"Fresh supply of Pop Tarts?"

"Never leave home without 'em," Duffy laughs.

"You bet your butt I am!" I shriek. "Play me a song, boys!"

Dave hits a button on the console of his motorcycle and Steppenwolf's "Born to Be Wild" screams through the speakers as I watch all five men pull leather vests off the seats of their bikes and put them on.

They turn their backs to me, ensuring I can see clearly what is emblazoned on the backs.

OFAPT

"Old Farts and Pop Tarts"

I laugh so hard tears run down my cheeks. My sides ache from the muscle spasms.

Colby turns me around and tips my chin up. "You're sure about this?"

I reach for his scruff and run my fingers through it and watch as his eyes close and he leans his cheek into my hand. *Oh yeah.* "The only thing I've ever been more sure of is saying, 'I do'. Let's go, husband."

He brushes his nose against mine and whispers, "I like that title."

"It looks good on you."

"What looks good on me," *kiss* "over me" *kiss* "under me", he says before dipping me and stealing a long, sensuous kiss, "is you."

"Uncle Morty's watching," I murmur against his mouth.

"I know," he says cockily.

I giggle. "You ready to ride?"

He nuzzles into the crook of my neck. "What are you offering?"

"Hey, loverboy!" my uncle growls from close by.

Colby raises his head slowly and antagonizes him with a smirk. "Yes, Uncle Morty?"

Laughter rings louder than if a dirty joke had been told amongst the guys and they huddle together like boys on a football team.

"Thank God Morty's gettin' laid," Grady mumbles. "This trip would be hell on earth if he didn't have some kinda release from the torture that boy is gonna rain on him."

"Don't count on much," Charlie tells him. "Maggie's only pullin' the stick from the front. He's still got that stick up his ass."

"Just so we remember what we're here for," Duffy reminds them.

"It's about Millie," Dave says. "Wipe out the old, ring in the new."

"Absolutely," Bruce agrees. "We gave them the boost they needed. Now we kick them out of the nest and let them fly."

Charlie squirrels his face as he looks at him, then shakes his head. "Six months on the road and now you say somethin' smart?"

Bruce shrugs sheepishly. "Didn't want to give you too much of me at once."

"We'd better hit the road before Morty hits Cheddar," Duffy warns. "Can't let him know we set the whole thing up. Let him go on thinkin' he's smarter than we are."

The huddle breaks apart and Grady calls out, "Time to get these wheels rolling."

We mount the bikes, strap the helmets to our heads, start the engines and a mighty roar echoes against the building. Thumbs up come from every driver, and we pull out onto the street and head for the highway.

"You doing okay back there?" Colby asks as we enter the interstate eastward bound.

I feel the rumble under my butt, the wind against my body, the freedom of the open road. "I've never been better. Thank you for everything."

"I love you, Millicent. This is only the beginning." He laughs. "We're just getting started."

The End

Thanks for coming along for the ride. It's been one of the sweetest journeys I've ever taken.

Please consider leaving a review on Amazon or Goodreads. It not only means a lot to your author, but gives you, the reader, a voice in the pages.

Other Books By This Author

<u>The Crew Series:</u>

<u>Run To Me</u>

<u>Wicked Lemonade</u>

<u>Find Another Hero: Just Make Sure He Can Dance</u>

<u>Tell Me Why, Jannie</u>

<u>The Fresh French Connection</u>

<u>Old Farts and Pop Tarts</u>

<u>Saari, Not Sorry</u>

<u>The Chauffeur: Phoenix Rising</u>

<u>Manipulation 101: Code of Ethics</u>

300

About the Author

A diehard laughaholic who has learned to take everything with a grain of salt, Annie Mick loves to dish it out with a good dose of sarcasm.

If you can giggle while you wiggle, it's added exercise and spares you ten minutes on the treadmill.

It is true that if you can laugh while you cry, the tears are saltier and it makes the margaritas taste better.

If you can find your hero in one of her books, therein lies her success. If you can find a bit of yourself in one her characters, therein lies her joy.

Life is too short to not get lost in a fantasy; if only for a day, if only in a book, one page at a time.

Sweet dreams.

www.ingramcontent.com/pod-product-compliance
Lightning Source LLC
Chambersburg PA
CBHW070525310726
48976CB00002BA/538